# Killer Words

# V. M. BURNS

KENSINGTON
PUBLISHING CORP.

www.kensingtonbooks.com

KENSINGTON BOOKS are published by

Kensington Publishing Corp.
119 West 40th Street
New York, NY 10018

All Kensington titles, imprints, and distributed lines are available at special quantity discounts for bulk purchases for sales promotion, premiums, fund-raising, educational, or institutional use.

This book is a work of fiction. Names, characters, businesses, organizations, places, events, and incidents either are the product of the author's imagination or are used fictitiously. Any resemblance to actual persons, living or dead, events, or locales is entirely coincidental.

To the extent that the image or images on the cover of this book depict a person or persons, such person or persons are merely models, and are not intended to portray any character or characters featured in the book.

Special book excerpts or customized printings can also be created to fit specific needs. For details, write or phone the office of the Kensington Sales Manager: Kensington Publishing Corp., 119 West 40th Street, New York, NY 10018. Attn. Sales Department. Phone: 1-800-221-2647.

The K logo is a trademark of Kensington Publishing Corp.

ISBN: 978-1-4967-2898-2 (ebook)
ISBN: 978-1-4967-2897-5

First Kensington Trade Paperback Printing: December 2021

10 9 8 7 6 5 4 3 2 1

Printed in the United States of America

**Praise for V. M. Burns and her Mystery Bookshop Mysteries!**

## A TOURIST'S GUIDE TO MURDER

"Colorful characters and just enough mystery trivia boost the fast-moving plot. Cozy fans are sure to have fun." —*Publishers Weekly*

## BOOKMARKED FOR MURDER

"This two-in-one mystery satisfies on so many levels, with this fifth in the series being as fresh and unique as the first."
—*Kings River Life Magazine*

"In the end, *Bookmarked for Murder* is a fantastic bookstore cozy murder book, and the 'Mystery Bookshop' series is an enthralling read that makes me smile and has me hoping my retirement will be just like Nana Jo's and the other characters'. This book is beyond entertaining. It's a page-turner that is filled with remarkable characters that have readers coming back for more." —*The Cozy Review*

## READ HERRING HUNT

"As good as any Jessica Fletcher story could be, Burns has a way with words and her characters are absolutely riveting. There is no doubt this is one series that will continue for a good, long time to come." —*Suspense Magazine*

## THE PLOT IS MURDER

"This debut cleverly integrates a historical cozy within a contemporary mystery. In both story lines, the elder characters shine; they are refreshingly witty and robust, with formidable connections and investigative skills." —*Library Journal* (starred review)

"*The Plot Is Murder* is a great addition to the ranks of cozy mysteries. Samantha Washington is a savvy and sympathetic sleuth and her crime-busting senior citizen posse all but steal the show. Two parallel plots make this book-within-a-book twice as much fun. I hope this debut mystery is the start of a long series to come."
—Laurien Berenson, author of *Pup Fiction*

"You'll love this delightful debut mystery with its charming and wacky cast of characters and a mystery within a mystery just to keep things interesting." —Victoria Thompson, *New York Times* bestselling author

"A charming read—with murder, romance and lots of mouthwatering desserts." —Laura Levine, author of *Murder Gets a Makeover*

## Books by V. M. Burns

*Mystery Bookshop Mysteries*
THE PLOT IS MURDER
READ HERRING HUNT
THE NOVEL ART OF MURDER
WED, READ & DEAD
BOOKMARKED FOR MURDER
A TOURIST'S GUIDE TO MURDER
KILLER WORDS

*Dog Club Mysteries*
IN THE DOG HOUSE
THE PUPPY WHO KNEW TOO MUCH
BARK IF IT'S MURDER
PAW AND ORDER
SIT, STAY, SLAY

Published by Kensington Publishing Corp.

To Coco and Cash aka Snickers and Oreo
Thanks for the warm hugs, kisses, and many laughs

# Acknowledgments

It took a village to get this book from idea to finished product, and I have been so fortunate to have a great village. Thanks to Dawn Dowdle, Blue Ridge Literary Agency, freelance editor, Michael Dell, Bev Cotton, graphic designer extraordinaire, virtual assistant Kelly Fowler, and Cassandra Morgan at CMBS Global. Thanks to Memphis retired policeman and author Ernie Lancaster for the crash course in ballistics. Big thanks to Abby Vandiver for the legal help and for putting on your sergeant's cap and pushing me to write when I didn't feel like it. And thanks to Alexia Gordon and Cheyney McWilliams for the medical advice. And thanks to all of the wonderful people at Kensington who have believed in me and supported my dreams: John Scognamiglio, Michelle Addo, and Larissa Ackerman.

Thank you to my Seton Hill University family, my tribe (Michelle, Patricia, Anna, Matt, Alex, Jeff, Gina, Jessica, Penny, Crystal, Kenya, Lana, Tyler), the Barnyardians (Tim, Chuck, Lindsey, Jill, Kristie, Sandy), my awesome team (Amber, Derrick, Eric, Carol, Lacy, and Jordan), and the best training team ever (Tena, Grace, Deborah, Jamie).

Shout out to Crime Writers of Color, Sisters in Crime, Angel White at Certified Book Nerd, Dru Ann Love, Colleen Finn, Kings River Life, Debry Jo Berkshire, Karen Kenyon, Lori Caswell at Dollycas, and all of the wonderful reviewers, book bloggers, and librarians who dedicate their time, effort and energy to helping authors. I appreciate all of the kind words, support, and for all you do to promote books.

I would not be able to do what I do without the love and support of my family, who have endured long conversations about fictional characters, murder, and poisons without complaint . . . well, without many complaints. Even when you just held the phone and let me babble, I appreciated it. Thanks to my dad, Benjamin, Jacquelyn, Christopher (Carson, Cameron, and Crosby) Rucker, and Jillian (Drew and Marcella) Merkel. As always, special thanks to my two partners in crime, Sophia and Shelitha. This would not have been possible without you two, and for that I will be eternally grateful.

# Chapter 1

"Bow chicka wow wow!" Nana Jo fanned herself with the newspaper she was reading. "This is some steamy stuff."

I cornered the dust bunny I'd been chasing with my broom for the last few minutes, swept it into my dustpan, and dumped it into the trash. Feeling like I'd just conquered Mount Everest, I strutted over to the seat where my grandmother was sitting and glanced over her shoulder. "What are you reading?"

"An article about the North Harbor Police Department. According to this, North Harbor is not only a hotbed of crime and vice, but the police department is in bed with the criminals." She turned around to look at me. "Literally, in *bed* with the criminals."

I read a paragraph and found myself gasping. "Who knew all of this criminal activity was going on in sleepy little North Harbor, Michigan?"

Nana Jo pointed toward an empty chair across from her. "Take a seat. I'm just about done with this page."

I glanced around the empty bookstore and realized I wouldn't be missed if I took a short break. I went to the counter and poured myself a cup of tea. I grabbed a plate of peanut butter cookies, placed the plate in the center of the small bistro table, and sat across from my grandmother.

She passed me the front page of the *North Harbor Herald*. Our local newspaper wasn't much bigger than the Sunday morning comics in big-city newspapers, but for a town of fifteen thousand, it was standard. I was so shocked by what I read that I found myself rereading it, so it took much longer than it should have.

"Close your mouth," Nana Jo said. "You're going to catch flies."

I hadn't even realized my mouth was open. "I can't believe what I'm reading."

"Shocking, isn't it?"

"It's not just the allegations of corruption and misconduct that are being presented; it's the allegations that aren't supported by facts. There's absolutely no evidence presented. These are . . . allegations and salacious innuendo that have been printed in black and white. It's . . ."

"The shoddy journalism you'd expect from supermarket rags, but not from a legitimate newspaper."

"Exactly."

"North Harbor's a small town, and the *Herald* is a small newspaper, but in the past, the writing was always very good and supported by evidence." Nana Jo pointed to the page she'd just finished reading. "Just take a look at all of that. I mean really, it's almost as though a grade schooler wrote it."

As a former high school English teacher, I noticed every misspelled word, misplaced comma, and dangling participle. "I noticed. I've tried to turn off my inner editor so I can read and enjoy books. Now that I have my first book published, I'm nervous about that."

Nana Jo patted my hand. "No need to stress about it. It's impossible to prevent some minor issues, but there's no way your books will have this many problems. I mean, there's one place where an entire sentence is missing."

I glanced over at the section she pointed to and cringed. There definitely seemed to be something missing. We spent a few minutes pondering what it could be until the bell on the front door chimed. I started to rise, but Nana Jo waved me down.

"You finish reading. I'll take care of the customer." She headed toward the front of the store.

I couldn't help but smile and say a quick prayer of thanks for my family's support. When my late husband, Leon, and I talked about our dream to open a bookstore that specialized in mysteries, I never thought the dream would actually come true or that when it did he wouldn't be here with me. However, it was Leon's death that gave me the push I needed to take a leap of faith, quit my job, sell my house, and buy a building. Opening a mystery bookshop was hard work, but I was blessed to have my mystery-loving grandmother helping most weekdays. When Nana Jo wasn't here, my nephews, Christopher and Zaq, were usually ready to earn extra pocket money. I've also become friends with some amazing students at Michigan Southwest University, MISU, what the locals referred to as Miss You, including my former high school student and local football hero Dawson Alexander, his girlfriend, Jillian Clark, and Zaq's girlfriend, Emma Lee.

I glanced up and saw my grandmother, who was nearly six feet tall and well over two hundred pounds, towering over a petite man who came into the store about once a week. He was fond of both psychological thrillers and culinary cozies. It seemed like an unusual combination, but when Nana Jo asked him about it, he said that he loved the heart-racing drama of the thrillers but also loved to cook and had found some great recipes in cozies. That was one of the things that I loved about crime fiction: there was something for everyone.

I glanced around at my store's bookshelves, which held everything related to crime fiction. I sold true-crime novels, like *In Cold Blood* by Truman Capote. Even though the book was first published in 1966, it was still very popular. I also carried noir fiction by authors like Raymond Chandler that tended to be darker. There was a substantial section of my personal favorites, cozy mysteries by Agatha Christie, Victoria Thompson, and Emily Brightwell. Filling shelves with my favorite books was just one of the perks of owning my own bookstore.

Nana Jo was extolling the virtues of Leslie Budewitz's Food Lovers' Village mystery series. As the person who first got me hooked on mysteries, Nana Jo was knowledgeable, and had a knack of helping customers find the right type of mystery. I watched as she sold the first two Food Lovers' Village Mysteries, along with thrillers by Tracy Clark and John Balducci. Nana Jo was a great salesperson, and my petite mystery lover walked out with a big bag and an even bigger smile.

Nana Jo came back and flopped into the chair she had recently vacated.

"Are you tired?" I said. "Things are really slow, and I can certainly handle—"

She waved away my protest. "I'm not tired . . . not exactly. I just feel . . . bored."

"I know exactly how you feel. Ever since we returned from England, I've been feeling the same way. I know every day isn't a mad dash tour across England, but . . . things in North Harbor have been incredibly dull."

"It's not just touring England but solving two murders. Don't forget that. We solved two murders and helped put a dangerous criminal behind bars."

"I know, but that was just a fluke."

"Fluke? Samantha, you have a knack for solving murders.

England wasn't the first time you've hunted down a murderer."

"I'd hardly call what we've done *hunting down murderers*." I sighed. "But I have to admit it was exciting to know that we helped piece the clues together and assisted the police to figure out whodunit and make sure that justice was carried out. Although that last time was a bit more excitement than I would have liked. I mean, we could have been killed."

"Pish posh. We had everything well in hand. Detective Sergeant Templeton just came in at the end and took all of the credit, but it was you, me, and the *girls* who got to the bottom of that one."

I smiled. My grandmother was biased, but we had played a major role in the case. "Don't forget Hannah Schneider."

"Hannah was invaluable. I just wish she lived here rather than in England. She would fit in well at Shady Acres."

Shady Acres was the retirement village where my grandmother and her friends lived. Although Nana Jo spent several days of each week with me, she had her own house at Shady Acres. It was an active facility for senior citizens that offered surfing, cooking, martial arts, and a host of other classes that Nana Jo and her friends took, and it was where they lived. "I think she's going to come for a visit in a few months. She said she wanted to visit her cousin in New Zealand, but she hoped it wouldn't be long."

"That'll be awesome."

"You're right. I love my bookshop, but it can be rather dull, especially after England, and I'll admit, I've been struggling."

She reached over and patted my hand. "Well, we just need another murder to stimulate your little gray cells."

"Nana Jo, we should not be hoping for a murder. That's awful."

"You know what I mean. Maybe we just need a little excitement."

"I know what you mean, but I think it would be best if I focus on solving the mysteries in the pages of my book."

"How's the editing going?"

"Slowly. I've looked at this manuscript so many times my eyes are crossed. I think after a while my brain just sees what it wants to see. I'm so afraid I'll miss something and it'll be just as bad as that article in the *Herald*."

"You'd have to work hard to make that many errors. Maybe you need to take a break. Let's go to the casino." She smiled. "Unless, of course, you and Frank have plans."

I tried to avoid smiling, but my mouth had a mind of its own when it came to talking about my boyfriend, Frank Patterson. It still seemed alien for me to have a boyfriend. Leon and I were married for more than thirteen years. When he died, I didn't think I'd ever want to be involved in another relationship. However, Frank helped me realize that my heart didn't die with Leon. Leon died, but my heart kept beating, and eventually I realized there was room for someone else. "It's Friday night, the busiest night at the restaurant. So, Frank and I aren't going anywhere."

"Great." Nana Jo whipped out her cell phone. "I kind of thought you might be free, so I told the girls you'd pick them up around seven thirty."

Despite a steady stream of customers, the time dragged. Normally, I enjoyed a slow, easy pace; however, today I just couldn't get into the groove. When the last customer left, I locked the door and took a few minutes to clean and get ready for tomorrow. When I was tired, sweeping, dusting, and restocking the shelves was harder. But getting to sleep an extra thirty minutes in the morning was well worth pushing through any fatigue I felt at night. Walking through the aisles, I admired the brightly colored books that lined the shelves. I inhaled the woody, citrus aroma of the wood cleaner I used on my bookshelves and smiled. It was a familiar scent that wrapped around me like a warm blanket.

"You going to keep sniffing that polish with that goofy look on your face all night?"

Nana Jo snapped me back to reality. I finished dusting while she swept. Before long, everything was ready for our next day.

One of the things I loved about the building I'd purchased in North Harbor was my commute. I walked upstairs to the converted loft that was now my new home. When Leon and I dreamed of owning this building, we knew there was a loft upstairs. We talked about renting out the space to help pay the mortgage and alleviate the pressure of having to pay the mortgage and make the bookstore successful. However, when Leon was dying, he knew that I was a creature of routine and needed a change. He suggested I sell the house where we'd lived together and move into the bookstore's loft. He was right. The house was filled with memories—too many memories. Leon knew I would have spent too much time in my past to move into my future. The new space was a large, open loft with beautiful oak hardwood floors, brick walls, seventeen-foot ceilings, and floor-to-ceiling windows. I worked with a designer and renovated the 2000-square-foot space, which now contained a nice kitchen area, two bedrooms, and two bathrooms.

At the top of the stairs, I was greeted by my two toy poodles, Snickers and Oreo. In the past, the dogs would have heard me coming upstairs and met me at the bottom. However, they were both getting older and enjoyed their daytime naps. Snickers was fourteen and the older of the two dogs. She stretched, yawned, and then did a full-body extension stretch that involved balancing on two legs and pointing her paws. Apparently, napping all day was exhausting.

At twelve, Oreo had also taken to enjoying long naps during the day, but he was still a playful puppy at heart.

We walked downstairs, and I opened the door to let them out into the enclosed courtyard. The building was on a corner. The previous owner had built a garage at the back of the property, and a fence connected the detached garage to the house and created a courtyard that was perfect for the dogs.

Even in the most basic of areas, the poodles were true to their personalities. Snickers stepped over the threshold, squatted, and quickly answered the call of nature. Within seconds, she was done, wiped her feet, and then came inside and stood beside me while we waited for Oreo. He bounded outside with a joy and exuberance that brought a smile to my face. A leaf blew across the yard, and Oreo spent a few minutes pouncing, barking, and tossing the leaf into the air. Snickers gave me a look that said, *Really?* Eventually, Oreo remembered why he was there. He walked to the edge of the garage and hiked his leg.

When he took an interest in a stick, I interrupted his second round of play. "Oreo, come."

He picked up his stick and trotted to the door. I didn't mind indulging his play, but I drew the line at bringing nature inside. I relieved him of his stick and tossed it as far away as I could and closed the door.

Back upstairs, I still had nearly an hour before I needed to go to Shady Acres. I fed the poodles and then fired up my laptop.

My e-mails consisted largely of spam proclaiming *I was already a winner* and that a prince of a small African nation wanted to give me millions of dollars to help get money out of his country. Despite my spam filters, my daily routine involved deleting fifteen to twenty e-mails. The three to five e-mails that were left were a lot less interesting. However, today my inbox included one from my agent. My heart raced whenever I saw e-mails from Pamela Porter of Big Apple Literary Agency.

I opened the e-mail. I read it multiple times and then read it again.

Nana Jo stuck her head in the room. "Squinting at the screen doesn't help."

"I'm trying to understand what 'building my brand' means."

"That's easy. It means you need to market yourself. You've got to get on social media. Tweet, blog, Instagram, and a host of other sites. Interact with readers and help them get to know you."

I stared at my grandmother. "What's my brand?"

"Your brand is you. It's what you write. It's like Coke or Pepsi. Samantha Washington, or you could use your initials like J. K. Rowling or D. H. Lawrence."

"What if I don't have a brand?"

"You have one. You just don't know what it is yet. Maybe you should hire a publicist to help you figure out what your brand is and how to market that."

I stared at the e-mail. "I need an author photo and a bio and . . . do all authors do this? Whatever happened to just writing a book?"

"An author photo shoot will be great. I'll bet Dorothy or her sister who runs the art gallery could hook you up with a good photographer."

"Hook me up? I don't need to be hooked up with a photographer. I can just have Christopher or Zaq take a picture."

"Samantha Marie Washington, this is your *author* photo. It will be on the backs of all your books, the books you've dreamed of writing most of your life. Don't you want to look your best?"

Since she put it like that, how could I disagree? *Oh, no. I want to look my worst?* "But Christopher and Zaq take great pictures." Even to my ears, I sounded whiny.

Nana Jo narrowed her eyes and stared. "I'll make a note to talk to Dorothy tonight." She made a few notes on her phone and then continued to analyze me. "You should go back to Jenna's stylist and let her do your hair and makeup before you get your picture taken."

"What's wrong with my hair?"

"Nothing. It's just that she did an excellent job cutting your hair before, and I just loved the highlights." She stared at me. "Besides, didn't you tell me earlier today that you needed to get your hair cut?"

"Yes," I said even whinier than before. I hated getting trapped.

"What's the matter with you? Isn't this what you wanted? To get your books published?"

"I know. I guess . . . now that it's happening, it's all a bit overwhelming. I mean, what if no one likes my books? What if no one buys my books? What if I'm a royal failure? I don't have the slightest clue what I'm doing, and I don't know anything about social media and brands and marketing." I put my head down on my desk.

Nana Jo patted my back. "That's just nerves. Your books will sell. The publisher wouldn't offer you a contract if they didn't think so. You just need to find the people who like British historic cozy mysteries. That's what discovering and marketing your brand will do."

"I honestly don't know the first thing about social media. Zaq created the website for the bookstore, and between him and Christopher, the site pretty much runs itself."

"Well, it's about time you learned. The twins are twenty-one and about to graduate from college. They'll be off to graduate school soon."

I put my head back down on the table.

"You can pay someone to run your website until you can get yourself up to speed."

I looked at my grandmother. "How am I going to learn all of this stuff?"

"You're in luck. When I was reading that ghastly article earlier, I happened across a continuing education course on social media." She pulled out her cell phone and swiped. "MISU is running the class, and they're giving discounts to senior citizens."

"I'm not a senior citizen . . . yet."

"I know you're not, but I am."

"You already know more about social media than I do."

"True, but there's always new stuff coming out. I don't think I do enough with Instagram, and I want to do more videos and get on TikTok."

"What's Tik—Oh, never mind. Where do I sign up?"

# Chapter 2

North Harbor was an economically depressed town on the shores of Lake Michigan in the southwestern corner of the state. The area had once been a manufacturing hub for parts that contributed to the Detroit automotive industry. However, when many of the manufacturing jobs moved to the South and overseas North Harbor's economy collapsed, and it never recovered. North Harbor's twin city of South Harbor, which shared the same Lake Michigan coastline, was a thriving tourist town with cobbled streets, lighthouses, and multi-million-dollar beach homes.

The drive from my bookstore in downtown North Harbor to Shady Acres Retirement Village was a straight shot on the road that ran parallel to the lake. At seven thirty, the sun was starting to set on the water. When I caught glimpses of the lake between the houses, I allowed its serenity and beauty to soak into my soul. Winters on the lake could be brutal, but the rest of the year made it worthwhile.

Shady Acres was a gated retirement community that provided apartments and single-family homes called villas. After my grandfather died Nana Jo had purchased a villa and got an excellent deal. Now her lakefront villa was worth five times what she'd paid for it. The great thing about Shady Acres was that they catered to an active community and offered activities on everything from surfing to belly dancing to martial arts. In fact, Nana Jo and her friend Dorothy were now black belts in Aikido and were working on jujitsu.

Nana Jo's friends piled into my Ford Escape and we headed off. They were an interesting and rather eclectic group of women. Dorothy Clark was about six feet tall, like Nana Jo, and just shy of three hundred pounds. She was a shameless flirt who sang like an angel. In contrast, Irma Starczewski was about five feet tall and one hundred pounds sopping wet. Her hair, which she wore in a beehive, was dyed jet black. About sixty years ago, Irma had been a beauty pageant queen who enjoyed wearing tight, short clothes and six-inch hooker heels. Dorothy liked to flirt, but Irma took flirting to an entirely different level. Ruby Mae Stevenson was my grandmother's youngest friend and my favorite. An African-American woman from Alabama, she spoke with a soft southern drawl and wore her salt-and-pepper hair pulled back into a bun. Nana Jo said Ruby Mae's hair was so long she could sit on it, but I'd never seen it down. She had nine children and a massive extended family. Everywhere we went, she met a great-nephew, a great-great-grandson, or a third cousin once removed.

The talk was nonstop from the moment the girls entered the car until I pulled up outside of the Four Feathers Casino. We had a routine that involved a drop-off at the front. They went to the restaurant while I parked the car. Regardless of the day or time, Ruby Mae's extended family always managed to rustle us a seat. When I walked into the restaurant, I realized today was no different. Despite a long line, Nana Jo and the girls were seated at a large table near the seafood buffet. There was a big man with a wide grin and a white chef's outfit and hat standing near Ruby Mae.

When I sat down, Ruby Mae beamed. "Sam, I want you to meet my grandson, Paul. He just started as the head pastry chef."

Paul and I shook hands and mumbled an appropriate greeting.

The server came over, and I recognized her as another of Ruby Mae's extended family. She brought beverages, including a Diet Coke for me, that Nana Jo must have ordered. I was definitely a creature of habit. Before we left to pile our plates, Paul promised us something special and told us to leave plenty of room for dessert.

However, no one short of a professional eater could have found room for the number of desserts that were brought out to us. Four-layer coconut cake, chocolate mousse, strawberry tarts with the flakiest crust I'd ever eaten, and shot glasses filled with custard. It was not only visually stunning but also delicious. We were stuffed but happy.

Trips to the Four Feathers had become a weekly event for us, although we usually made the trek on Tuesday nights, which was ladies' night, but occasionally we changed plans and came on other days. Our trips to the casino always started with dinner at the buffet. Even though the buffet didn't allow doggie bags, Ruby Mae's relatives always made sure we had food for later. I worked off the indulgent meals by hauling the doggie bags to the car. After dinner, we split up and went our separate ways, following our own vices. Irma didn't waste much time gambling. Her evening would be spent picking up men in one of the bars. Dorothy enjoyed playing blackjack in the high-stakes room, while Nana Jo played poker. Ruby Mae gambled less than Irma and usually spent the bulk of her time sitting near the massive fireplace at the entrance, knitting and talking to her relatives. I had never been to the casino before my husband died and I started hanging out with my grandmother. I typically spent my time playing penny slots, and then I would find a quiet corner where I could write.

I enjoyed the walk to the car with the bags and was grateful that I hadn't found a closer parking space, which added a few extra steps toward working off all the desserts I'd eaten. When I finished my errand, I still felt like my pants had shrunk, but I wasn't miserable.

Fifty dollars was my gambling limit, which can go a long way when you're playing penny slots. I took my money and found a seat at a machine I'd played before that would stop and play songs by the Beatles periodically. Unfortunately, tonight wasn't my night, and after losing half of my gambling allowance I cut bait and ran.

Rather than finding another machine, I decided writing might be more productive than gambling. The Four Feathers not only was a casino but also included a hotel and conference facility. From experience, I knew the hotel side would be quieter with less smoke. Not far from the front desk was an area I'd used before, and thankfully, it was empty.

Parked in my comfy chair, I pulled my notepad out of my bag and escaped into the British countryside.

**Wickfield Lodge, English Country Home of
Lord William Marsh
Late August 1939**

"Clara, please, you've just got to come to dinner tonight. If you don't come, it'll ruin absolutely everything."

Lady Clara Trewellan-Harper stared at her overly dramatic American friend, Kathleen Kennedy, Kick to her friends. In appearance, the two women looked very similar. Both were slender with dark hair and dark eyes. Clara wasn't vain, but she knew she was prettier than her friend. Kick wasn't stunningly beautiful, but she was bright, with a sharp mind. She had a fun, vivacious personality that drew people to her and had led to her being declared *"the debutante of 1938."* Clara couldn't put her finger on what it was, but Kick had a fun, fresh, engaging personality that made people notice her.

"Honestly, Kick, I can't understand what possible difference it could make if I'm there or not. Your father's the ambassador, and he'll have all of his political friends there. I'm sure he won't miss me at all. Besides, if Billy Cavendish is coming, which I heard he will, you'll be occupied the entire time."

Kick blushed. "That's just it. If you and your handsome policeman don't come, then the duke won't let Billy come either because we'll be the only younger people there."

"What possible difference could it make to Lord Cavendish if I attend?"

Kick pouted. "He's on to us. He knows that Billy and I are serious, and he's opposed." Kick folded her arms and paced across the study. "He doesn't want his son marrying an American, especially not a Catholic. And every time my mother thinks about me marrying outside of the Catholic faith, she bursts into tears." She turned and faced her friend. "Can you believe it? This is the twentieth century, but to listen to our parents you'd think we were still back in medieval times." She flopped down in an armchair.

"It is rather silly, but I still don't see why my coming to dinner will make any difference one way or another."

Kick sat up. "If there are other young people, then it's not like Billy and I are alone together. My family is perfectly okay with me hanging out with a group of friends."

Realization dawned on Lady Clara. "Oh, I see. All of your other friends have bailed, and if Peter and I don't come, then . . ."

Kick nodded. "Exactly. Oh, Clara, it's not that I don't want to see you. I do, but I love Billy, and our families are making things impossible."

Lady Clara sighed. "Kick, I want to help, I really do, but I've got a friend coming tonight. Marguerite and I were classmates at CLC."

"What's CLC?"

"Sometimes I forget you're American and weren't born here." She smiled. "Cheltenham Ladies' College. Margie was my closest pal. She's studying to be a barrister, and she's got a break and is coming down to spend a few days here. I can't abandon her."

"Bring her along. The more the merrier. Perhaps your policeman has a friend. Or I can ask Billy if his brother Andrew or one of his other friends can come." Kick poked out her lip, clasped her hands together, and dropped to her knees. "Please?"

Lady Clara held up her hands in surrender. "All right, I'll come, but you'll owe me one. I can't imagine a more boring evening."

Kick hopped to her feet and grabbed Lady Clara in a bear hug. "I promise tonight will be a night you'll never forget."

# Chapter 3

The alarm I set on my phone vibrated and brought me back to the present. Unless prearranged, our routine included settling up and leaving around midnight. So, I put away my notepad and headed toward the main entrance. Time flies when you're having fun.

I headed around the corner toward the hallway that led away from the hotel toward the casino. My head was probably still seventy years in the past, because I wasn't paying careful attention and nearly ran into a couple who were engaged in a very intimate and passionate moment.

"Excuse me."

"Watch where you're going," a tall man with dark hair and eyes and chiseled features said, practically spitting the words at me.

Recognition caused me to hesitate. However, I collected myself. "Sorry," I mumbled, and hurried away. I forced myself not to turn and look back.

I made it to the entrance, where I met up with the others. Another part of our casino routine involved settling up. This was something Nana Jo and the girls decided on before I started accompanying them. At the end of the night, everyone split their winnings. They said this made it more fun. Unfortunately, I only had the twenty-five dollars left from my gambling allowance, so it meant five dollars for each of us. Most of the others hadn't fared much better; however, Irma surprised us when she reached inside her bra and pulled out a wad of bills.

"I don't think I want to know what you had to do to get that money," Nana Jo said.

"I won it fair and square. I met this really nice guy in the bar. His name was Harry. Well, Harry wanted to play craps, so we went to the table. I gave him my money. He bet it for me, and I won." Irma laughed and waved her money.

"Well, I'll be jiggered," Nana Jo said.

I walked to the garage to get the car, amazed that I was leaving two hundred dollars richer than when I arrived, thanks largely to Irma.

I picked everyone up and drove them back to Shady Acres and then drove home. I pulled into the garage and was about to get out when Nana Jo stopped me.

"Okay, what's wrong?"

"What do you mean? Nothing's wrong."

She gave me that *You can't fool me* look. "Sam, if you don't want to talk about it, that's fine. But I know you, and I know something is bothering you. You barely said five words all the way from the casino. Did something happen?"

"No. Everything's fine." I didn't sound convincing. I took a deep breath. "Nothing's wrong. I promise." I told Nana Jo about what I'd seen.

"Are you sure it was him?"

"Yep. He's so Hollywood handsome that he's hard to mistake."

"You got that right." She paused. "And you're sure the woman wasn't his wife?"

"She certainly wasn't the woman we've seen on the news by his side, although I feel like I've seen her somewhere before." I thought for several moments but couldn't recall where.

"Disappointing that here's yet another bull of a politician who can't just graze in his own field." Nana Jo opened the car door. "This is the twenty-first century. You'd think they would realize that there are cell phones and cameras everywhere, especially in a casino."

"I didn't even think about that. There must be hundreds of cameras all over the casino. You'd think he would have chosen a place a bit more private."

We got out of the car, I heard barking and knew that Snickers and Oreo had convinced Dawson to take them in.

The previous owner of the building had created a loft space above my garage that I rented out. Dawson Alexander was one of my former students when I taught high school English. He was now a student at MISU and my assistant at the bookstore. A door opened at the top of the stairs, and Snickers and Oreo ran down to the garage.

We let them out to the backyard and waited while they took care of business.

I could tell by the tilt of her head and the way she bit her lower lip that Nana Jo was deep in thought. Eventually, she said, "I read up on him when he threw his hat in the race for mayor. He's part of the Pontolomas, the tribe that owns the Four Feathers. So, I'm sure he gets special privileges."

"I've heard the entire Pontoloma tribe shares the revenue from the casino. If he's a member, then he must be—"

"Privileged. Maybe he feels he can get special treatment at the Four Feathers. You know, talk to the other members and 'wink-wink. Keep my infidelity under wraps.'"

"I suppose so," I mumbled.

Snickers finished early, and Oreo finally hiked his leg at his favorite spot. We went inside.

Nana Jo turned off the alarm. "He's certainly able to afford a hotel in some isolated, out-of-the-way spot. Maybe his wife doesn't care about his . . . dalliances, but I'll bet you his opponent in the election will absolutely care."

Once we were all inside, Nana Jo reset the alarm, and we all went upstairs.

"I suppose what he does in his personal life should be personal. I mean, his wife is the only person who really has anything to say about it. If it doesn't matter to her . . ." I shrugged. "It shouldn't matter to me either. After all, the United States has had countless presidents that had affairs, and they were still able to do a good job running the country."

Nana Jo stopped and turned to face me. "You're right to a certain extent, but I think it's time we had a higher standard. It's not the fact that they are adulterers. That bothers me, but it's what committing adultery means that matters more. It's the fact that they made a vow to be faithful and then broke that vow. That's what bothers me. Your grandfather and I stood in a small church in front of God and swore to be faithful. Neither one of us were willing to violate that vow." She stopped. "Of course, your grandfather also knew that if he did violate it, I'd take my Peacemaker and make sure it was the last vow he ever did break."

I smiled. "Leon and I felt the same way. I mean, I know people change over time and marriage is hard. If the marriage isn't working, then get a divorce. I know it isn't easy, but . . . you just don't cheat."

"Right; so if John Cloverton is having an affair, which it sounds like he is, then he can't be trusted."

"If the allegations in the newspaper are true, then neither of the candidates for mayor are to be trusted. Either we vote for someone who ignores his marital vows and cheats on his wife or someone who may be misappropriating funds. Sounds like a choice between Scylla and Charybdis from Greek mythology."

"The choice between a six-headed monster and a whirlwind? Yeah, not much of a choice. I'm not sure which one is the lesser of the two evils."

"I can understand why people don't bother voting when those are your choices, but—"

"Samantha Marie Washington, you bite your tongue. Voting is a right that men and women have fought and died for so you could cast a ballot and make decisions for yourself. Regardless of the options, we are going to march down to the voting booth on election day and cast our ballots. Then we'll get involved and attend those boring council meetings so we are informed on the issues. We are also going to write petitions, make phone calls, and hold those elected officials' feet to the fire. By golly, I'm not going to stand by and allow these candidates to get away with anything other than the highest standards."

I laughed. "I was just going to say I understand why people don't want to vote, but I'm thankful that I live in a democracy where I can vote. I didn't mean to get you riled up."

"Well, I'm riled. In fact, I think I'll write a letter right now."

"Nana Jo, it's almost two o'clock in the morning. Maybe you should get some sleep first."

"It'll be stronger while my feathers are still ruffled." She marched to her bedroom.

I glanced down at Snickers and Oreo, who were watching Nana Jo with a *Who stole her biscuit?* expression.

"I think those two men are going to wish they had thought twice before running for office in North Harbor, Michigan. Nana Jo is going to eat them for breakfast."

# Chapter 4

For years, Sundays have always been time spent with my mom. The day typically starts with church service and then brunch, shopping, or whatever. Last Christmas Eve, my mom remarried, and I wondered if things would change. I didn't exactly relish these Sunday excursions, but it was yet another part of my routine—familiar. I loved my mom, but I was willing to forgo the weekly guilt-fest. *"Why don't you dress better . . . lose weight . . . visit more . . . sit up straight . . . watch your posture . . . find a cure for cancer?"* I'm only slightly joking about the cure for cancer. *"Surely, if you put your mind to it, you could do just about anything."* I loved my mom, but the extended time spent with her had the same effects as a mood-altering drug that worked in the wrong direction. Monday through Saturday, I was a happy, positive, successful business owner, soon-to-be-published writer, and somewhat confident adult. However, after hours spent with my mom, I was usually left feeling frumpy, downcast, and lazy, with the confidence of a teenage schoolgirl. When my mom married Harold Robertson, a man who adored the ground she walked on, I expected these Sunday outings to change. Harold and my mom were usually inseparable, except on Sundays. Not wanting to "take away from our time together," Harold rarely attended the early service, and allowed my mom and me to go together. My sister, Jenna, said he probably needed the break, but Harold's devotion to my mom knew no limits.

Despite my late night, I got up early, since my mom preferred the earliest church service. Most of the time, it was just me and my mom. However, I was happy when I heard Nana Jo stumbling around. It was always easier to cope with Nana Jo there as a buffer between my mom and me.

Showered and dressed, I followed the rich nutty aroma of coffee into the kitchen. Nana Jo sat on the barstool sipping coffee and reading the Sunday newspaper. She was awake, but the look on her face told me she wasn't ready for dialogue yet, which was fine with me. Without coffee, my conversation was barely fit for Snickers and Oreo.

I poured a cup of the magical elixir into my favorite mug and led a procession of poodles downstairs and outside. Snickers wasn't a morning dog either, but she did what was necessary. Oreo bounded around but finally completed his routine.

Nana Jo and I drove to pick up Mom, who had a villa in South Harbor. I was surprised when she and Harold chose to live there, given the fact that he was wealthier than King Midas and could probably have afforded one of those big McMansions that were popping up around town and blocking the Lake Michigan shoreline. Harold's family had owned Robertson's Department Store. When I was young, Robertson's was the nicest store in our area. Although I hadn't been able to afford anything beyond their Bargain Basement, it was still a treat to go inside and walk out with a shiny black bag with the Robertson's name printed in gold cursive. In our area, that bag was as special as the Tiffany blue box. Harold hadn't followed in the family business, choosing instead to study aeronautical engineering. He had spent close to half a century working at NASA. When his beloved wife was dying from cancer, he retired from NASA to care for her. After she passed, he returned to Southwestern Michigan.

Mom climbed into the back seat of the car, and we headed to church. Eight o'clock service was generally attended by the older, more conservative members of the congregation and the music was tailored accordingly. Rather than upbeat, jazzy tunes played by a full band, the early service stuck to tried and true traditional hymns. After service, Mom wanted to have brunch at a fancy downtown hotel called The Avenue.

South Harbor was referred to as the twin city to North Harbor. They were side by side and shared the same Lake Michigan shoreline. However, South Harbor and North Harbor were about as different as two cities could be. North Harbor was economically depressed, while South Harbor was a flourishing tourist town. North Harbor city government had gone bankrupt, and the school system had some of the worst standardized test scores in the state. While the South Harbor government thrived and the schools were highly sought after, North Harbor had deserted, burned-out buildings with empty holes where glass windows once stood. South Harbor had quaint brick brownstones on cobblestoned streets lined by fudge and ice-cream shops and stores selling shell necklaces, gaudy lighthouse miniatures, and other trinkets for tourists. In much the same way, my mom and Nana Jo were related opposites. Nana Jo was tall, tough, and sturdy, while my mother, Grace, was petite and dainty. At barely five feet tall and less than one hundred pounds, my mom bore little physical resemblance to her mother. Nana Jo, on the one hand, had been raised on a farm and learned to farm, shoot, and utilize the healing power of plants; she was resourceful. My mom, on the other hand, had what my sister, Jenna, called a princess complex. As Nana Jo's only child, she was spoiled by her father and coddled and protected by mine. Now she was remarried to yet another man who was perfectly content with catering to her every whim. The physical differences were vast, but lately I'd noticed that my mom had an inner strength that, when called upon, showed maybe she had inherited a lot more of Nana Jo's spunk than I'd realized.

The Avenue sat atop the bluffs and looked out over Lake Michigan. At one time, The Avenue had been the grandest hotel for miles. However, like a Monet painting, appearances can be deceptive. From a distance, the hotel still presented a grand and impressive façade, but when you looked closely its image of elegance and wealth blurred. Despite these shortfalls, the grand staircase that greeted guests at the entry was still quite impressive.

"Grace, you're unusually quiet," Nana Jo said. "Are you okay?"

"Of course. I'm just thinking."

Nana Jo and I exchanged looks. My mom wasn't exactly a profound thinker, preferring instead to leave the heavy work to someone else. However, if she had something on her mind, we'd find out about it soon enough.

I pulled up to the front and allowed Nana Jo and Mom to get out, and then I drove around the side of the building and parked before joining them inside. I found a parking space next to a black Mercedes that looked like my sister Jenna's car, but I pushed the idea out of my mind. I wasn't a fan of eight o'clock service, but my sister, Jenna, was vehemently opposed to anything that required her to get up on her weekends at the same time that she had to be up on weekdays.

Upon entering the building from the front, I arrived at a large landing. The stairs leading up went to the lobby and reception desks. To the left and right, the wide curved marble staircase led down to the dining room.

Since both staircases led to the same place, I turned left and headed down. At the bottom of the stairs there was a large crowd of people waiting for brunch. I muscled my way to the host station, but before I could give her my name and ask how long the wait would be I heard my name.

I turned toward the voice and wasn't surprised when I caught sight of Harold standing at a large round table and waving for me to come over.

Mom was already seated in the most comfortable chair with the best view. When I saw my sister, her husband, and their two kids, I knew Mom's thinking earlier must have been pretty serious if she'd managed to convince Jenna out for breakfast.

"Hi, Harold. I didn't know we were having a party."

"Just family." Harold helped me remove my jacket and handed it to a waiter who hovered nearby.

I waved good morning to my brother-in-law, Tony Rutherford, and hugged my nephews, Christopher and Zaq, before taking a seat between Nana Jo and Jenna. I leaned toward my sister and whispered, "What's going on?"

Nana Jo and I weren't morning people, but Jenna was in a completely different league. My sister shot me a look that would have silenced a lesser mortal or someone who hadn't spent their formative years learning to counter the Frost Queen.

I stuck out my tongue, crossed my eyes, and made the silliest face I could muster.

For nearly a minute, my sister held her frosty stare; Princess Elsa had nothing on my sister. However, when I poked out my lip, her eyes softened and the corners of her mouth twitched.

"You'd better stop or your face will get stuck like that." She took a sip of tea to hide her smile, but everyone could feel the temperature of the room had just increased significantly.

I uncrossed my eyes and relaxed my facial muscles. "You might be right." I massaged my cheeks. "That hurt."

The waiters wore red livery with gold braids and black pants, and this one appeared to be about thirteen, with flaming red hair, freckles, and a look of pain in his eyes. He reminded me of Opie from *The Andy Griffith Show*. He stood very straight and looked so serious it was almost laughable.

I leaned close to my sister. "What's this about?"

Jenna shrugged. "I have no idea. I got a call saying our presence was requested."

Harold didn't keep us in suspense long. Opie and a slightly older waiter, who reminded me of Eddie Haskell from *Leave It to Beaver*, took our orders. Once the orders were placed, Harold stood up.

"Ladies and gentlemen." He smiled at each of us. "Grace and I are so pleased to have our family here."

Mom sniffed, and Harold handed her a handkerchief. He took a few moments to make sure she was okay before he continued. "We've asked all of you here to tell you that after long and careful consideration . . ." He babbled on about how concerned and sensitive Mom was.

Nana Jo leaned toward me. "Is he still talking about Grace?"

I shrugged.

"I think he's drunk," she said, glancing around. "And I'm going to need a drink if I've got to sit here and listen to any more of this love-sick drivel. All this syrup is making my blood sugar rise."

We listened quietly as Harold extolled Mom's virtues and Nana Jo tried to get our waiter's attention. Eventually, she caught his eye and beckoned him over.

Opie hurried to the table, and Nana Jo ordered a whiskey.

"I'm sorry, but we can't serve hard liquor this early on a Sunday," Opie said.

"No worries. Bring me a deconstructed Bloody Mary." Nana Jo smiled. "I'll put it together myself."

Opie left to get Nana Jo's drink.

Harold droned on.

"What's he talking about?" I asked Jenna.

"I have no idea, but order me whatever Nana Jo just got. I'm going to need something stronger than this tea."

The Eddie Haskell waiter hovered too close to the table, and Nana Jo tried to grab his coattail but missed. He yelped and turned beet red.

The twins lost control. Christopher tried to swallow a laugh and nearly choked. Zaq spat out his orange juice.

Harold didn't seem to notice the commotion. He merely took a long, loving look at Mom and then announced, "We'll be leaving for Australia on Sunday."

"Australia?"

"Wait, what?" I looked from Harold to my mom. "Where did this come from?"

Mom gave me a look that shouted, *I knew you weren't listening*. "Yes, dear. That's what Harold has been explaining. We're going to save the koala bears."

I felt like I'd just been pranked. "Koala bears?"

Opie returned with a tray of tomato juice and another glass with a clear liquid that could only have been the vodka, along with a small dish of olives.

Nana Jo tossed back the vodka. "I'm going to need another of these."

"Best make it a pitcher," I said.

Opie turned to leave, but Nana Jo stopped him. "Skip the tomato juice this time. We've got plenty."

Opie hurried away, making sure to leave a wide berth between him and Nana Jo.

Mom frowned. "Samantha, isn't it a bit early to be drinking?"

I guzzled down the mimosa I'd ordered. "Nope. Actually, I think I should have started sooner."

Nana Jo squinted at Harold. "Let me get this straight. You

and Grace are planning to chuck everything and move to Australia to save the . . ."

"Koala bears," I said.

Harold held up a hand to ward off Nana Jo's questions. "Now, Josephine, I'm sure you're concerned about your baby, but I can assure you—"

"Baby?" Jenna whispered. "Mom is in her sixties."

Harold continued. "We aren't really chucking everything. We're going to keep Grace's villa, for now. We'll need a place to crash when we come back for a visit, and don't you worry, there will be plenty of those."

"Oh, goody," Jenna mumbled.

"We're thinking about buying a little place on the ocean."

"Ocean?" I said. "What ocean? We live on Lake Michigan."

Jenna nudged me. "He's talking about Australia."

"Well, it started as a little bungalow," Harold said, "but then Grace wanted to make sure we had plenty of room for all of you to visit, so by the time we finished . . ." He smiled at Mom "We ended up with a pretty big place."

"It's got eight bedrooms," Mom said, "and it's right on the beach, so there will be plenty of things to do when you all come over to visit." She turned to Harold. "Show them the pictures."

Harold pulled out his cell phone, made a few swipes, and then slid it across the table.

Since I was between the two biggest stakeholders, I picked it up while Nana Jo and Jenna leaned close. Tony and the twins stood behind us, and we all crowded together to look at the pictures together.

"You've already bought a house?" Jenna asked.

Harold nodded. "Wired the money to Sydney on Friday."

I swiped the pictures of a massive beach estate that included a wine cellar, a boat dock, and the most amazing views ever. When we'd gone through the pictures several times, I slid the phone back to Harold.

He reached in his pocket and pulled out a paper. "Before we leave, I wanted to get one of these attorneys to help with a few legal things."

Both Jenna and her husband were attorneys. Jenna was a criminal defense attorney, while Tony practiced corporate law in the nearby town of River Bend, Indiana.

"Oh, God," Jenna said, and she reached over and gulped down the mimosa Opie had just placed on the table to replace the one I'd finished.

"We want to get our wills drawn up properly," Harold said. He held up a hand. "Not that either one of us intends that anything will happen, mind you, but we want to make sure all the t's are crossed and the i's are dotted anyway."

Nana Jo turned to Opie. "Better keep them coming."

"First, we want to set up a trust for the boys." He gazed lovingly at my mother. "I'd like to call it the Grace Robertson Family Trust."

"Oh, Harold," Mom gushed.

He smiled. "I put a million dollars for each of the twins to cover graduate school, if they decide they want to attend, and to help them get started in life."

Christopher's eyes were as big as half-dollars. "A million . . . *dollars*?"

"Each?" Zaq squeaked.

Harold smiled and nodded.

Both of the twins nearly leaped out of their seats. Christopher got up so quickly he knocked over his chair. They both ran over and hugged Harold and Mom.

Christopher and Zaq were twenty-one. Tall and thin, like their dad, they were identical twins, but each had their own unique personality, which made them easy to tell apart. Christopher was into business and marketing and tended toward an ultraconservative look. Zaq was a technology geek with an eclectic style who embraced his inner nerd. So, while Christopher looked immaculate in khakis, a button-down shirt, and a tie, Zaq wore jeans with red Converse All-Stars and a T-shirt that read:

*01000111*
*01100101*
*01100101*
*01101011*
*If you can read that, you are too*

"What's Zaq's shirt say?" I asked.

"It's binary code for 'geek,'" Nana Jo said.

I gazed at my grandmother with admiration, but she shook her head. "Don't be too impressed. I asked him."

Both Christopher and Zaq towered over Mom and Harold, but my nephews embraced their grandparents with tenderness and affection. It brought a tear to my eye.

When the boys sat down, Jenna and Tony thanked both Grace and Harold.

Harold cleared his throat and gazed at me. "I know Dawson couldn't make it today, but I haven't forgotten him. I have a million dollars for him too. Although we all know he's going to be a hugely successful professional football player, maybe one day when he is ready to start that bakery he'll have a nest egg."

Now it was my turn to get choked up. Leon and I never had children of our own, but Dawson Alexander was probably the closest thing I had. I hugged Harold and my mom. I knew it was all Harold's money, but it was his love for my mom that made this happen.

Nana Jo wiped away a tear. "That boy has had a rough life. I'm glad he's getting a break."

I thought Harold was done, but he had more. "Lastly, I have to say that I will never forget what you all did to help me in my time of need." He had to swallow and take several deep breaths before he was composed enough to continue. "When the police believed I'd killed that woman . . . you all came to my aid, and I want to pay it forward. So, I'd like to set up a sleuthing fund to be run by the Sleuthing Seniors."

The Sleuthing Seniors was the book club that Nana Jo and the girls established when I opened my bookshop. "What's a sleuthing fund?" I asked.

"I'm going to set aside five million dollars that can be used to help support the Sleuthing Seniors in the pursuit of justice. I certainly don't want to dictate how you spend the money, but I'm sure you may need to hire additional staff to help out at the bookshop once the twins leave for graduate school and Dawson leaves for the NFL. Or if you have to pay for a private investigator or, well, any expenses." He glanced at Jenna. "Plus, Grace tells me that Jenna has wanted to set up her own practice. Good lawyers don't come cheap, and Jenna wouldn't accept payment from me even though she worked so hard on my case, but I hope this fund could be used to help pay for the best legal defense in Southwestern Michigan."

For the first time in my life, my sister was stunned silent. Eventually, she stood, walked around the table, and hugged Harold and Mom. "I'd be honored."

The rest of the meal consisted of eating, celebrating, and planning for the future. Between the Bloody Marys, mimosas, and excitement, we were all pretty giddy. When we noticed the line for tables expand, we hurried to finish up.

Harold refused to allow us to pay. He didn't even look at the tab before giving his credit card to Opie. After he signed, he pulled a few bills out of his wallet and stuck them in the leather pouch for our waiters. After a few moments, a wide-eyed Opie returned, trailed by the Eddie Haskell look-alike.

"Sir, did you intend to leave this?" Opie held up two crisp one-hundred-dollar bills.

Harold nodded.

Opie grinned and pumped Harold's hand. "Thank you. Thank you so much."

Eddie was so overcome with emotion, he actually hugged Harold, but then he immediately pulled away. "I'm sorry."

Harold laughed. "No problem. You two were excellent waiters, and we appreciate all that you did to make our meal so enjoyable."

I stood up. "I'd better go get the car."

Everyone started to make their way toward the stairs.

Nana Jo was walking slightly ahead of me. She stopped abruptly, and I bumped into her. "Sam, isn't that Mayor Carpenter?"

I followed her gaze over to a table in a corner near the back of the dining area. Mayor Carpenter was a short, fat bald man with a large mole on the side of his head. He was leaning across the table whispering with a man I recognized as the chief of police.

"That sure looks like the mayor in deep conversation with the chief of police."

Jenna walked up and whispered, "Is that Stinky Pitt standing over by the kitchen door?"

I glanced over in the direction she indicated and sure enough, there stood Detective Bradley Pitt of the North Harbor Police Department. Detective Pitt, short, fat, and balding with a bad comb-over, stood near the door with his hands folded in front of him. He wore mirrored glasses, and an earbud for a cell phone hung from his ear.

"What's he supposed to be?" Jenna asked.

"I think he's security. You know, like when the Secret Service is protecting the president."

Nana Jo frowned. "The Secret Service try to blend into

the environment. Stinky Pitt stands out like a prostitute at a Baptist camp meeting. And with all of that polyester, I would think it would be a fire hazard to have him standing so close to the kitchen."

Detective Pitt's wardrobe did tend to draw attention to himself. He was fond of polyester, and today he had on white polyester pants that were too tight and too short, exposing bright orange socks. He wore a polyester shirt with huge tropical flowers that stretched across his chest, straining the buttons that looked ready to pop.

Chief Zachary Davis was medium height with a medium build. The most distinct thing about Chief Davis was his large head of thick dark hair, which looked like a mop, and a thick dark mustache that sat like a spider under his nose and covered his mouth.

"Five dollars says they're plotting how to deal with the negative media attention. I'll bet—"

I never got to find out what Nana Jo was betting because John Cloverton, followed by a reporter I recognized from the local news and a man with a video camera, burst through the door. The news crew followed Cloverton downstairs and filmed him as he pushed his way to the back of the restaurant.

Mayor Carpenter held up a menu to block his face, while Chief Davis stood and used his body to shield the mayor from the camera and the reporter.

Cloverton faced the camera and hurled accusations at the mayor faster than a major-league pitcher firing a fastball. "Why are you hiding in a corner of the restaurant? Why won't you talk to your constituents? The people want to know how their tax dollars are being spent."

Detective Pitt rushed from his post near the kitchen and shoved Cloverton backward.

Cloverton stumbled before tripping and falling to the floor.

Stinky Pitt fumed. "You get out of here or so help me God I'll—"

"Or you'll what?" Cloverton shouted. "The people have a right to know. Are you threatening me?"

I didn't think Detective Pitt's face could have gotten redder, but it did. It turned from red to purple, and the vein on the side of his head pulsed. He looked ready to explode. He took one step forward and looked as though he intended to pummel Cloverton, but Chief Davis grabbed his arm and pulled him back.

From the floor, Cloverton continued his verbal barrage. He taunted and baited the detective, although his taunts changed and became less political and more personal. Stinky Pitt fell hook, line, and sinker.

"Want to pretend you're a big man, hiding behind your boss," Cloverton said. "But we both know the truth, don't we?" He smirked and then whispered something that was intended for Detective Pitt only.

Like a bull preparing to charge, Stinky Pitt shoved the chief of police aside, leaned forward, grabbed Cloverton by his lapels, and pulled him to his feet. Then he hauled back and landed a quick punch to the gut and followed it with a left cross that dropped the would-be politician like a sack of potatoes.

Chief Davis grabbed Detective Pitt and pushed him back against the wall.

The commotion generated a crowd, and the hotel management and security forced their way toward the front. The manager spent a minute checking on Cloverton, who now had a bloody lip and a bruise that indicated a black eye within twenty-four hours.

Cloverton waved away the manager's assistance and got to his feet. He turned to the cameraman. "Did you get that? I hope so because I intend to sue." He turned to face the diners who stood in shocked amazement. "You're all witnesses to the police brutality that I just endured."

The manager and the hotel security escorted Cloverton and the reporters out. Once the reporters were gone, one of the managers led the mayor through a back passage. Chief Davis gave Stinky Pitt a look that would have wilted lettuce before following the mayor's path.

Stinky Pitt stood against the wall a moment before tucking his head and walking out.

"I wouldn't have thought Stinky Pitt had it in him," Nana Jo said. "That was a pretty darned good left hook."

I wouldn't have thought Detective Pitt had it in him either. I wondered what Cloverton could have said that sent him into such a rage.

Nana Jo interrupted my wonderings. "Hey, you gonna get the car?"

"Sure." I headed outside.

At the side of the building, Cloverton had just finished an interview, and based on his smile, he was extremely pleased with himself. As the reporters packed up their gear and loaded their van, I saw Cloverton giving a high five to the woman who I believed was his wife. She was definitely *not* the woman I saw him fondling at the casino just a few hours ago.

# Chapter 5

I was excited to see that Dawson was back from football practice when Nana Jo and I got home. As soon as I opened the door, I was greeted by the smell of cinnamon, apples, and spices. The delicious aroma drew us upstairs like a dog on a leash.

We found Dawson in the kitchen baking, while Snickers and Oreo scoured the floor for crumbs.

Dawson Alexander was tall and skinny, although he had been instructed to "bulk up" by his coach, so he'd put on some weight since he'd started playing football for the MISU Tigers at Michigan Southwest University. He was an excellent quarterback and had a promising career ahead.

Nana Jo took a big whiff. "Hmmm, that smells wonderful."

Dawson frowned. "I've been trying my hand at these apple pie tartlets I found in a recipe book, but my crust isn't flaky enough."

"Why don't you let me be the judge of that." Nana Jo popped one of the tartlets in her mouth and moaned.

"Sounds like Nana Jo approves," I joked.

"Delicious." She covered her mouth and chewed. "The only thing missing is a cup of coffee to wash it down. Why don't I make that while you have a seat? Sam has something to tell you."

"Okay." He gave me a sideways glance but put a plate of tartlets on the dining room table and took a seat.

Shocked doesn't even begin to scratch the surface of the look Dawson gave me when I told him about the trust. He stared at me with his mouth open for nearly a minute. Eventually, a tear ran down his face, and he placed his head on my shoulder and cried. I held him for several moments while we both sat and cried. He didn't have to speak for me to understand the emotions. Dawson's mother had died when he was a kid, leaving him to be raised by a father who abused not only alcohol but also his son. Football provided Dawson with an opportunity to break away. He was getting not only a great education but also a future. When the tears slowed, he sat up.

Nana Jo handed us paper towels, and all three of us wiped our faces.

"I can't believe it. I mean . . . I can understand the trust for Christopher and Zaq. They're family, but I'm just—"

"You're as much a part of our family as Christopher and Zaq, and don't you forget it." I blew my nose.

"That's right," Nana Jo said. "Now, what are you going to do with all of that money?"

Dawson shook his head, but there was something in his eyes that looked like fear.

"You do want the money . . . don't you?" I asked.

"Are you joking? Who wouldn't want a million dollars? It's just . . . I wouldn't have to tell anyone about the trust, would I?"

"You'll probably have to tell the university, but I'll be happy to go with you. Or we can have Jenna go as your attorney. Since your scholarship is for football, I don't think it will impact that. You'll still get to play if that's what you're worried about." I stared hard to understand where his hesitancy was coming from.

"I'm not worried about football or the university." He lowered his eyes. "I was thinking about my dad. He won't have to find out, will he?"

"I don't know. You're still a minor, so I'm not sure how that will work. We can ask Jenna tomorrow."

"It's not that I wouldn't want to help my dad, but . . . if he found out I had that kind of money, he'd just figure out a way to get his hands on it, and then . . . he'd just get in more trouble." He hung his head.

I glanced at Nana Jo, who patted him on the back. "I'm sure Jenna can make sure that the money is tied up so your dad can't possibly get his hands on it. You just leave it to us."

Dawson took a deep breath. "Wow. I can't believe it."

I could see the wheels turning inside his head. "You have an idea. I can see it on your face. Spill it. You planning to buy a fancy sports car or a big house on Lake Michigan?"

"Actually, I was thinking it would be nice if I could create some type of scholarship for other kids . . . you know, like me. Kids who want to do something with their lives, but maybe they aren't too smart."

"What do you mean, kids like you?" Nana Jo gave him a swipe. "You're very smart. Last time I looked you had a B average."

"Sure, I have a B average *now*, thanks to you and Mrs. W. tutoring me. If it hadn't been for the two of you, I would have flunked out of school after my freshman year and ended up losing my scholarship."

"Sam and I simply helped explain things. You did the hard work yourself. You took the tests. You wrote the papers, and *you* brought your GPA up to where it is."

"You should be proud of yourself," I said, patting his hand. "I know we are."

"I am proud, but every kid isn't going to break into your building and hide out in your bathroom. Man, I can't imagine what would have happened if you had called the police." He glanced down at Snickers, who had wormed her way into his lap and was lying on her back while he scratched her belly. "Or let this little beast rip me to shreds like she wanted to when you found me."

"Actually, I think it was Oreo who tried to rip your pants clean off your body." I laughed. "You were hungry and scared and . . ." I got choked up remembering the bruises and scars on his body that his father had given him.

"So, you fed me, patched me up, gave me a place to stay, and tutored me so I could stay in school. And, when the police thought I'd murdered my ex-girlfriend, you protected me, got Mrs. Rutherford to represent me, and tracked down the real killer. I owe you so much." He looked at me and Nana Jo. "All of you."

"Fiddlesticks," Nan Jo said. "That's what families do." I could tell by the husky tone in her voice that she was feeling emotional.

"Nana Jo's right. That's what families do. They look out for each other, and you're part of our family." I reached over and squeezed his arm. "Now, before I ruin what's left of my makeup, what were you thinking you'd like to do with your trust?"

"I want to set up some type of scholarship. Maybe there's a kid who needs to get out of a bad situation. . . . I want to use this money to help. Do you think Mrs. Rutherford could help me set up something like that?"

"I'm sure she can. We'll ask first thing tomorrow, but are you sure you don't want to buy a new car?"

He shook his head. "Nah, I have my old beater. That's good enough for running from here to the college. If I'm fortunate enough to get drafted, then hopefully I can earn the money to buy a car. But . . . I know that I can't play ball forever. Lots of football players get hurt. One day, when I can't play ball anymore, I'd like to go to cooking school. I'd like to make the flakiest crusts in North America." He grinned.

I took an apple tartlet from the plate and ate it. The crust was flaky and buttery and everything a crust should be. The apples, cinnamon, and spices were perfectly balanced and gave me a warm feeling inside. "I think your crusts are pretty darned good right now. Although I do think there's something . . ."

He glanced at me expectantly, with a slight look of disappointment in his eyes.

I snapped my fingers. "Ice cream."

"I think I can fix that." He grinned, stood up, and headed for the freezer.

Just as we sat down to eat, my phone rang. I glanced at the face on the screen and smiled. "It's Lexi and Angelo."

Lexi and Angelo Gelano were two orphans we'd met a few months ago when they ran away from an abusive foster home in Chicago. They'd made it as far as North Harbor when Frank found them asleep in the back of his restaurant. Frank Patterson's connections with the government were able to track down their relatives in Italy who had been searching for the children ever since they'd received word of their parents' deaths.

I grinned and waved frantically at the screen. "Buongiorno."

Angelo giggled. "It's afternoon, not morning, silly. You mean *buon pomeriggio*, not *buongiorno*." Angelo was a vivacious four-year-old with blond curly hair.

His older sister, Lexi, gave him a shove. "Angelo, you're the one being silly." She was twelve going on twenty-five and had long dark hair. Both were nicely tanned and looked happy.

Dawson and Nana Jo crowded around my phone, and we all spent five minutes talking, laughing, and getting caught up. Lexi and Angelo had moved to Italy to stay with their grandparents, and they both looked happy. They were surrounded by family who loved them and I was glad, but I still missed them. I was thankful they were allowed to call us on Sundays so we could stay in touch.

Five minutes went by way too fast. Before I knew it, our time was up and we were saying our good-byes. Once their faces were gone, I felt sad. Dawson, Nana Jo, and I talked for a while longer, and then Dawson said he had better get started on his homework. Nana Jo said she was going to finish a thriller, *Without Sanction* by Don Bentley. I went to my bedroom and decided to spend a little time in the English countryside.

Lady Clara walked out onto the balcony and stood for a moment staring at the tall, thin figure of Detective Peter Covington of the Metropolitan Police force, better known as Scotland Yard. He must have felt her eyes on him because he turned.

"I was just getting some fresh air."

She moved next to him. "I'm sorry for dragging you here. I knew it would be horrible, but when Kick asked . . . I just couldn't say no."

Detective Covington shook his head. "I just can't stand all that defeatist talk. England won the Great

War, and as far as I'm concerned, we're still the greatest nation on the sea or in the air, but to listen to those . . . those . . . politicians, England might as well roll over and hand Hitler the keys to Buckingham Palace without even trying."

She rubbed his arm. "I know."

"You'd think the ambassador and Lady Astor would want to fight. I mean, they're Americans. I thought they were supposed to be about independence and freedom, but to listen to them talk, England doesn't stand a chance." He paced across the small balcony. "And Ribbentrop is so arrogant. Did you hear him talking about how superior their Aryan soldiers are? Well, I for one don't intend to let England go down without a fight. I intend to—"

Lady Clara gasped.

He stopped pacing and stared at her. "Darling, I'm sorry. I didn't mean to spring it on you like this." He pulled her into his arms.

"I knew. I knew as soon as the Military Training Act passed Parliament that you would sign up for your six months of military training. I just hoped we'd have more time."

"You're shivering." He took off his tuxedo jacket and draped it around her shoulders and pulled her close. "Perhaps we should go back—"

"I'm not cold. I'm just . . . afraid. I don't know what I'd do if something happened. If you—"

The detective clasped Clara in his arms and kissed her. He pulled away and gazed into her eyes.

He was just about to speak when someone stepped outside.

"Oh, I'm sorry." Marguerite turned to head back inside.

"No, please. We were just . . . getting a breath of air."

Marguerite Evans was a strong, sturdy farm girl with soft brown eyes and thick red hair. "I believe the men are looking for you. They said something about port and wanting to play billiards."

Clara handed him his jacket. "You'd better go. We'll be in shortly."

His eyes spoke volumes before he turned, nodded to Marguerite, and went inside.

Lady Clara took several steps forward to go inside, but she was stopped when Marguerite grabbed her arm.

"Clara, I need to talk to you."

"Of course. I'm sorry about all of this." She waved at the house. "It's just that Kick sounded so desperate, and she needed young people or her father wouldn't let her come."

Marguerite shook her head. "That's all right. I don't mind. In fact, if it weren't for those . . ."

Lady Clara smiled. "Politicians."

"If that's a sampling of the type of people running the country, then it's a wonder the British Empire has survived as long as it has." She crossed her arms and paced.

Lady Clara noted how similar her friend was to Peter, who had paced and said virtually the same things just moments ago.

Marguerite ranted for several minutes. Once her wrath was abated, she turned to her friend. "I'm sorry. I didn't mean to get so worked up, but hearing all of that hogwash just makes my blood boil."

"It's perfectly understandable." She gave her friend a shy glance. "Although I'd hoped that maybe something . . . or someone else might make your blood boil."

Marguerite laughed. "Your detective's friend, Ollie, is nice."

"Nice? Puppies are nice. I think he looks like Errol Flynn."

"He's certainly handsome, but I don't have time for romance . . . not right now, anyway."

"What are you talking about?"

Marguerite glanced around to make sure no one was watching; then she pulled her friend close. "I shouldn't be telling you this, but I have to tell someone." Marguerite's normally jovial face was serious.

"Tell me what?"

"First, you have to promise not to tell anyone." She gave her friend a hard stare.

"I promise."

Marguerite took a moment and then made up her mind. "You know, I've always been really good at languages."

Lady Clara nodded. "Top of our class."

"I've been recruited to help with some important, top-secret things. I don't know all of the details, but I'm going to be working for the government."

"What are you going to be doing? I mean, there isn't a war."

"Not yet, but when it comes, and it will, England needs to be ready, and I'm going to help."

"How?"

"Mostly translating documents, but it could involve more dangerous work if things don't go well. I was contacted by some people from a secret agency, and they interviewed me and several other girls.

They said we could help our nation, but it could be dangerous."

"Dangerous? How?"

"I couldn't tell you all of the details, even if I knew them. I've been sworn to secrecy. In fact, I shouldn't be telling you anything. I can't even tell my parents, and . . . if I ended up leaving England, no one would know. I just couldn't go away without anyone knowing. I can take whatever they did to me . . . at least, I hope that my courage will hold up. However, there's just something about the thought of dying in a foreign country and no one knowing where I was that I couldn't take. I lie awake at night thinking about it until I feel like I'm going mad. That's when I realized I had to tell someone. I needed someone who knows me to know. That's when I thought of you." She stared at Clara. "You understand, don't you?"

"Yes, I understand."

Marguerite released a breath, and her shoulders relaxed. "Somehow, I knew you'd understand. I think I can endure anything now."

Lady Clara hugged her friend. She felt the tears sting the backs of her eyes and tried to swallow the lump that rose in her throat. She blinked away the tears and forced down the lump that threatened to choke her, but no amount of blinking or swallowing could erase the feeling of doom and the dark cloud that settled over her.

# Chapter 6

Monday morning, I woke up feeling energetic despite my late-night writing. Once I had showered and dressed, I took Snickers and Oreo downstairs. I had a missed message from Frank and smiled as I opened it. He was letting me know he made my favorite soup and would have it waiting for me.

Frank owned a café down the street from my bookstore. He was an excellent cook and I loved eating, so we were a perfect match.

When the poodles were finished, we went back upstairs.

Nana Jo was sitting at the breakfast bar drinking coffee and reading the *River Bend Tribune*. North Harbor was so small that the local newspaper, the *North Harbor Herald*, only came out on weekends. Anyone wanting the news on weekdays bought papers from River Bend, Kalamazoo, or Chicago. River Bend capitalized on this by including a section called "Michiana News," which included news from North and South Harbor.

"You seem engrossed," I said.

"They have an article about the spectacle at The Avenue." She pointed to the article, and I read over her shoulder.

"Poor Stinky Pitt."

She gave me a look that said, *You must be joking.* "Poor Stinky Pitt my . . . big toe."

The article stated the facts and the facts didn't show any of the public officials in the best light, but Stinky Pitt looked exceptionally bad, especially in the picture of him standing over John Cloverton.

"That picture reminds me of Muhammad Ali standing over an opponent he'd just knocked out." Nana Jo took her cup to the sink and stretched. "Don't forget our class starts tonight."

I must have looked as confused as I felt, because she added, "Don't tell me you forgot already?"

Still, no bells rang. I sipped my coffee hoping the caffeine would ignite my memory, but I must not have been fully caffeinated, because nothing came.

"Social Media for the Novice."

*Clang. Clang. Clang.* The bells sounded in my head. I tried to play off my memory lapse. "I didn't forget."

"Sure, you didn't forget, and pigs can fly."

"I remembered I signed up for the class; I just didn't know it was tonight."

"Well, it starts at six thirty. It's a good thing I thought to ask Dawson to cover so we could go."

"Thank you."

We went downstairs and got things ready. The business was steady, and we stayed busy until noon, when Nana Jo told me she was hungry enough to start gnawing on her arm. That's when I left to go to North Harbor Café to pick up lunch.

I walked down the street with a smile on my face and a spring in my step. Monday is the busiest day at North Harbor Café and I know Frank needs to focus on his business, so I try not to bother him . . . well, not much.

Today was no exception. The restaurant was as crowded as ever. Every table was filled, and a large crowd stood near the hostess station waiting for seats. As usual, Frank was behind the bar filling drink orders.

I pushed my way through the crowd.

The hostess looked up, recognized me, and smiled. "Hello, Mrs. Washington." She glanced at the bar. "I'm afraid there aren't any seats, but if you want to go over, I'll find one from the back—"

I waved her away. "Thanks, Mary, but I won't be long. Please don't bother. I don't mind standing." I walked over to the edge of the bar.

Frank was at the other end, but when he saw me he smiled. Frank Patterson was in his forties. He cut his salt-and-pepper hair in a way that screamed former military. He had soft brown eyes and a lovely smile.

I leaned against the edge of the bar. I didn't have long to wait. Frank came down, stopping long enough to take a pitcher of lemon water from the freezer and getting a glass. He poured my glass and set it in front of me before he leaned close. "Hello, beautiful."

I could feel the heat rise up my neck and grinned. "Hello, handsome."

He glanced around as though unsure who I was referring to but then leaned across and gave me a quick kiss.

I took a deep breath and inhaled. Frank always smelled of an herbal Irish soap, red wine, coffee, and bacon.

He chuckled. "You only love me because I smell like bacon."

"Not true. I also love you because you make the best corn chowder soup I've ever eaten."

He smiled. "I'll take whatever I can get."

Before he left, I ordered a sandwich for Nana Jo, and he hurried to the back.

I didn't have long to wait before he returned with a box of food.

Normally, we would spend a few minutes flirting, but he was busy, so we made our good-byes short.

"Dinner tonight?"

"Oh, I'm sorry. I can't. I signed up for a class on social media. How about tomorrow?"

"I suppose I can wait one more day, although . . . there is a charge for canceling reservations at the last minute."

"Add it to my tab." I gave him one last smile before I left.

Nana Jo and I took turns eating lunch, and the rest of the afternoon went by quickly. Dawson got back around five. He brought his girlfriend, Jillian Clark, and her roommate, Emma Lee. Both were students at MISU, and Emma and my nephew Zaq had become quite the item.

"Hi, Mrs. Washington." The girls dropped their bookbags on the counter and immediately started helping check out customers.

At five feet tall and barely one hundred pounds, Emma Lee had long dark hair that she wore pulled back into a pony-tail. She had dark, almond-shaped eyes and a southern drawl that made you smile.

My eyes expressed the question that I didn't want to voice.

She read my look perfectly. "Nothing yet, and the waiting is driving me to eat. I've gained five pounds in two months. I've been stress eating like a sumo wrestler."

Jillian and I exchanged looks that Emma intercepted.

"Don't start on how you can't see the weight gain, because I can definitely feel the extra pounds when I try to zip my pants. Just because I'm not five hundred pounds doesn't mean my struggle isn't real." She took a bite of a sugar cookie.

"Your MCAT scores were amazing," I said, trying to re-assure her.

Jillian folded her arms over her chest. "Plus, you've gotten acceptance letters from five different medical schools, any one of which most students would sell a kidney to get admitted to."

Emma blushed. "I know, but I really, really want to go to Columbia or Northwestern. Those are my first choices. They have amazing pediatrics programs, and . . . I just really want to get accepted."

Jillian hugged her friend. "I know you do, and I'm confident that you will get accepted. They'd be fools not to accept you."

The two friends pulled apart. I glanced around to make sure Dawson wasn't within earshot before I asked Jillian, "What about you?"

Jillian's eyes got bigger. "I'm so nervous. My audition is Wednesday, and every time I think about it, I get a horrible feeling in the pit of my stomach and want to throw up."

Both Emma and Jillian were extremely talented. Emma was a straight-A student and destined to be a leader in the medical profession. Jillian was an amazing singer, dancer, and actress. She was preparing for an audition with the Bolshoi Ballet Academy's summer program. It was highly competitive. She was a star at MISU, but she'd have to compete against dancers from all over the country. If she was accepted, she'd spend six weeks in New York City getting trained by teachers from the prestigious Bolshoi academy. There was also a chance at earning a scholarship for further training in Moscow.

"I have nightmares about it and wake up in a sweat. They're going to think I'm too old."

"You're only twenty years old." I knew this was important to her, so I forced myself not to laugh at the idea of twenty as old.

"You don't understand. I'll be competing against much

younger dancers for that scholarship. They only take a small number of girls every year."

"I'm sure you'll do just fine." I squeezed her and searched my brain for something even remotely helpful. Life had created so many calluses that I struggled to remember what it felt like to be so young and tender, where I felt like the entire world balanced on whether I passed a test, got invited to the big dance, or kissed *the boy*. "When I was teaching high school, I took the class "Seven Habits of Highly Effective People" by Stephen R. Covey. It was one of the best classes I've ever taken, and it completely changed my life."

She looked at me. "How?"

"Well, I guess I was in a place where I was ready for a change, but one of the activities you do in the class is to write a personal mission statement."

"A mission statement like companies have on their website?" Emma asked.

"Yep, but this was a mission statement we wrote for our lives. 'Why are we here? What do you want to accomplish?' That was more than fifteen years ago, and I still remember my mission statement."

Jillian hesitated but finally asked. "Would you share it?"

"It's short, just six words. 'Live well. Enjoy life. No regrets.'" I stared from Emma to Jillian. "Life is short, and the older I get the more I realize that there are so many things that are outside of our control. You've practiced and practiced. Go to the audition and give it your best. That's all you can do. After that, it's up to the judges, but at least you'll know that you've given it your best shot. No regrets."

She thought for a few minutes. "No regrets. I like that."

Emma smiled. "Me too."

"Good. Now, shouldn't you both be studying or practicing or something?"

They shook their heads.

"I've practiced until my feet hurt. My dance teacher made me promise to take the evening off."

"And I have one paper to write, but I need a change of scenery. When Dawson told us he was working here for a few hours, I begged him to let me come. I need some poodle love to help me through." She reached in her backpack and pulled out two sticks of string cheese. "Zaq said they loved these."

I laughed. "They do love them, but not too much. Remember, they each weigh less than ten pounds."

She crossed her fingers over her heart. "I promise. Besides, I'll probably end up eating them before I even get upstairs."

The store was in good hands with Dawson, Jillian, and Emma, so Nana Jo and I headed to MISU for our class.

MISU was located in North Harbor Township and was a beautiful, sprawling campus, especially in the spring and autumn. The beautifully landscaped lawns with mature trees looked like a college brochure.

The class was being held in the Hechtman-Ayers Performing Arts Center. I know a lot of people in the community weren't fans of the contemporary look of the steel, concrete, and glass building. It was definitely a contrast to the traditional ivy-covered brick and limestone buildings that dotted the campus. It was flooded with light and was open and airy, accommodating everything from sculpture and metalsmithing to painting and dance studios, along with three performance spaces. Apparently, the building also had a few meeting rooms too, because that's where our class was being held. Thankfully, Nana Jo had asked Jillian for directions before we left the bookstore, so it didn't take long to find the room listed on the e-mail confirmation.

Despite being located inside of a building dedicated to art, the meeting room was a plain white box.

"They should have gotten some of the art students' paintings and hung them on the walls," Nana Jo mumbled as she stared at the smooth white walls. "This color is blinding."

"Actually, it's a digital display room."

I turned to see where the voice had come from and nearly gasped when I recognized the woman John Cloverton had been fondling at the casino. She was young and thin with dishwater-blond hair. Today, she had on a short skirt that made her legs look like they went on for miles. I didn't realize my mouth was open until Nana Jo closed it.

"You're gonna catch flies."

I whispered, "That's her. That's the girl I saw at the casino."

It took Nana Jo a moment to connect the dots, but I could tell when the light came on. She turned back to get another good look.

The girl went to a console at the front of the room. After a few moments, the lights in the room dimmed, a projector of some type came down from the ceiling, and then the room was transformed into a tropical paradise. Flowers were everywhere, and what was once the front of the room was now a huge waterfall that flowed down the wall and pooled on the floor.

"What in the Sam Hill just happened?" Nana Jo asked.

A woman standing in the middle of the room squealed and nearly tripped as she stared in amazement at the pool of water.

John Cloverton marched into the room. "I see my assistant is playing with the controls." He was devilishly handsome and dressed in a dark suit. The only blemish being a black eye. He smiled. "Chastity likes to play with all the buttons."

"Chastity?" Nana Jo whispered. "Now that's a misnomer if ever I heard one."

The assistant giggled but flipped the switch, and suddenly the room was back to its boring white normal.

"What just happened?" Nana Jo asked. "That was . . .

amazing, like when you go to the movies and put on those three-D glasses and it looks like King Kong is going to step right on top of you."

Cloverton turned to the young girl. "Chastity, perhaps you'd like to explain."

"It's a new technology developed by teamLab Borderless in Japan. It's a collective that creates art that isn't defined by canvas or rooms, buildings, or . . . well, anything. You aren't just in a room looking at a stagnant painting on a wall. You're in the art. It's moving and flowing and changing. This technology is cutting edge. It'll change the world."

Cloverton walked to the console. "As you can see, Chastity's very passionate about art."

Chastity gave him an adoring look, and their gazes met and held for a few seconds longer than necessary. Chastity reached out and pulled a hair from his shoulder. It was a simple gesture, but there was a certain measure of intimacy that went beyond that of a teacher and an assistant.

"It would seem art isn't the only thing Chastity is *passionate* about," Nana Jo whispered.

Mildred Cloverton walked to the front and forced a computer printout and a pen into the young girl's hands. "Chastity, perhaps you could *assist* us by taking attendance."

The spell was broken. The glow that moments earlier had illuminated the young assistant's face was extinguished. Chastity tucked her head, mumbled a response, and moved toward the first person in the room with her sheet and pen.

Something flashed across John Cloverton's face, but it was gone before I could identify what it was. He smiled. "While Chastity takes attendance, I'll take a moment to introduce myself." He took more than a moment. He told us about his entire life history from birth to the present, and he didn't just talk about himself. He had a slide presentation. He shared cute baby pictures, his college years, his experiences as a businessman in North Harbor. When he came to the current decade, he included a wedding picture. He turned to Mildred and gave her his dazzling white smile. "One day, I walked into a pharmacy and met the love of my life. This lovely woman has been my rock. I don't know what I'd do without her." His voice cracked, and he rubbed his eye. "I think I've got a bit of dust in my eye."

There were a few *aww*s from the class. Nana Jo whispered, "I think I might gag."

John Cloverton pulled out a handkerchief and wiped his eyes dry and returned to his presentation. By the time he finished the decade, we knew pretty much everything there was to know about him. He glanced at his watch and announced it was time for our fifteen-minute break.

The class was small, only nine people in total. Seven of them were women, and when you added Chastity and Mildred it was overwhelmingly female. Without saying a word, Nana Jo and I followed the women like lemmings out of the classroom, down the hall, and around the corner to the ladies' room. There were, of course, only two stalls, so we got in line.

"Just once, I wish there were a queue for the men's room and that an architect would build a bathroom with four times as many stalls for women as for men," Nana Jo complained.

We answered the call of nature, washed, and returned to the room. I was able to take a good look around at the other students.

Nana Jo stood next to me. She tilted her head toward a group of four middle-aged women who were together. "They're all friends who get together every Tuesday night and play cards. They want to know what their kids are doing online, so they signed up for this class."

"Do you know them?"

"Of course not."

"Then, how did you find all that out?"

"We met in the bathroom." She shook her head as though to imply I should have known that. After all, doesn't everyone make new friends when they go to the bathroom?

She directed my attention toward an older couple who were standing at the front of the room talking to John Cloverton. "That's Doris and Edgar Malone. Doris is infatuated with John Cloverton and convinced her husband to come along simply so she could meet him."

I stared at my grandmother but refrained from asking how she knew that. I'd seen Doris in the line for the bathroom too.

"Who's that?" I glanced to the side where the youngest member of the class sat. He looked to be in his early twenties, and if his face was any indication, he was furious.

She shrugged. "I walked over to introduce myself, but he merely grunted."

John Cloverton finally resumed class, and for the last forty-five minutes he talked about the various types of social media. The information was so incredibly rudimentary that even I found it useless. Mildred interjected from time to time to tactfully correct or clarify a point that John had flubbed. She was subtle in her corrections, but they were definitely corrections. It was clear that John was the pretty face while Mildred was the brains behind the operation.

Just as they were about to wrap up, the door to the classroom burst open. Everyone turned to see who had entered.

"Stinky Pitt?" Nana Jo said. "What are you doing here?"

Detective Pitt's face turned red, but he ignored Nana Jo and walked over to John Cloverton. He looked at Mildred Cloverton, and his face turned from a pink lemonade to a turnip. He nodded. "Mildred."

John Cloverton flashed a big smile. "Stinky Pitt?" He chuckled.

Detective Pitt reached inside his pocket and pulled out a

piece of paper. He slapped it on the desk. "John Cloverton, I have a warrant for your arrest."

Cloverton turned to the class. "Can someone videotape this abuse of police power? This is the same officer who assaulted me just yesterday." He pointed to his eye. "Please let it be known that should anything happen to me, the people to blame will be none other than the mayor, his henchmen from the police, Chief of Police Zachary Davis, and their executioner, Detective Brad 'Stinky' Pitt."

Detective Pitt pulled out a pair of handcuffs and wrenched Cloverton's arms behind his back.

Mildred reached out a hand. "Is that really necessary? Surely, this can wait until we dismiss our class."

"This is merely an attempt to embarrass and humiliate me in front of my students," Cloverton yelled. "It's just like all of the other underhanded tricks our cowering mayor tries to use to silence the one voice of truth in this community. I'm the only person brave enough to speak out against him, but just like his other attempts to silence me, this too will fail."

Detective Pitt secured the handcuffs onto Cloverton's wrists and then dragged him from the room.

Mildred grabbed her purse and hurried after them.

I turned to Nana Jo and noticed that she, like most of the class, had her phone out and was, indeed, videotaping the arrest. "Nana Jo. What are you doing? You can't honestly believe that Detective Pitt intends to harm him."

"No, but then you never know."

Chastity's face was white as a sheet, and she was visibly shaking. The rude guy who grunted at Nana Jo walked over to her and reached out his arm, but she merely stared at him like a scared rabbit and then ran from the room.

The class stood around talking about what we'd just seen, but since no one could provide any answers, we gathered our belongings and left.

When I pulled into the garage, there was no light in Dawson's apartment. However, I found him, Emma, and Jillian at the dining room table. Snickers was asleep on Emma's lap and barely lifted an eyelid when I approached. Oreo gave me a sniff and then quickly returned to his perch on Dawson's lap.

"Traitors," I said.

Snickers yawned and then used her paw to guide Emma's hand to the spot that made her eyes roll back in her head.

"How was your class?" Jillian asked.

Nana Jo filled them in on the good, the bad, the boring, and the exciting climax.

We answered what questions we could, but eventually, we both headed to our rooms leaving the younger crowd to their studies.

During Cloverton's boring lecture, it had taken everything in me to stay awake. However, now that I was home and finally able to sleep, my mind wouldn't slow down. So, instead of fighting it, I moved to my desk and took a stroll back in time.

Lady Nancy Astor patted the seat cushion next to her. "Lady Clara, you must come over here and tell me all about your handsome bobby."

With a herculean effort, Lady Clara avoided rolling her eyes. Good breeding meant she couldn't tell the viscountess and member of Parliament for Plymouth Sutton what she wanted. Instead, she sat on the seat Lady Astor indicated and said, "Actually, he isn't a bobby. He's a detective inspector, but being an American, I'm sure it's not easy to understand the difference."

Lady Astor's right eye twitched, and Clara knew the American-born politician recognized the dig, no matter how sweetly delivered. How could she not? The papers were quite fond of reminding her that despite her marriage to a member of the British peerage and her election to the House of Parliament, she was still an outsider.

Lady Clara blushed. She had once liked the spunky American who could stand toe to toe with the likes of Winston Churchill, known for his quick wit and keen mind; however, rumors of her outdated ethnic and religious views were troubling. She smiled. "You know, Winston Churchill is my cousin. Did you really tell him if you were his wife, you'd put poison in his coffee?"

Lady Astor laughed. "I did."

Marguerite Evans sat in a chair across from Lady Astor. "What did he say?"

Lady Astor sat up tall, pushed her chest out, and responded in a blustery manner. "He said, *'Nancy, if I were your husband, I would drink it.'*" She paused for a moment and then let out a deep laugh.

Lady Astor sipped tea and regaled the ladies with humorous stories from her life in Great Britain. She looked across at Kick, who was standing by the fireplace. "You know, dear, we Americans need to stick together. When I first came to England, all the women hated me. They thought I wanted to take their husbands."

Kick smiled. "Well, did you?"

Lady Astor laughed. "Ha. If they knew the trouble I had getting rid of my first husband, they wouldn't have asked."

The doors to the drawing room opened, and Ambassador Joseph Kennedy entered with his arm around the German foreign minister, Joachim von Ribbentrop. They were followed by Geoffrey Fordham-Baker, Philip Henry Kerr, the 11th Marquess of Lothian, and Billy Cavendish, who was talking to John Cairncross and Donald Maclean. Peter Covington and Oliver Martin brought up the rear.

Billy made a straight line to Kick Kennedy's side.

Joseph Kennedy moved to the fireplace and pulled a cord. A servant entered with a tea cart. He pushed the cart toward Kick, who stared at it as though it were a snake.

"Would you like me to pour out?" Lady Astor asked.

Kick released a sigh and nodded.

Lady Astor poured tea and passed cups around. "You surprise me, Ambassador. I never would have taken you for a teetotaler."

"Why? Because I'm Irish? That's a horrible stereotype that all Irishmen are alcoholics." Joseph Kennedy sipped his tea.

"Actually, it's because you've made your fortune importing liquor and, some say, bootlegging." Lady Astor continued to pour.

"That just shows why women should stay out of business. They have no head for it. My import businesses are just that, business. I import alcohol to make money, and I've made lots of it. It's pure economics—supply and demand. When Prohibition ended, I knew there would be a big demand for the stuff. So, I invested heavily in Scottish distilleries. History proved me right, and I made a fortune. That doesn't mean I have to drink the stuff."

Lady Clara glanced at Peter and noted a vein pulsing on the side of his head. He appeared wound like a tight spring, ready to pop at any moment. She reached over and slipped her hand in his and squeezed it. "This will be over soon."

"Not soon enough," he whispered.

The German foreign minister glanced around the room and nodded. "True. When I lived in Canada, I too established a business, importing German wine and champagne. The Führer was just saying to me the other day how much he enjoyed my champagne."

"Really?" Lady Astor said. "I was under the impression that Hitler didn't drink?"

Ribbentrop colored slightly and gave the MP a knowing look. "Ah, that is true, but one cannot drink tea when one is celebrating." He stood. "And we are celebrating, no?"

"What exactly are we celebrating?" Lady Clara asked.

"We should have champagne to celebrate our alliance between Germany and Britain." He gave Joseph Kennedy a gleeful look.

The American ambassador got up and rang the bell again. When the servant who had brought the tea moments earlier returned, the ambassador instructed him to bring champagne.

Ribbentrop clapped like a schoolboy and stood smiling, blind to the emotional turmoil he was creating.

The servant returned with a tray of glasses and several bottles of champagne.

The ambassador picked up a corkscrew and prepared to plunge it into the bottle, but Ribbentrop interrupted him. "Perhaps you will permit me."

Kennedy frowned, but he quickly conceded and handed over the corkscrew.

Ribbentrop placed the corkscrew on the tray. He picked up a different bottle from the tray and held it up. "Most people do not know the *proper* way to open champagne. You must first remove the foil. Like so." He ripped the foil from the top of the bottle and placed it on the tray. "Next, you remove the wire cage." He held up the bottle for everyone to see the wire that held the cork in place and then unwound and removed it. "Lastly, is the cork. Many people erroneously believe that a corkscrew is needed, but you risk getting bits of the cork into the bottle. The *best* way is simply to grasp the cork with one hand and hold it and then twist the bottle." He demonstrated, and after a few moments a slight *pop* was heard. He held up the cork for all to see. Smiling broadly, he bowed.

The ambassador smiled with his teeth clenched and mumbled, "Arrogant little—"

Ribbentrop turned to the ambassador. "Excuse me, did you say something?"

Ambassador Kennedy waved his hand. "No. Carry on."

Ribbentrop poured champagne into a fluted glass. "Next, you must pour just a small amount into the glass. It's important to pour slow and steady and then stop to allow the bubbles to settle before continuing."

"Dear God, I didn't think anyone could make champagne boring," Covington whispered.

When all of the glasses were poured, John Cairncross stood. "Since you poured, the least I can do is serve." He took a glass in each hand and distributed them. When he came to Oliver Martin, he tripped and spilled the champagne. "I'm terribly sorry. Here, why don't you take mine? I haven't touched it."

Martin accepted the glass. "Thank you."

"Now, if everyone is served," Ribbentrop said, "I would like to propose a toast." He stood straight, held his glass high in the air. "To the Führer. To Germany and her allies." He smiled and sipped his champagne.

Lady Clara placed her untouched glass on the coffee table. She noted that she was not the only person who didn't drink. None of the young people present drank. Lady Astor, a teetotaler, touched her lips to the glass out of politeness but didn't drink and then placed the glass on the table.

"Allies?" Geoffrey Fordham-Baker said. "I didn't realize Germany had any allies. Can I quote you?" Well on his way to inebriation, he sat up straight and pulled a pen and a notebook from his pocket. "For the record?"

Geoffrey Fordham-Baker was an editor at the *Times* newspaper and was always on the hunt for a story. As the fourth son of the 2nd Viscount of Lampton, he traveled in circles that would normally have been closed to members of the press. He was short, fat, and bald, and his face was red from overindulging on wine with dinner, port after dinner, and now champagne. He was the only party member who hadn't dressed for dinner, and his dark tweed suit was worn and rumpled. Yet, for all his faults, Lady Nancy Astor liked him, and he was a frequent guest for her weekend parties at Cliveden, her country estate, and was considered a member of her tight-knit friends, who were referred to as the Cliveden Set.

The German foreign minister bristled. "Britain would do well to reconsider their position. Those who oppose Germany . . . well, let's just say, they don't do well."

Lady Astor rose. "I believe if we could sit down and talk like rational adults, we could come to a resolution that would be mutually beneficial to all parties."

"Agreed," Ambassador Kennedy said. "God knows England isn't ready for another war, and I have it on good authority that the United States will remain neutral. Britain won't be able to rely on the U.S. to bail them out again."

Billy Cavendish looked as though he would explode. Kick coaxed him toward a corner of the room and whispered soothing words to him.

"If it comes to war, Mr. Ambassador, I can assure you that England will be ready," Lady Clara said. "We won't stand idly by while Germany runs roughshod across Europe. We don't like bullies who prey on weaker nations."

John Cairncross stood and applauded. "Well said."

Joachim von Ribbentrop gave her a snide smirk. "You would rather see your fine British countryside overrun with communists and Jews?"

"As opposed to Nazis?" Lady Clara said. "Yes."

Marguerite stood by her friend's side. "Absolutely."

Ambassador Kennedy laughed. "Young people. So much energy and enthusiasm."

Billy Cavendish stepped forward. "We are young, Ambassador, but that doesn't mean we're wrong. It's the young who will step in and clean up the mess created by antiquated, prejudiced minds. And, when it comes time to fight, and the time will come, it's the young who'll do it. We're the ones conscripted into service. We're the ones that will defend this great empire and all of her citizens to our dying day."

Kick gasped. Lady Clara turned and saw the blood rush from her face. However, after a moment she pulled herself together and moved to stand by Billy's side.

"This is better than the flick I was planning to see," John Cairncross said, flopping into a chair and grinning at his friend. Donald Maclean scooted to the edge of his seat and glanced from one side of the room to the other, as though waiting for the next ball to be served at Wimbledon.

"You young people don't understand," Phillip Kerr said. "The Treaty of Versailles was unfair. If we can come to an agreement that will help Germany regain her strength, then there will be no need for war."

"Exactly, appeasement is what we need. That will keep everyone safe." Lady Astor nodded and turned to walk away, followed by the ambassadors, Kerr, and the editor.

"Why?" Oliver Martin asked.

Phillip Kerr turned. "What?"

"Why? Why should we appease Germany? They lost the war."

Marguerite gave Martin an encouraging nod and moved to his side.

Joseph Kennedy fumed. "Now listen here. You don't have any idea—"

Peter Covington moved forward. "Ollie's right. If Germany felt the terms were unfair, then they shouldn't have signed the treaty, but it's the law. Governments create laws to ensure the safety of their people. We all must abide by those laws." He shook his head. "I'm just a dumb policeman, but I have sworn an oath to defend the law, not to appease those who break it."

Lady Clara gazed at Peter with pride. She stood taller and held her head higher.

On one side of the room stood the older crowd, on the other, the young. In the middle of the divide sat John Cairncross and Donald Maclean. For a few moments, the air crackled with tension. The stalemate was broken when Cairncross leaped from his chair and shouted, "All hail Britannia."

Joseph Kennedy glanced at his daughter and then turned and escorted the older set out of the room.

The door closed, and the tension released. Kick and Billy went out onto the balcony.

Detective Covington hung his head and moved to a quiet corner of the room, but Lady Clara followed him. "What's the matter?"

"I'm sorry. I was determined to keep my bloody mouth closed and not say or do anything to embarrass you, but—"

Lady Clara lifted his head and gazed into his eyes. "But what? That was bloody brilliant, and I've never been prouder of you."

"Really?" His eyes searched her face, and seeing the truth in her eyes, he flushed. "Bloody Cavendish beat me to the balcony this time."

Lady Clara smiled. "I know another way out. Come with me." She grabbed his arm and pulled him from the room.

Marguerite stood near Oliver Martin, but when she was forced to repeat herself for the third time she turned to walk away.

He grabbed her arm to stop her. "I'm sorry. I've been abominably rude. It's just that . . ." He gazed to where Donald Maclean and John Cairncross were sitting. "I feel sure I recognize them, but I can't remember where."

She smiled. "Perhaps you've arrested them."

"No, I don't think so."

"I find it helps me remember if I don't force myself. Think about something else. Get your mind off of them and you'll remember. Tell me about your work. How long have you been a policeman?"

"Only a few months. I was a student at Cambridge until my dad had a heart attack." He hesitated. "Bad ticker. It runs in the family. First my grandad and my uncle and then my dad. When my dad died, I came home and got a job. You know, to help out."

"I'm sorry to hear about your dad. What were you studying?"

"Physics. I wanted . . ." He turned back and stared at the two men.

"You've remembered. I told you it would work."

"Yes, I've remembered." He frowned. "Please excuse me. I need to go. I need to . . . Can you tell Peter I had to go? I have . . . I don't know what to do, but I have to tell someone." He gulped his drink and then hurried from the room.

From the hallway, there was a large crash.

Everyone rushed to see what had happened. Oliver Martin lay on the floor by the front door. He clutched his chest.

Marguerite screamed, "Someone call for a doctor!"

The servant who brought the champagne earlier picked up the telephone and dialed.

Peter Covington rushed to his friend.

Oliver Martin lay still on the floor with one hand clutching his heart and the other balled in a fist by his side.

Covington felt for a pulse.

Lady Clara stood over his shoulder. "Is he . . . ?"

Covington shook his head. "He's dead."

# Chapter 7

The next morning, my bed shook so violently I thought we must have been having an earthquake. I jolted awake only to find Nana Jo holding up a newspaper.

"Sam, wake up. It happened."

"What?"

"John Cloverton was murdered, and according to the newspaper, Stinky Pitt killed him."

As though doused with cold water, I was shocked awake. I sat up and stared. "You can't be serious."

Nana Jo tossed the newspaper at me. "Read that. I'm going to get dressed, and then I'll tell the girls to meet us at Frank's for lunch."

I didn't register what she'd said until she left the room. It was too early in the morning, and I hadn't had coffee yet. My brain wasn't firing on all cylinders. However, the second problem was resolved when Nana Jo returned with a cup of coffee and placed it on my nightstand.

"Bless you," I mumbled.

According to the *River Bend Tribune*, John Cloverton was arrested by Detective Bradley Pitt on Monday night and was taken to the police station. The police claimed that Cloverton was fingerprinted and arrested. He posted a five-hundred-dollar bond a few hours later and was released. However, Mildred Cloverton claimed that when her husband failed to come home she grew concerned and went to the police station, where she was told he had already been released. She stayed at the station for several hours demanding to talk to the chief of police. Eventually, when she returned home, she found her husband dead on the floor. There was no information about the cause of death, but then it was pretty early for that.

The newspaper included a brief summary of the allegations that John Cloverton had made against the mayor and the chief of police, along with the encounter with Detective Pitt at The Avenue. They included the photo of Detective Pitt standing over John Cloverton after he punched him along with a photo that looked like a selfie of his black eye. Either Cloverton had sent the photo as a follow-up or Mildred had paused her mourning long enough to send it.

I read the article again and finished my coffee.

Nana Jo opened my door. "You're not dressed yet? You'd better get a move on."

I glanced at the time. "What's the big hurry? The store doesn't open for two hours."

"We've got to go down to the police station to see Stinky Pitt before we open the store."

"Why?"

She looked at me as though I'd suddenly started speaking a foreign language. "Because we're going to need to hear his side of the story if you're going to figure out who killed John Cloverton."

"Wait, what? Why do I have to figure out who killed Cloverton? That's the police's job." She started to talk, but I held up a hand to stop her. "Look, in the past, we've helped solve some murders because Detective Pitt was . . . well, he can be a bit shortsighted. However, he won't be the one working on this case. So, why don't we leave this one to the professionals?"

"First, we don't know that whoever the North Harbor police assigned to the case is any better than Stinky Pitt. Second, it doesn't sound like the police intend to look any further than Stinky Pitt. He's going to be the fall guy for this murder."

"We don't know that for sure," I said.

"John Cloverton has only been dead a few hours, and they've already arrested Stinky for the murder. Now, what does that tell you?"

I frowned. She was right.

"So much for innocent until proven guilty."

"Well, maybe he is guilty. Maybe they have clear and compelling evidence that proves beyond a shadow of a doubt that he did it." I knew before the words left my mouth that they weren't true.

"Then, we'll find that out when we speak to him." She sighed. "Look, I know Stinky Pitt isn't the brightest bulb in the pack. The sharpest knife in the drawer. Or the swiftest gazelle in the herd. But that doesn't mean he should be used as a scapegoat for a murder he didn't commit." She put a hand on her hip and gave me the stern look that said she meant business. "I taught him math in grade school, and I know what he's capable of doing and what he isn't, and I'm not going to leave him to fend for himself when he needs help. Now stop arguing. Get up and get dressed." She turned her steely gaze to the poodles and commanded, "Come on, let's go potty outside."

Normally, Snickers takes a few minutes, as she goes through her stretching routine, but not even she opposed Nana Jo. Today, she skipped her routine, climbed out of her bed, and hurried along.

"Smart dog," I murmured as I got out of bed.

I didn't dawdle in the shower and made quick work of getting clean and dressed. In less than thirty minutes, I was heading downstairs to the car.

The drive to the jail and courthouse was quick. North Harbor was too small and too poor to have its own police station, courthouse, and fire department. Instead, there was one station that served the county and the buildings were combined. The county police station and courthouse were attached and comprised a sprawling complex located on an area that sat on a small street in between North and South Harbor.

When you entered the courthouse there were security cameras and metal detectors. I couldn't approach those metal detectors without thinking about the first time Nana Jo and I came here after Stinky Pitt had arrested Dawson for murder. Before we approached the detector, I stopped and turned to Nana Jo. "You didn't—"

"I'm not packing heat if that's what you're wondering." She placed her purse on the conveyor belt and walked through the device without a blip or beep. No guns were drawn, which was a major improvement.

I released a sigh and followed her example.

We picked up our bags and approached the door we knew led to the police station. Inside, we gave our names to the desk sergeant and told him we were here to see Detective Pitt, and we were instructed to take a seat.

After a few minutes, I was surprised to see my sister, Jenna Rutherford, coming through the doors. "What are you doing here?"

She frowned and pointed to Nana Jo. "I got a call this morning ordering me to come."

I turned to my grandmother, who shrugged. "Well, Stinky Pitt is going to need a good attorney to get him out of this mess."

"Did it ever occur to you that Detective Pitt might not want me to defend him? Maybe he wants to get his own attorney." Jenna's tone indicated she hadn't had enough of her morning caffeine, but she wasn't a coffee drinker and required a strong cup of tea before she was capable of civility.

Nana Jo reached in her purse and pulled out a square packet, which I recognized as an English Breakfast tea bag. "Here, you can get some hot water in the break room."

Jenna stared at the tea bag. I could see the corners of her lips twitch. "I don't suppose you've got a cup in that suitcase?"

Nana Jo gave her a look that would have withered someone with less spunk, but my sister wasn't called the pit bull for nothing. Still, Jenna held up her hands in surrender and walked to the front desk. She pulled out her wallet and showed her identification, which got her buzzed inside the gate. In less than five minutes, she returned with a Styrofoam cup with the stringed tab hanging over the top and a spiral of smoke drifting up through the plastic lid. She blew on the liquid through the small opening. After a few sips, my sister mellowed like an addict getting a hit of their drug of choice. I watched as her shoulders dropped a quarter of an inch and her eyebrows went down a fraction. Her lips, which moments earlier were set in a straight line, were now softer, with the indication that an upward curve was possible. She leaned back in her chair, and a sigh escaped.

Nana Jo nodded. "Good. She's got her caffeine. Now maybe we can stop thinking about personal needs and focus on helping our friend."

Jenna raised a brow. "Friend? Are we still talking about Stinky Pitt? The man who has tried to arrest Sam, you, Dawson, Harold—"

"You've made your point," Nana Jo said. "And yes, we're still talking about Stinky Pitt."

I whispered, "She was his math teacher."

"That was elementary school."

I shrugged.

"It doesn't matter how long ago it was," Nana Jo said. "He's a man in need. Surely, you two can stop thinking about yourselves long enough to show some compassion to a fellow human being in need of assistance?"

"If you're going to put it like that." Jenna sipped her tea. "However, I have to be in court in an hour."

"Well, good thing you're here. The courthouse is just down the hall, so you don't have far to go."

Before Jenna could reply, a short, stocky woman came out. I'd seen her around when I'd come to visit Detective Pitt in the past. "My name's Sergeant Matthews."

We followed the sergeant down a narrow hall to a small conference room. There were two chairs and a small conference table. Sergeant Matthews left and came back with one folding chair and one chair she'd obviously borrowed from someone's desk. She left, and just a short while later she returned with Detective Pitt.

He looked old, tired, and pathetic. The hairs that usually covered his bald dome were standing at attention. He sat in the chair behind the table. Sergeant Matthews left the room, closing the door behind her.

For a few moments, Detective Pitt seemed confused. "Why are you here? They told me my lawyer was here."

"You have an attorney?" Jenna said. "That's good." She grabbed her briefcase and stood. "I certainly don't want to infringe on another attorney's turf."

"I don't have an attorney . . . not really. The police union sent someone over, but he wants me to take a deal." He wiped the back of his neck. "I'm innocent. I don't want a deal, but he said if I go to trial, then things will be worse. He was going to try to get me into one of those low-security prisons. With good behavior, it might be two to three years."

"You mean, he wants you to plead guilty?" Nana Jo asked.

He nodded.

"Is that what you want?" Jenna asked.

He thought about it. Finally, he shook his head. "What I want is to go home. I want this whole nightmare to be over." He took a deep breath. "But I want a chance to tell my side of the story, to clear my name, even if that means I have to go to trial." He sighed. "Anyway, I was going to have the public defender's office send someone over." He glanced toward Jenna. "I can't afford to pay you, so no use wasting your time." He stood.

Jenna sat. "Well, if you want to use a public defender, that's fine too. If there's someone particular you'd feel more comfortable talking to . . . I understand."

He bowed his head. "Maybe you missed the part where I said I can't afford to pay you."

Jenna took a deep breath. "Well, then today is your lucky day."

He grunted. "Lucky? You call this lucky?"

"I was given a special grant so your legal defense is covered if you want me to represent you."

He narrowed his eyes and scowled. "What type of grant?"

"What difference does it make?" Nana Jo said. "Stop being difficult and sit down and tell us what happened."

Detective Pitt may have been a police detective, but he recognized the authority behind my grandmother's words and sat.

"Wait," Jenna said. "I'm a lawyer, and if I represent you, then anything you tell me is confidential." She pointed to me and Nana Jo. "They are not your lawyers and are not protected. They could be subpoenaed to testify against you. Anything you say in front of them could be used against you. If you'd like them to leave I—"

I grabbed my purse and stood up but was surprised when Detective Pitt waved a hand.

"I don't care if they stay. I don't have anything to hide. I didn't kill John Cloverton."

I sat down.

"Didn't I tell you?" Nana Jo said to me.

Detective Pitt gave me a look that made me feel a need to defend myself. "I never said he killed anyone."

Jenna glanced at her watch and then pulled out a small tape recorder from her briefcase. "Do you mind if I record this? I don't have much time, and I don't want to miss anything."

He shook his head, and Jenna turned on her tape.

"Interview with Detective Bradley Pitt." Jenna continued with the date and indicated that both I and Nana Jo were present. For good measure, she asked again if Detective Pitt wanted us to leave. He said no, and she placed the recorder in front of him and asked him to tell her what happened.

Detective Pitt took several deep breaths. "I drove to MISU and arrested him." He pointed a finger at Nana Jo and me. "They were there. They saw everything."

"Why did you arrest him? What were the charges?"

Detective Pitt squirmed.

"And why did you go to the campus to arrest him?" Nana Jo said. "Why not wait until after the class?"

"I'll ask the questions," Jenna said.

"I wanted to embarrass him a bit," Detective Pitt said, "the way he'd embarrassed me on Sunday at The Avenue."

I leaned forward. "What did he whisper to you that made you so angry that you punched him?"

I saw the color rise from his neck up to his face, but he clamped his mouth shut and remained silent.

Nana Jo and I were former teachers, and Jenna was an attorney. We understood the value of silence, and we used it.

Detective Pitt held out for quite some time, but just like everyone else, he eventually caved in to the endless silence. "It was personal."

Again, we waited.

The silence circled him like a shark circling its prey until he rolled his eyes, leaned forward, and whispered, "He commented about . . ." He coughed. "He commented on the size . . . He questioned . . ." He squirmed, and his face turned red. Finally, he sank back in his seat and mumbled, "He questioned my manhood."

Stunned, Nana Jo and Jenna exchanged glances. Eventually, I leaned forward. "I'm sorry, and it's really none of my business, but . . . well, how would he know? I mean, if you two were . . . well, a couple, then that would—"

"Whoa, Nellie. Hold up. A couple? Who? Me and John Cloverton? Are you out of your mind?"

"If you're not gay, then why was he questioning your manhood?" Nana Jo asked.

"She must have told him."

I saw the same confusion I felt reflected on the faces of both my grandmother and my sister. This time, it was Jenna's turn to break the silence. "She? Who is she?"

"Mildred."

"You were . . . ah, intimate with Mildred Cloverton?" I asked.

"Of course. We were married for over ten years." He stared at us. "Mildred Lynn Cloverton was my wife."

# Chapter 8

I don't know if I was more shocked by the fact that Mildred Cloverton was Detective Pitt's ex-wife or the fact that Detective Pitt ever had a wife. I asked Nana Jo, but while she'd once been Pitt's teacher, she'd lost touch with him until much later, so she'd been as shocked as me. I tried to shake it off, but it was a struggle. I'm not sure I remembered much more of his interview after that. My mind kept drifting back to *Mildred Cloverton had been Mrs. Stinky Pitt.*

Jenna must have gotten what she needed, because she turned off the recorder and packed up her notepad. After instructing Detective Pitt not to talk to the police or anyone else without her present, she hurried off to court.

I must have driven back to the bookshop, because Nana Jo and I were there, but my mind was stuck in a loop and kept replaying the message, *Stinky Pitt was married.* Thankfully, the morning at the bookstore didn't require a lot of mental energy. When customers knew what they wanted, it was merely a matter of helping them check out and bagging purchases. I could manage that on autopilot. Nana Jo tackled the few people who needed recommendations, which was perfect. She had a flair for helping people who were new to mysteries find the subgenre that appealed most by asking a few questions like, *"What's your favorite color?" "Favorite movie?" "Favorite drink?"* I had no idea how she did it, but time and time again, customers came back and told me how spot-on her recommendations were.

Just before noon, the twins came to help out.

"How did you know I needed help?" I asked my nephews.

Christopher held up his phone. "Nana Jo sent a text."

Once again, I was grateful my grandmother hadn't been mesmerized by the idea of Stinky Pitt being married and had arranged coverage so we could meet the girls for lunch.

Shady Acres had a van that made trips to downtown North and South Harbor multiple times each day, but I wasn't surprised when we arrived and didn't see the girls. The same hostess who had greeted me the day before told us that they were upstairs.

I glanced behind the bar and was disappointed when I didn't see Frank mixing drinks. Instead, his assistant, Benny Lewis, stood in Frank's spot. He glanced up and waved.

I climbed the stairs that led up to the second floor. Unlike my building, which was just down the street, Frank's restaurant didn't have living space upstairs. His second floor would eventually be more dining space, but it wasn't open to the public yet. Generally, he only opened the space up for private gatherings. I was going to ask our hostess where Frank was, but my question was answered when we got to the top and I saw him serving drinks.

I wasn't surprised to see Irma, Ruby Mae, and Dorothy since I knew Nana Jo had arranged for them to meet us here. What was a surprise was seeing Dawson, Emma, Jillian, my mom, and Harold.

"Looks like the whole gang's here," I said.

Nana Jo looked around. "Just about."

Jenna hurried up the stairs. "Am I late?"

"I thought you were in court?" I asked.

"Even lawyers get a lunch break." She glanced at her watch. "I've got to be back in less than two hours, so we need to make this quick."

Everyone took their seats. I sat next to Jenna, and I was pleasantly surprised when Frank sat on the other side of me.

"I can't believe you're going to join us."

"It's not often that I can take time off from work, especially during the noontime rush, but when I saw the article in the paper, I knew you'd be on the case. And I wanted to show my support. Detective Pitt may not be the best example of our boys in blue, but he isn't a murderer."

I leaned over and kissed him.

"What was that for? Not that I'm complaining, mind you."

"For being . . . you."

He grinned and was about to say something when Nana Jo spoke.

"Listen up. We don't have a lot of time, so let's get this party started." She pulled her iPad out of her purse. "Now, you all read the article in the newspaper. The police have arrested Detective Bradley Pitt, and he's being held at the county police department." She turned to Jenna. "I'm not sure how much we're at liberty to talk about, so I'll let Jenna summarize the case."

"Detective Pitt believes he's being framed for the murder of John Cloverton. He claims that he arrested Cloverton, who posted bond at midnight. Detective Pitt says he went home not long after that and never saw John Cloverton again."

"What kind of evidence do the police have on him?" Frank asked.

"What's his motive?" Harold asked.

"Those two questions are pretty much one and the same.

They believe the motive was jealousy. Detective Pitt's ex-wife is Mildred Cloverton."

Based on the group's reaction to Jenna's statement, it was clear that I wasn't the only person who was shocked to learn that Stinky Pitt had been married.

Nana Jo waved her hands to quiet the group. "I know we're all surprised that some woman was willing to risk spontaneous combustion from all that polyester."

"I'd be more worried about going blind from staring at all those crazy colors," Dorothy said.

"They say there's someone for everyone," Ruby Mae said.

"The fact that Pitt assaulted him just one day earlier isn't going to go over well if we end up going to trial," Jenna said.

Nana Jo quickly brought everyone up to speed on what we'd witnessed at The Avenue on Sunday, although they'd already read about the incident in the newspaper. Nana Jo turned to Jenna. "Anything else?"

"I'm waiting for the report from the coroner for the official cause of death, but there were gun casings found at the scene, and it looks like Cloverton was shot with a nine-millimeter bullet. I'll give you three guesses as to the type of bullets Detective Pitt uses."

"Nine-millimeter?" Mom said.

Jenna nodded.

"Were they able to run the ballistics on Pitt's gun to see if it matches the ones that killed Cloverton?" Frank said.

Although he rarely talked about it, Frank Patterson had spent many years in the military and working for the government. He spoke multiple languages, had amazing connections, and when asked about his past generally responded with, "*That's classified.*" So, I wasn't surprised by his question.

"They're doing the ballistics today, but I'd bet my new Jimmy Choo boots they find a match," Jenna said.

"You don't believe—"

Jenna held up a hand to stop me. "Detective Pitt may not be a rocket scientist, but I find it hard to believe that even he'd be dumb enough to use his own gun and then leave the gun at his house to be found. He's a cop. He has access to all kinds of weapons."

"Not even Stinky Pitt could be dumb enough to leave the gun in his house when he could have chucked it into Lake Michigan," Nana Jo said.

"Of course, the district attorney will just say he didn't have time to get rid of the gun, so I've got my work cut out for me." Jenna sighed.

I leaned close to my sister and whispered, "What's wrong? You look worried."

She took a moment before responding. "Honestly, I am worried. There's a lot of circumstantial evidence. If we can't figure out who really killed John Cloverton, Detective Pitt could end up in prison . . . or worse."

I stared at my sister and saw the concern. "Then, I guess we'd better get busy."

# Chapter 9

"Sam," Nana Jo yelled.

"Sorry, I was thinking."

"Well, I hope you're thinking about assignments, because we need to get busy trying to figure out who killed John Cloverton. Now, what do you want us to do?" Nana Jo asked.

"I think there are two things we need to figure out. First, who wanted John Cloverton dead, and who wants Detective Pitt to pay for it."

"Cloverton wanted to be mayor and those articles in the newspaper accusing the mayor and the police chief of misappropriation of funds and abuse of power stirred up a lot of dirt," Harold said.

"So, maybe the mayor or the chief of police wanted to shut Cloverton up," Nana Jo said.

"My cousin Abigail is Chief Davis's secretary," Ruby Mae said, looking up from the knitting, which I suspected helped her think, just like writing helped me. "Maybe I can find out if there's any truth in the allegations that Cloverton was throwing around."

"Great," Nana Jo said.

"The mayor and I golf at the same course," Harold said. "Maybe Grace and I can take time away from packing to get in a round of golf."

"Mom plays golf?" Jenna asked.

I shrugged.

I took a few minutes and shared what I'd seen at the casino.

"Chastity?" Jillian said. "You don't mean Chastity Drummond?"

"Tall, skinny, with legs that are taller than me?" Emma asked.

I nodded. "Sounds like the same girl. Do you know her?"

"She's a student at MISU. I've seen her around campus. We could ask around about her if you want?" Jillian looked from Emma to Dawson. They all nodded.

I always worried about the younger folks getting involved in our investigations. There was a murderer on the loose, after all. They must have noticed my concern.

"We promise not to do anything dangerous. We'll just ask a few friends, that's all." Jillian used her finger to draw an X across her heart.

Emma held up three fingers. "Girl Scout's promise."

Dawson smiled. "I promise to keep an eye on both of them."

"Okay, but please be careful. If Chastity is a murderer, then she could be extremely dangerous."

"I met a guy who works in security at the casino," Irma said. "I'll bet with a bit of enticement he might be able to give me some information on Cloverton." She patted her beehive hair. "I might have to go to some extreme lengths, but I'm willing to make the sacrifice."

Nana Jo rolled her eyes. "Freddie's son, Mark, is with the

state police. He might be able to help tell us if there was anyone at the police station who wanted to set up Stinky Pitt.
Maybe he could go through some of his cases and tell us if
there was someone that might want to see Pitt in prison for
murder."

Freddie Williams was Nana Jo's boyfriend and a retired
cop. Between him and his son, they would be able to tell us
about the general gossip going around the police department.

Dorothy Clark raised her hand. "I have a friend who used
to work with Cloverton when he was running his public relations business before he decided to go into politics. He might
be able to provide some insight into Cloverton's character."

"Perfect," Nana Jo said. She turned to me. "What about
you?"

"I think I'd like to find out more about Mildred Cloverton. She obviously knew both men. I don't know that she
wanted to see either one of them dead, but she may know
someone who would want to see her husband dead."

With our assignments in place, we ordered lunch and ate.
I ordered meals for Christopher and Zaq, and Jenna offered to
drop them off before she headed back to court, which left
more time for us to talk over the case.

I felt as though I was being watched. I turned around to
see Frank staring at me. "What?"

"Nothing. I'm just waiting for my assignment."

I smiled. "Well, I did have something I thought you might
be able to look into."

"I thought so."

"It's just that when we were in Cloverton's class the other
night and listening to him drone on and on about his life, he
mentioned that when he graduated from college he spent a
couple of years in the military."

"I'll be happy to check around, but is there something

specific that you want me to check into? I mean, a lot of people served in the military." He gave me a hard stare. "What specifically about him is bothering you?"

"I don't know. It's just the way he looked when he was talking about it. It reminded me of the way you are when you talk about being in the military."

He frowned. "I don't really talk about it."

"I know. It was the same with him. For a moment, he got that same look that you get sometimes. Then he forced a fake smile on his face and glossed over it."

He stared at me for a long time. "Sam, depending on when he served, he may have seen a lot of horrible stuff—stuff that will make you wake up in the middle of the night with cold sweats years later. Nothing can prepare you for seeing . . ." He swallowed. "It might not have anything to do with his murder."

"I know, but it reminded me . . . it reminded me of a Sherlock Holmes mystery I read."

The corners of his lips twitched, but he did not roll his eyes, so I continued. "I know you're going to say I'm being ridiculous, but . . ."

He shook his head. "I wasn't going to say anything. Tell me about the book."

Before I got a chance, one of the servers came up to tell Frank that there was a problem downstairs.

"I've got an emergency in the kitchen. How about you tell me tonight. We're still on for dinner, right?"

I nodded.

By the time I got back to the store, the twins had finished eating and were taking care of customers along with Dawson, Jillian, Emma, and Nana Jo.

"Shouldn't they be studying?" I asked Nana Jo.

"I asked them the same thing. They're either done studying or in desperate need of a break."

"There really aren't that many customers, and I'm sure you and I could handle it."

"I told them the same thing. They don't want to go." She looked around. "I think they like spending time working in the bookshop. Plus, it's a diversion from . . . other concerns."

I frowned. "What concerns?"

"Christopher and Zaq have interviews tomorrow, and I think they're both a bit nervous."

I smacked myself. "Oh, and Jillian has the audition with the Bolshoi for their summer program tomorrow."

She nodded. "Emma still hasn't gotten a letter from her top two medical schools, and Dawson seems to be sweating bullets about his chemistry test."

"I guess they need a diversion for a few hours."

"I say we give them a couple of hours and then we send them packing."

"Agreed."

Nana Jo decided to use her time to talk to a research librarian she used to know quite well. I decided to spend mine writing.

⌒⌒⌒

"Cootchie-cootchie-coo." Lady Daphne Browning made faces and smiled broadly into the face of the well-wrapped bundle she held in her arms.

"If you girls keep cooing and spewing out that drivel, that poor child won't be able to speak two words of the King's English when he's old enough to talk," Lord William Marsh said. His eyes danced, and despite his words, his tone was light.

"You just ignore your grumpy great-uncle. Everybody knows babies understand baby talk perfectly well, don't you?" She sat on the sofa and rocked the baby in her arms.

Lord William turned to James Browning, the 15th Duke of Kingsfordshire. "Can you talk sense into your wife? She won't listen to reason."

James glanced at Daphne as she cradled the baby in her arms and made kissing noises He smiled and shook his head. "Afraid not. She was your niece long before she became my wife. If you weren't able to talk sense into her, then I fear it's much too late now."

Daphne looked up. "How can anyone do anything but coo at this perfect little bundle of joy?" She rocked him. "I'm going to be the best aunt ever."

As Lady Elizabeth Marsh sat nearby on the sofa she smiled at her niece and knitted. "I have no doubt you will, dear. Penelope and Victor are already grateful for the opportunity to take a nap."

Daphne looked up. "When does the nurse arrive? I'm sure James and I could have delayed our trip a day or two and taken care of little Pippin." She smiled. "I'm so glad they named him after Father. I think he would approve."

"Penelope wanted to name him after all of the men she loved, but Victor felt that would be too much to saddle the young earl with," Lady Elizabeth said. "So, they decided to go with the grandfathers." She smiled at her husband.

Technically not a grandfather, Lord William had raised his nieces, Daphne and Penelope, from the time they were barely able to walk and their parents, Peregrine and Henrietta Marsh, had died in an automobile crash. Never having children of their own, Lord William and Lady Elizabeth poured all of their love and affection into their nieces. He sniffed and wiped his nose with a handkerchief. "Yes. Good deal, that. Lord Peregrine William Nevil Carlston will be a blessing to us all."

Lady Elizabeth returned her attention to her knitting before answering. "The nurse, Miss Jane Martin, will be here tomorrow. She was here for the birth, but the poor girl's brother passed not long after her father died. It was just too much for her poor mother to handle alone. I knew between you and me, plus Mrs. McDuffie, Gladys, and Millie from downstairs, we could care for the little one until she returned."

"I'm surprised Mrs. McDuffie is allowing either of us to even hold him," Daphne said.

Lady Clara came into the library. She wandered over to the window and stared out across the lawn.

Lady Elizabeth looked at her young cousin. Based on how she stalked the post office, Lady Elizabeth assumed the girl was having trouble of the heart and waiting for a letter. She was just about to ask when the door opened and the housekeeper entered.

"Beggin' your pardon, your ladyship, but it's time for Master Carlston's next feeding."

"Already?" Daphne whined. "I've barely had a moment with my nephew."

Practically on cue, the previously sleeping and well-behaved lord opened his mouth and squealed. His face turned red, and he stiffened his little body as he mustered up enough energy for a massive squall.

The stout, freckle-faced housekeeper smiled and marched over to Lady Daphne and reached for the screaming baby.

"Oh, can't I at least carry him up to Penelope?"

Mrs. McDuffie had loved both Penelope and Daphne from the moment they came to stay with their aunt and uncle, and she had rarely been able to deny Daphne anything. She smiled. "Of course you can. Come along."

Daphne carefully stood up and followed the housekeeper out of the room.

Lord William reached in his pocket and pulled out his pipe, along with a leather pouch that normally carried his tobacco. He opened the bag, but it was empty. He stood up and shuffled out of the room, mumbling about tobacco, leaving Lady Elizabeth, Lady Clara, and Lord Browning alone.

Clara spun around. "James, isn't the chief inspector at Scotland Yard a relative of yours?"

"Not exactly a relative. Chief Inspector Buddington is my godfather. Why do you ask? Don't tell me young Covington has gotten fresh."

Lady Clara smiled, but it didn't reach her eyes. "No, of course not. It's nothing like that. It's just . . . I don't know what to do." She folded her arms across her chest and heaved a sigh. "But it's just not fair, and someone should do something."

"What's not fair, dear? Unless you want to tell James privately, in which case I can—" Lady Elizabeth stood.

"Oh, no. It's nothing that you can't hear, Aunt Elizabeth." She motioned for her to stay.

Lady Elizabeth returned to her seat. "Then, why don't you sit down and tell us what happened."

Lady Clara hesitated a moment but made up her mind and hurried to the sofa and sat next to Lady Elizabeth. "It's just that things have been so bizarre ever since Oliver Martin died."

"Oliver Martin?" Lady Elizabeth asked.

"Yes, he's that friend of Peter's who died at the

American Embassy when we were there for dinner a few weeks ago."

James Browning leaned forward. "Maybe you should tell me about it."

Lady Clara recounted the events, from her friend Kick's request to the death of Oliver Martin in the foyer of the American Embassy. "The poor man had just told Marguerite that his family had heart trouble, and then he died. Unfortunately, Victor didn't believe it was his heart. He thought it was murder and wanted to launch an investigation, but between the American ambassador, the German foreign minister, and Lady Astor, there was just too much red tape."

"Wait, the German foreign minister, Joachim von Ribbentrop, was there?" James asked.

"Yes, the arrogant fool." She looked up. "I'm sorry, but he was just so cocky, I just couldn't stand him."

"I'm glad to hear it." He smiled. "But maybe you could step back and tell me everyone who was there and what was said."

Lady Clara thought back and gave him the full guest list and recapped most of the conversation that she remembered. "I'm sorry I don't remember much more. Honestly, everyone was just so dull that I blocked out as much as possible."

Lady Elizabeth stopped knitting and walked over to a desk. She rifled through a few letters until she found the one she wanted. She removed the letter from the envelope and glanced at it. "I thought it was too much of a coincidence. The nurse Penelope hired was the sister of the young man who died, Oliver Martin."

James Browning exchanged a glance with Lady Elizabeth before returning his gaze to Lady Clara. "So,

Oliver Martin appears to have a heart attack and dies, but Peter thinks he was murdered?" He stands up and paces in front of the fireplace. "Did anyone else come in during the party? Anyone outside of those invited?"

Lady Clara thought back and then shook her head. "No, only the servant who brought the champagne."

"For Oliver Martin to have been murdered, the murderer would have had to be one of the guests."

Lady Clara shrugged. "I suppose so."

"But what's the problem?" Browning asked. "What's happened to Peter?"

"Well, first he was up for a promotion, but he didn't get it. He scored higher than anyone on the exam." She flushed slightly. "He has a friend that works in the department that administered the tests, and he told him." She took a deep breath. "But he was passed over. They gave the promotion to someone else. Then he got reassigned."

"Reassigned?" Lady Elizabeth asked. "Where?"

"Buckinghamshire. It was hard enough for us to go out when he was working in London, but now that he's all the way in Buckinghamshire, we'll never see each other, and it's not like we have very much time. We—"

"What do you mean, dear? Why don't you have time?"

"He signed up for military training. Peter's sure there'll be another war, and he'll go and serve." Lady Clara hung her head, and a tear dropped from her eye and landed on her hand.

James Browning passed her a handkerchief, and she wiped her face.

"And just when I finally got him to stop being silly about me having a title and him being a policeman and being seen with me in public. Now this." She stamped her foot. "It just isn't fair."

James Browning looked as though he was lost in thought for several moments. Eventually, he asked, "Did they say why they transferred him to Buckinghamshire?"

"No, they didn't. That's what I was hoping you could help with. I thought maybe you could ask your godfather about it. Obviously, they think Peter's done something wrong." She narrowed her eyes and scowled. "I'll bet it was Lady Astor. She didn't like it when Peter stood up to her when she and the Marquess of Lothian kept talking about how we needed to appease Germany." She huffed. "You'll do it, won't you?"

James Browning nodded. "I'll ask, but I can't guarantee he'll give me answers."

Her face lit up. "I'm sure he'll tell you. Thank you." She took a deep breath and then hurried to the door. "I'd better dash if I'm going to see the baby before they put him to bed." She rushed from the room.

Lady Elizabeth picked up her knitting and returned to her seat. She sat quietly for several moments.

James Browning broke the silence. "What are you thinking?"

She frowned. "Probably much the same thing that you are. That Peter's gotten himself mixed up in a murder involving a lot of very influential people." She knitted. "He's lucky if they just reassigned him to the countryside. Things could have been a lot worse."

James Browning smiled. Lady Elizabeth's instincts

were sharp as a whip. They'd helped her solve several murders in the past. "Still, I wonder why they chose Buckinghamshire?"

Lady Elizabeth stared at her nephew. To most, the wealthy, athletic aristocrat was just part of the landed gentry. He owned a large estate in Kingsfordshire, drove an expensive car, and traveled abroad often. The idle rich. However, she knew differently. She was part of a small, select group of people who knew what he was and what he did. The concern she saw etched across his face was more than just the concerns for a friend's career. No, there was something more worrying him. She prayed that Peter Covington, whom she'd grown quite fond of, would come out all right. Both for Clara's sake and for his.

# Chapter 10

Nana Jo hadn't returned yet when I went downstairs to the bookstore. However, the store wasn't crowded. It certainly wasn't anything I couldn't handle alone. Once the store was empty, I called everyone together.

"Listen, I appreciate all of the help. I really do. However, I know you all have studying to do, papers to write, interviews to prepare for." I turned to Jillian. "And you need rest before your audition." I saw the objection rising from her gut, but before it made it out of her mouth I held up a hand to stop it. "I completely understand the nerves, but you need to try some deep breathing, relaxation, yoga, or something that will help you relax."

She took a deep breath and nodded.

"I truly appreciate each and every one of you, but your first priority is school, so it's time to get busy."

They grabbed their backpacks and headed out.

I stood for several moments and allowed the silence and serenity to seep into my soul.

"Don't tell me you've taken to sleeping on your feet."

I opened my eyes and stared at my grandmother. "How long have you been standing there?"

"Long enough." She glanced around. "You sent everyone home?"

"They need to study."

"It's not very busy. I'm sure I can handle it if you have some sleuthing you want to do."

"Not really. In fact, I was going to make the same offer to you. Don't you have a date tonight?"

Nana Jo glanced at her watch. "Freddie is picking me up here at closing, and we're going dancing."

"I've got this. Why don't you go upstairs and relax? I'm pretty sure I can handle things alone." I spread my arms to indicate the empty store.

"All right, but I'll be upstairs if you need me."

It had been quite some time since I'd worked the store alone, and I have to admit that I enjoyed the solitude. It was a way of reconnecting to the store, the customers, and the dream that sparked the store in the first place.

Between customers, I tidied the shelves, dusted, restocked, and set up a table display featuring culinary cozy mysteries by Nancy Coco, Leslie Budewitz, Ellen Byron, and Libby Klein. I stacked the books and placed a plate of Dawson's cookies in front of the display, which I knew would attract traffic. When I finished, I stepped back to admire my handiwork.

"Are those real? I'm worn-out and starving."

I turned around to see my sister staring at the cookies with a gleam in her eyes that reminded me of the Cookie Monster from *Sesame Street*. "They're real, but they have raisins in them." I knew my sister's taste did not extend to cookies with raisins or chocolate chips.

"Darn!"

"I think there may be some sugar cookies left in the back."

I walked to the back of the store where we had a small café area. I had a few bistro tables and a bar where I kept the elaborate espresso machine my sister had bought when I opened the store but still couldn't figure out how to work. Next to it was a single-cup brewer and an electric teakettle. Jenna complained that non-tea drinkers couldn't taste when coffee had been brewed through the single-cup brewer, so I bought the electric teakettle, which surprisingly was getting quite a bit of use.

Jenna sat at the bistro table while I got two teacups and a plate of sugar cookies. When I sat down, I noticed that she'd eaten three cookies. She shoved the fourth cookie in her mouth and said, "Don't judge. I'm starving."

"I don't judge where cookies are concerned." I slid the plate with the remaining two cookies in front of her and took a sip of my tea. "What brings you here?"

"Sam, things aren't looking good for Detective Pitt."

"Why?"

"The ballistics confirmed that the bullets that the coroner removed from John Cloverton were fired from Detective Pitt's gun."

I don't know how long I sat staring. When I was able to talk, I said, "How is that possible? Where did they find the gun?"

"That's the bad part. It was the gun he kept in his nightstand beside his bed."

"But . . . I just don't believe he shot that man."

She took a deep breath. "Frankly, I don't either, but that doesn't change the fact that he had animosity toward Cloverton. The D.A. is going to say he was jealous because Cloverton had taken his wife from him."

"Did he?"

She nodded. "Apparently, John Cloverton and Mildred

had an affair. She divorced Pitt to marry Cloverton." She paused. "Then there's the fact that he hit him in front of an entire restaurant filled with people. The D.A. is going to say he had a short fuse."

"But he was antagonized. Cloverton goaded him into hitting him so that he could make Detective Pitt look bad. Surely, he can see that. Why else would he have shown up at the restaurant like that with a camera crew in tow?"

"Agreed, but you have to admit it worked."

She sipped her tea in silence, making me ask, "What else?"

"There's talk going around that the mayor and the chief of police intend to sacrifice Detective Pitt. They need a scapegoat to get the heat off them. Detective Pitt will take the fall for killing Cloverton, whether he's guilty or not."

"But I thought the police always stuck together? What happened to their blue wall of brotherhood?"

"That wall has closed, and Detective Pitt is on the outside."

"It's not fair. But if he's not guilty, they can't really hurt him, right?"

She hung her head. "It means the police and the D.A. stop investigating. They believe they have their man. So, rather than looking for the real killer, they focus on finding evidence that will link Pitt to the murder." She sighed. "Sam, I don't know what I can do. I might not even be able to get him out on bond."

"But that's not fair. What about his cousin? He was the former chief; can't he vouch for him?"

She shook her head. "Refuses to get involved. The fact that he won't speak up will come across like he knows his cousin is guilty. It'll be just as bad as if he got on the stand and testified against him."

"I can't believe they're doing this to him. I mean, Detective Pitt may not be the best detective on the force, but surely he deserves better than this."

Jenna finished her tea. "Agreed." She stood up. "Now I'm going home to soak my feet and try to come up with some miracle which will at least get Detective Pitt out of jail long enough for you and Nana Jo to figure out whodunit." She grabbed her briefcase and headed for the door.

# Chapter 11

After Jenna left, I sat at the bistro table for several minutes. Detective Pitt's gun was the murder weapon. He certainly had a reason to be angry with John Cloverton. I thought about Leon, and I know that if he'd had an affair and cheated on me I'd have been furious. We made vows, and as far as I knew, we'd both honored and kept them. My mind drifted to Frank. We weren't married. There was nothing tying us together. If he wanted to date other women, he was free to do so. I was free to date other men, but . . . I didn't. We didn't. At least, I didn't think so. I shook my head to erase the images and uncertainty that had slipped in. This wasn't about me. I needed to focus on Detective Pitt. He'd punched John Cloverton and given him a black eye. Only a man who still cared, still had feelings, for his ex-wife would have done that. Right? That meant he had a motive. Detective Pitt could have followed John Cloverton when he left the police station. According to his testimony, he left for home not long after Cloverton. His gun was the murder weapon. Motive, means, and opportunity. He had them all.

"Samantha," Nana Jo yelled.

I nearly jumped out of my seat. "Nana Jo, you scared me."

"Well, I'm not sure where your mind was, but I called you three times."

I took several deep breaths to steady my heart. "I'm sorry; I was . . . lost in thought."

"Freddie will be here any minute. I fed the dogs and let them out, so they should be good, but . . ." She scowled at me. "Aren't you and Frank going out tonight?"

"What time is it?"

She looked at her watch, but before she could respond, Frank Patterson walked in the front door.

"I saw the lights on, so I came to the front."

"I must have forgotten to lock up after Jenna left."

"Jenna was here?" Nana Jo asked.

I took a moment and updated her on what Jenna had said. Nana Jo was furious. "Why, those lily-livered cowards. If they think I'm going to stand by in silence and let them get away with railroading Stinky Pitt to take the fall for them, they've got another think coming."

Freddie Williams walked into the store. One glance at Nana Jo and he stopped and asked, "What's got Josephine so worked up?"

Frank opened his mouth, but before he could speak, Nana Jo interrupted. "I'll tell you why I'm so *worked up*. It's these two-bit politicians who think they can get away with running roughshod over an innocent man, that's what."

I hurried to lock the front door. "We won't solve it tonight. I need to change, and you two are going dancing."

Freddie was in his seventies and had a full head of silver hair. Between his superstraight posture, authoritative walk, and haircut, which was short on the sides and in back but longer on the top in a variation of the army's high and tight, he broadcast his roots as former military or ex-cop. At six feet, he was slightly taller than Nana Jo, and he had kind eyes and a heart the size of Lake Michigan. The fact that he loved my grandmother showed he had excellent taste, and I liked him.

Despite the fact that Nana Jo was still ranting about government corruption, Freddie managed to get her outside and away. I hoped a good meal and a night of dancing would calm her down.

When they were gone, Frank helped me lock up and make sure the store was ready for the next day. Then we headed upstairs.

"It'll just take me a few moments to get ready. I just need to—"

Frank held up a hand. "Why don't we just stay in tonight. We can order in and watch a movie."

"Are you sure?" I searched his face but didn't see any signs of disappointment.

He removed his jacket. "Absolutely."

Frank was a bit of a food snob, which was understandable considering he owned a restaurant. We'd been dating long enough for him to know my likes and dislikes, so I was happy to let him handle the restaurant selection and the food recommendations. He chose Italian from a restaurant we'd visited many times before. I smiled at the thought of digging into my favorite spicy pasta dish and the most amazing cheesecake I'd ever eaten.

Even though the food would arrive in plastic containers, I pulled out china, glassware, and real utensils. Just because the meal wasn't prepared in my kitchen didn't mean we couldn't enjoy it in style. Frank made a call to his restaurant, and within moments one of the waiters was downstairs with a bottle of wine.

It didn't take long for the food to arrive, and we sat down and enjoyed it in the comfort of home. Apart from intense stares from the poodles that watched each and every bite in case something dropped to the floor, it was wonderful to have the formality of a delicious meal with none of the work.

The cheesecake was lighter and fluffier than I remembered, and I moaned when I ate it. When I opened my eyes, Frank was laughing at me.

"What?"

"Nothing. I was just wondering if you wanted a moment alone with that?"

I stuck out my tongue and took another bite and another and another until I was scraping up the graham cracker crust with my fork to get every crumb.

When we were done, I loaded the dishes into the dishwasher. I turned around to find Frank staring at me. "What? Do I have crumbs on my face?"

He walked over, took me in his arms, and kissed me. When we parted, we were both breathing hard. "Samantha, I have a question for you."

"Okay."

"Do you think you could ever . . . I mean, have you ever thought about maybe one day remarrying? Because if you do, I'd like to apply for the job."

I took a deep breath and sorted through my thoughts. "When Leon died, I never dreamed that I would even consider the idea of getting married again. I was devastated. I loved him." The light I'd noticed in Frank's face moments ago went out. I continued. "I never thought I would ever even date anyone else, but then . . . I met you, and being with you felt right. No one will ever be able to take Leon's place, but I've also learned that my heart is bigger than I first thought. Leon will always be there, but that doesn't mean that I don't have room for someone else . . . for you." The light flipped back on, and his eyes shone. "However, marriage is a big step. There's a lot of adjusting, compromises. I'm a creature of habit. I like routines. I'm not sure I'm ready for change quite yet, so if you're asking me . . . could I have a little time to think about it?"

"That's a fair request, and for the record, I am asking."

My heart skipped a beat, and my pulse raced. "I just need a little time."

I was afraid the rest of the evening would be awkward, but it wasn't. Rather than watching a movie, we talked. We talked about Detective Pitt, John Cloverton, and the allegations Mildred Cloverton threw at their door.

"Do you think there's any truth in them?" I said.

"I can be very cynical and tend to believe where there's smoke there's fire." He paused in thought. "What's that quote about power corrupting?"

"'*Power tends to corrupt, and absolute power corrupts absolutely. Great men are almost always bad men, even when they exercise influence and not authority, still more when you superadd the tendency or the certainty of corruption by authority.*' It's a quote from Lord John Dalberg-Acton, first Baron Acton, thirteenth Marquess of Groppoli."

He whistled.

"He was a British politician, historian, and writer. I've researched so many dukes, earls, and marquesses for my books, I've become a font of useless facts about the British aristocracy."

"Speaking of writing . . . how's my favorite, soon-to-be-published author?"

I sighed. "It depends on what part of writing you're asking about. If you're talking about the book, that's fine. I've murdered a young man at the American Embassy at a dinner party hosted by Joseph Kennedy."

He looked impressed. "I'd forgotten that the elder Kennedy had been the American ambassador to Great Britain."

"He was until he became such an embarrassment to Roosevelt that he was called home."

"What scandal did the senior Kennedy do that got him called home?"

I held up a hand and ticked off his offenses one by one. "First, Joseph Kennedy was anti-Semitic. Not only did he disapprove of war with Germany, but he openly supported Neville Chamberlain's policy of appeasement."

Frank groaned.

"Oh, it gets worse. Several times he tried to arrange a meeting with Hitler without the approval of the State Department to try and bring about what he called '*a better understanding between the United States and Germany,*' and—"

"There can't possibly be more."

"He argued against providing military and economic aid to England."

"Wait, please tell me this wasn't while he was still the ambassador."

"He not only did all of that while he was the ambassador to the United Kingdom, but he did it openly in front of British citizens and the media."

Frank stared at me with his mouth open. "It's a wonder someone didn't murder him."

"I'm sure Roosevelt wanted to, but Joseph Kennedy was wealthy by this time, and he'd donated a lot of money to get Roosevelt elected. Of course, he did it in the hopes that he would one day be president himself."

"I knew he wanted his sons to be president, but I never knew he wanted to be president."

"I suppose when he realized he would never be a viable candidate he turned his attention to his sons. It's fascinating stuff."

Frank smiled. "I love that even though your books are fiction, you do so much research to make them realistic."

I smiled. "Thanks. I love researching. I guess it's the teacher in me. I love adding elements from real life into the books whenever I can, but the interesting person in the Kennedy family for me wasn't Joe, but his daughter Kathleen. Everyone called her Kick."

He shook his head. "I don't think I remember hearing anything about her."

"Few people know her full story. While the family was in England, she met and fell in love with William John Robert Cavendish, the Marquess of Hartington. His father was the tenth Duke of Devonshire. Unfortunately, their union wasn't supported by either of their families."

"Why? Because her father was so . . . ?"

"Actually, it was because she was Catholic and he was Church of England."

He rolled his eyes. "You have got to be joking."

"I wish I were. Back then, Catholics weren't looked upon very favorably. Her family and her mother, in particular, felt if she married outside of the Catholic faith that she would be damned for all eternity. While his family . . . well, you know there was a long history of opposition to Catholicism in England ever since the fifteen-hundreds when Pope Clement the Seventh excommunicated Henry the Eighth and refused to annul his marriage to his first wife, Catherine of Aragon, so he could marry Anne Boleyn."

"Hard to believe four hundred years later people still had a problem with interfaith marriages. So, is that one of the great tragedies of the Kennedy family? Kathleen never married her marquess?"

"Oh, but she did. She went against her family's wishes and married the man she loved."

He stared at me. "Then why do you look so sad?"

"They married on May 6, 1944 . . . he was killed four months later, fighting in World War Two."

A tear rolled down my cheek. Frank gently wiped it away.

"I'm being silly. Here I am crying over someone I never met. It's just, she was so young. Her wedding day should have been the happiest time of her life. They got married in the registry office and not in either of their churches, and the only member of her family who attended the wedding was her brother JFK. Then, four months later, her husband was dead."

Frank pulled me close, and I put my head on his shoulder and wept for Kick Kennedy and Billy Cavendish. I couldn't help but think about all of the obstacles that Kick and Billy had to overcome just to get married, and even then, they had such a small amount of time together before they were torn apart by war. Here I was waffling about giving up my freedom to marry a man I loved when Leon's death reminded me of how short life was.

"You're not Kick Kennedy," Frank said, "and I'm not Billy Cavendish."

"What?"

"Don't make a decision based on something that happened to other people. You wanted time to think about it, and I want you to think about it. I don't want you to marry me because you feel bad for these other young lovers." He stared into my eyes. "Take your time and think about it. I'm not going anywhere."

He kissed me, and that put an end to the conversation and all rational thought until his phone rang.

He glanced at the number and then answered. "Is the restaurant on fire? Because if it's not, this is not a good time." He listened for several moments. "Okay, I'll be there in five minutes."

"Is the restaurant on fire?"

"No, but we do have a major plumbing problem, and I

have to go." He stopped. "Hey, you were going to tell me about Sherlock Holmes and how it tied into my assignment."

"It's nothing; just one of Holmes's clients was hiding something from his past, and his former military buddies came looking for him."

"You think Cloverton was hiding something?"

"I don't really know. It's just a feeling I got when he was talking."

I walked downstairs with Frank and took the opportunity to let the poodles out. We took a few moments and said our good-byes. Then he left. Snickers and Oreo had been asleep when I woke them to go potty. So, they were quick about taking care of their business. I set the alarm for the store and went upstairs.

Frank had given me a lot to think about and I knew I wouldn't sleep, so I sat down at my laptop.

*

"Welcome home. Welcome home. I hope you're done gallivanting all over Europe and are ready to settle down. Speaking of which, how's that beautiful wife of yours?" Inspector Buddington asked.

Everything about Chief Inspector Albert Buddington was large. His height and his girth both stood out as above average. Beneath his large nose was a large mustache that twitched when he talked. Big, bushy eyebrows that seemed to have a mind of their own, with each individual hair moving in a different direction, framed his eyes. To the detectives he supervised, his demeanor could be frightening, especially when he frowned, the two brows came together, and his voice boomed. However, to his godson he had always been kind.

"Daphne's wonderful," James said, smiling. "I'm a lucky man."

"Ha!" Inspector Buddington said. "Indeed. That you are. You are indeed, and I hope she won't let you forget it." He chuckled. "Tea?" He didn't wait for a reply and picked up his phone and requested tea for two. He leaned back in his chair. "Now, what brings you to the Metropolitan Police? You're not in any trouble, are you?"

James smiled. "No, sir, I was just wondering if one of my friends was in some kind of trouble."

"A friend, eh? I hope it's not a case of murder, like the last time you came down to the Met."

There was a knock on the door.

"That'll be our tea. Come in!"

A young man entered carrying a tray with tea. He set the tray on the inspector's desk and then hurried out of the office, closing the door behind him.

Inspector Buddington poured tea into both cups and then handed one to James. Cup in hand, the inspector leaned back in his chair and stared at his godson over the steaming cup. "Now, why don't you tell me who is this friend that's gotten himself into trouble, and let's see what can be done."

"Detective Inspector Peter Covington." He watched his godfather's face.

"Ah, yes, I thought that might be what brought you down here. Although . . . well, I had wondered if you didn't have a hand in . . . well . . . difficult situation, that."

"I understand there was a murder."

Chief Inspector Buddington took a deep breath and held it for several moments. "A young man named . . . a British policeman, Oliver Martin, died suddenly at the American Embassy. There's no evidence that it was murder. His father had a bad ticker . . . the blasted thing runs in the family. There's no way to prove he didn't just have a heart attack."

"But Peter didn't believe it."

"No. Detective Inspector Covington believed the young man was murdered."

"Surely, after all of his years working for you and solving countless murders, he deserved the benefit of the doubt." James stood up and paced. "I can't believe you wouldn't trust his instincts."

"Who said I didn't?"

James halted. He spun around and looked at his godfather. "What?"

"I never said I didn't believe him. Covington's a good lad. When it comes to murder . . . well, he knows his onions."

"Then why? Why was he passed over for a promotion and banished to Buckinghamshire?"

Chief Inspector Buddington stood and looked out his window. "Politics. That's what's at the heart of this mess." He turned and faced his godson. "The American ambassador, German ambassador, a member of Parliament, a marquis, and a duke. Oh, and that cousin of yours who happens also to be related to the king. Good gawd. The murder, if there really was one, and there's no scientific evidence that there was, wasn't even on British soil. The American Embassy is considered part of America, and I have no authority to investigate, even if I hadn't been ordered by the highest authority to drop it."

James was taken aback. "The highest authority?"

Hands behind his back, Detective Inspector Buddington's eyebrows came together, and his mustache twitched. "King George the Sixth himself."

"I've been out of the country; I didn't realize he was back from . . . I thought he and the queen were on their way to New York."

"Barely back in England a full day when he called me." He flopped into a chair. "I'm not used to getting telephone calls from royalty. Fairly rattled my insides, that did."

James's lips twitched.

"Oh, you can laugh . . . you being a duke and all, you're used to rubbing elbows with royalty, but I can tell you for a lowly copper, it's a shock to get a call like that."

"What did he say? I can't believe the king would trouble himself with the death of a policeman."

"He made it clear that we were to drop all talk of murder and we were not to start an official investigation . . . but he suggested that Detective Inspector Covington might be best able to serve his country from a more remote posting, like Buckinghamshire."

James rubbed his chin. "I see. So, it was the king who suggested Buckinghamshire?"

"It was indeed. I didn't even know there was an opening, but the next day a notice came across my desk with all of the paperwork that normally takes weeks to get completed, already approved, signed, and nothing left for me to do but dispatch young Covington."

"I see; well, that changes things."

"I wish you'd explain it to me. I'd like to know why I'm losing a good detective to a county with a population that's an eighth the size of London with a fraction of the crime."

James was silent for several moments. "I think King George may very well be right. It may be the best way for Peter to serve his country." A smile came to his face. "In fact, the more I think about it, the more I agree. Your idea to post Detective Inspector Covington to Buckinghamshire is brilliant."

"My idea? Why, I didn't . . . this isn't—"

"Oh, yes, if anyone asks, it was your idea, and I have to say, it's bloody brilliant. It may just be the most brilliant idea ever." James leaped from his seat and hurried to the door. "Thanks, Budgy. Thanks for everything."

# Chapter 12

When I awoke to my bed shaking, it felt like déjà vu. "Seriously, what is it now?"

"It's time to get up. How can you sleep when we have so much to do today?"

That woke me up. "What do you mean? What is there to do?"

"We've got the bookstore, and then we need to go down to city hall. I have a few things I want to say to the mayor. Then, there's the bail hearing for Detective Pitt." Nana Jo whipped the covers back. "Come on, shake a leg."

I stared at the spot where my grandmother had been and thought of a host of things to say, but none of them were fit to be uttered at—I glanced at my alarm clock—six o'clock in the morning. I flopped back onto my pillow and muttered, "You *have got to be kidding me.*"

Unfortunately, she wasn't kidding. "Samantha, get up and get dressed."

I wanted to rebel, but with my family, resistance was futile. I kicked the covers off my legs and forced myself to stand.

Gravity made the call of nature sing louder, so I hurried to answer its demand and perform my morning routine.

I dressed and took care of the poodles before I sat down to coffee.

"Why are you so happy?" Nana Jo said.

"What?"

"Something's different about you. Did Frank finally pop the question or something?"

"I don't know what you're talking about," I mumbled, and tried to hide my face with my coffee mug, but I'm a terrible liar. I could feel the heat rising up my neck, and between that, my inability to make eye contact, and Nana Jo's uncanny ability to read me like the *River Bend Tribune*, I knew she would figure it out.

"He did propose." She smiled. "Wait, please don't tell me you turned him down."

I took a deep breath and gave up on hiding behind my coffee and put down my mug. "I didn't decline. I just asked for a little more time." I braced myself for the tongue-lashing I felt coming.

"Good." She poured the cream in her coffee.

"Wait, you're not going to scold me?"

"Me? Scold? Never."

"Ha!"

"Marriage isn't easy. In fact, it's downright hard work. Sure, it has its advantages." She smiled. "But there's a lot of compromises. It's a constant balance of give and take. Trust me. There's a good reason why when I told Freddie he could move into my villa that I only go home for long weekends. When you've been on your own for any amount of time, you get accustomed to your freedom."

"That's it exactly. It's not that I don't love Frank. I do. It's just, I've gotten accustomed to being on my own now. At first, it was hard, and I missed Leon so much it literally hurt. I still miss him, but I have also enjoyed being here." I spread my arms to indicate the entire space. "I enjoy my new life. I even love going to the casino with you and the girls. Marriage will change things. I'll have to make a lot of adjustments. We both will, but am I being selfish?"

"Not at all. Marriage is a big step. You won't be as free as you are now. There will have to be compromises on both sides. Marriage is not a state that should be entered into lightly, no matter what age or stage you're in. I think you're being smart."

I was pleasantly surprised that Nana Jo wasn't giving me a hard time.

We talked a bit longer and then headed downtown.

City Hall wasn't located in the same building as the courthouse and the police station. It was actually in an old brick building that screamed 1970s architecture and was located on Wall Street, which aside from the name had nothing in common with New York City's famous financial district.

The building housed the fire department and several other small government agencies. Since the building had only two stories, we bypassed the elevator that looked older than me and opted for the stairs.

The mayor's office took up one entire side of the building. We opened a door with gold letters on the glass and walked inside. A young woman sat behind the desk. She looked to be in her early twenties and was grinning into the face of a young man who was leaning against a file cabinet. He was wearing the uniform of a delivery service. The woman glanced in our direction but continued her conversation—bad move.

We stood in front of the desk for a full minute while the woman flirted.

Nana Jo glanced around and spotted the office with the mayor's name on it. She turned and marched toward the door.

That got the girl's attention. "Hey, where do you think you're going? You can't just—"

However, she was wrong. Nana Jo could, and she did. She flung open the door and marched inside.

The mayor was seated behind the desk on the telephone. He stared up into Nana Jo's face. "What's the meaning of this? Who are you?"

"I'm a taxpayer, just one of the people who pay your salary and the salary of that lazy waste of time." She pointed at the secretary. "What kind of office are you running where citizens are kept waiting while your secretary ignores them to flirt with delivery drivers?"

The girl blushed and stammered, "I wasn't flirting . . . I was merely—"

The mayor waved away her protest. He spoke into the phone and said, "I'll call you back later." He glanced up at the girl. "That'll be all, Marla."

Marla looked as though she wanted to claw Nana Jo's eyes out, but she received a stare back from my grandmother that said, *Try me.* Marla must have thought better of it. She turned and walked out, giving the door a firm slam behind her.

The mayor smiled at Nana Jo. "Now, how may I help you?"

"You can tell me what you think you're doing by trying to make Detective Pitt into your scapegoat, that's what."

Mayor Carpenter shuffled papers on his desk. "I have no idea what you're talking about."

"For a politician, you sure are a bad liar." Nana Jo leaned across the desk. "My name is Josephine Thomas, and I was a schoolteacher for . . . almost as many years as you've been alive. I taught Detective Pitt, and he's a lot of things, but he isn't a killer."

"That's for the courts to decide."

"Yes, it is, and with my granddaughter's help, Detective Pitt will have his time in court. He'll get a chance to tell how he was sent like a vestal virgin on a Roman altar to deflect attention away from governmental corruption."

"Madam, I have no idea what you're talking about."

Nana Jo started to speak, but suddenly all the wind left her sails and she flopped into the chair. "I feel . . . faint."

Mayor Carpenter's face looked stricken. He stood up. "Are you having a heart attack? Do I need to call an ambulance?" He reached for the phone.

"No . . . I think I just need some water. Perhaps you'd be kind enough to get me a glass of water. I thought I saw a water fountain in the hallway."

For a large man, the mayor was able to move surprisingly fast. "Of course." He hurried out of the office.

As soon as he was gone, Nana Jo hopped up and started rifling through the papers on his desk.

I stared at my grandmother. "What on earth are you doing?"

"I'm snooping through these papers looking for evidence." She pulled out her phone and started snapping photos.

"You can't do that. It's illegal . . . I think. What if he comes back and catches you?"

"Get by the door and be my lookout."

I hurried to the door. "This is crazy. You're going to get both of us put in cells right next to Detective Pitt." I saw a large shadow approach the door. "They're coming."

Nana Jo rushed back to her seat, just making it before the door opened and the mayor hurried back in with a small paper cup of water. He ran to Nana Jo. "You do look flushed. I think I should call the paramedics to come and have a look."

Nana Jo did look flushed, but it was because of her mad dash to get seated before the mayor returned. Her purse was on the desk. She leaned forward and fumbled inside. She managed to dump most of the contents onto the mayor's desk. "Oh, dear me. Forgive me. I was just trying to get my pills." She pulled out a small pill container that I knew contained a vitamin and some dietary supplements.

She opened the container, took out a pill that looked a lot like Fred Flintstone, and popped it in her mouth. She took several deep breaths.

Mayor Carpenter hovered around her, staring as though waiting for her to keel over.

"I feel much better now. Thank you." She gulped back the last of the water. "I know I shouldn't get worked up, especially at my age, but when I think of poor Detective Pitt stuck in that prison cell . . . well, it makes my heart race."

Mayor Carpenter looked as though he could have used a heart pill. "Madam, I can assure you that Detective Pitt isn't being sacrificed for me or anyone else. He will get the same fair trial that is given to all citizens of this country."

"Great. I'm glad to hear it." Nana Jo grabbed her purse. "Come along, Sam. We've got to run if we want to make it down to the courthouse." She all but pulled me from the office.

The delivery driver was gone, but the secretary was apparently still a bit salty about being embarrassed in front of her boss. She filed her nails and glared at Nana Jo, who looked as though she wanted to leap over the desk and beat the girl to a pulp.

Once outside, Nana Jo was back to her usual self. I had to run to catch up to her.

At the car, she was practically giddy. "That was stimulating."

"That was wrong. What did you find?"

She smiled and pulled out her cell phone. "Looks like our mayor is planning on skipping the country. I found a receipt for a two-way ticket to Portugal, a brochure for some retreat, and it looks like he's been moving money from one account to another. He's probably been siphoning money from the city."

"Is Portugal a country without extradition agreements with the U.S.?"

"I don't know. I didn't have time to read through them carefully, so I took as many pictures as I could. I'll look over everything more carefully later." She swiped through the pictures she had taken. "Did you notice how when he heard that I was there about Detective Pitt he tried to hide those papers? That's what gave me the idea."

"I wish you'd give me a heads up before you feign a heart attack." I pulled out of the parking lot. "Or you're going to give me one."

The trip to the mayor's office took longer than we expected. I dropped Nana Jo off at the courthouse and then went back to open the bookstore. Christopher and Zaq were both interviewing for jobs at the same technology company. Christopher was going for a job in marketing, while Zaq was trying to get into programming. The company was headquartered in Chicago, so if they got the jobs they would just be a couple of hours away. They were coming to help me in the store after lunch.

I glanced at the time and said a quick prayer for Jillian, who would be auditioning for the Bolshoi summer program in just an hour. When I pulled into my garage, I sent a text message to let her know that regardless of what happened, I was proud of her for following her dreams.

When I got inside, Dawson had already opened the store for business.

"What are you doing here?" I said. "Shouldn't you be studying? Or taking a test?"

"I've crammed as much as I can. I can't look at another chemical symbol. It's to the point when I close my eyes, all I see is the periodic table. I need to get my mind off chemistry."

"Do you want to go upstairs and bake? I know that always helps you relax."

"I've already baked four dozen cookies, and I even decided to try my hand at bread. It's rising in a ball on the counter." He rubbed his eyes, which looked red and tired. "I think I just need a couple of hours of shelving books, helping customers . . . doing something other than studying. When you were teaching, I remember you telling us that our brains were like sponges."

I nodded.

"Well, I feel like mine is so full that if I try to soak up anything else, it's just going to run out."

"Then you definitely need a break."

We worked in the bookstore in perfect harmony for the entire morning. Dawson replenished the shelves and the treats, while I mostly took care of customers. He wasn't a big fan of mysteries, so he wasn't great at helping people who didn't know what they wanted. However, over time he'd learned some of the basics of mysteries, which helped in a pinch.

At noon, Christopher and Zaq stopped by, both professing that they thought their interviews went well, but these were highly coveted jobs and the company received thousands of applicants every year.

I ordered lunch and left money to pay and then hurried back to the courthouse. I'd told Nana Jo to text me when Detective Pitt was called up and I hadn't received a message, so I took that as a good sign.

At the courthouse, I was elated when I passed through security without a hitch. I was used to going to the police station side of the building and felt awkward going to the courthouse, but I did it. Inside, I stood for a moment and looked around until I spotted Nana Jo. She stood and waved at me as though she were trying to land a plane.

I squeezed down the aisle and plopped into the seat next to Nana Jo. I leaned close and whispered, "What did I miss?"

"Absolutely nothing. They haven't called Stinky Pitt's name yet. Jenna is back behind one of those doors." She flung her hand around to indicate the doors that were around the front of the court. "You'd think this would be exciting. Jenna said it wasn't a trial, so I wasn't to expect Perry Mason, but I was at least expecting Judge Judy. It's taking all my strength to stay awake."

The judge was a black woman with long braids, which she wore pulled back into a bun. She had on a black robe and sat in the position of prominence, raised up above everyone else.

I leaned toward Nana Jo and whispered, "I wonder if Ruby Mae is related to her."

"She is. I sent Ruby Mae a text message. Pictures aren't allowed." She pointed to a sign on the wall. "She said she was a great-niece by marriage."

I shook my head. "That woman has more relatives than anyone on the planet."

I pulled out my notebook, expecting that unlike Nana Jo, maybe there would be something I could use in one of my books. Unfortunately, Nana Jo had been right. The proceedings were, indeed, quite dull. Before long, I too found my attention drifting and my eyelids felt like lead. Before I realized what I was doing, I wandered off to the British countryside.

Lady Elizabeth, Lord William, and Lady Clara sat in the wood-paneled arched drawing room in front of a large stone fireplace.

Lady Daphne walked over to the wall and rang a bell. "I'm so glad you could all come."

James Browning passed Lord William a leather pouch.

Lord William pulled out his pipe. "Thank you. I meant to replenish the supply before I left, but . . . well, we got your request and took off at once."

James puffed on his pipe and returned to his seat. "It was all very sudden."

"I've heard a lot about Chequers Court, but I've never been here before," Lady Elizabeth said, looking around the room. "I don't usually run in the same circles as the prime minister."

James smiled. "Usually, neither do I, but when Mr. Chamberlain asked if we could stop in and look after a sick friend, well . . . we just couldn't say no."

Thompkins, the prim and proper butler who served the Marsh family, entered. He rolled a tea cart to Lady Daphne, gave a stiff bow, and turned to leave.

"Aunt Elizabeth, would you mind?" Lady Daphne asked.

Lady Elizabeth placed her knitting aside. "Not at all, dear."

Thompkins rolled the cart in front of Lady Elizabeth, bowed, and left.

"I can't tell you how grateful we are that you were able to spare Thompkins," Lady Daphne said. "The prime minister usually brings his staff with him, and since he's not here . . . we were in dire straits. We called an agency and arranged for a cook, maids, and the other staff, but a good butler is invaluable."

Lady Clara hopped up and paced. "It's very isolated out here, isn't it?"

"Yes, it is," James said. "I hope you won't find it too dull, but Sir Hugh Sinclair bought a mansion and fifty-eight acres of land. He's opening a . . . sort of hospital, and I thought perhaps Clara might want to work there." He glanced at his young cousin.

"I'm not particularly skilled, but I guess it's time I started earning my living. What kind of place is it?"

"It's an asylum of sorts for overworked government officials."

"An asylum?" Lord William said. "Do you think that will be appropriate? Will she be safe working there?"

"Oh, perfectly safe," James said. "It's more a place for rest and relaxation . . . a rest home of sorts. There are lots of young women from all over the country. Sir Andrew Franklin-Burns's daughter, Winifred, is there along with Lord Augustus Hampton's daughter, Eugenie." James rattled off the names of several other daughters of the aristocracy.

"Sounds like all the debutantes in England are working at this asylum," Lady Elizabeth said. "Rather curious that so many young women from society are all here tending to the infirm in a remote corner of the British countryside."

"In these trying times, the young ladies of the aristocracy want to do their part to aid the government," James said.

Lady Clara shrugged. "Well, I don't suppose it matters much what I do."

"Great. I can take you down first thing tomorrow. I'm sure they'll be glad to have you. Maybe we can stop by the local pub, the Shoulder of Mutton, to grab a bite. It's quite popular with a number of the locals here in Buckinghamshire."

"Buckinghamshire?" Lady Clara's face lit up. "Is that where we are?"

Lady Daphne laughed. "Didn't you know? You silly goose."

Lady Clara rushed and threw her arms around James and then Lady Daphne, and then she gave James another squeeze. "You are the most amazing . . . Buckinghamshire. How wonderful."

"When I heard of the opening, I thought of you immediately," James said. "I knew you were well suited for it."

Lady Clara could barely contain her excitement. After a few moments, she turned back to the duke. "What was the name of that pub?"

* * *

"Sam, pay attention." Nana Jo reinforced her request with a sharp elbow.

"Ouch." I glanced up and saw that Jenna and Detective Pitt had just arrived and taken a seat at the front, facing the judge.

The court clerk and judge went through the same process I'd witnessed multiple times already. "Have I only been here an hour? It feels longer."

"I've been here all day, so you'll get no sympathy from me."

The district attorney was young and handsome.

Nana Jo nudged me. "That suit must have cost a small fortune."

"He's very handsome."

"And he knows it too. I don't care for a man with highlights in his hair. Or mousse. I'll bet he wears expensive cologne too."

"You just don't like him because he wants to prosecute one of your former students."

"Wrong." She shook her head. "I don't like him because he looks like a model who wants to prosecute one of my former students *and* he is going up against my granddaughter. Now be quiet so I can hear."

The district attorney painted a picture of Detective Pitt that made him look about one step away from Jack the Ripper, and he finished the character assassination by asking the judge to deny bond.

"Why, that dirty little weasel," Nana Jo said.

Next, it was Jenna's turn. I don't think I've ever seen my sister in her natural habitat.

"Your honor, Detective Bradley Pitt has born and raised right here in North Harbor, Michigan." She then talked about his many years of service on the police force and as a member of the North Harbor Madrigals.

"Stinky Pitt can sing?" I asked.

Nana shrugged. "I guess so."

My imagination refused to even try to picture Detective Pitt as a singer, but . . . it must be true.

"Detective Pitt isn't a flight risk. In fact, my client is looking forward to an opportunity to lay his case before a jury of his peers, who we know will find him innocent. I would ask your honor to waive bond for someone who has dedicated his life to serving this community."

I glanced at Nana Jo, and her eyes reflected the same pride that I felt. She turned to the man who sat on the other side of her, and said, "That's my granddaughter."

Nana Jo and I may have been impressed, but the judge took a path down the middle. She didn't waive the bond, nor did she deny. She set bond at one million dollars, banged her gavel, and then called for the next case.

Nana Jo and I quietly left the courtroom. Once we were

free of the quiet, I turned to her. "One million dollars is a lot of money."

We found a bench outside and waited. Eventually, Jenna appeared from around the corner.

Nana Jo hugged her. "I was so proud of you. You were amazing."

"I'm rather surprised things went as well as they did."

"You call that well?" I asked. "Does Detective Pitt have a million dollars lying around?"

"He doesn't need a million. He only has to put up ten percent."

"Okay, I'll play. Does Detective Pitt have a hundred grand lying around?"

"He can put up his house as collateral. It's called a surety."

A tall man with a long beard, his hair pulled back in a ponytail, and wearing all leather approached. "Mrs. Rutherford?"

"Excuse me, here's my bail bondsman now." She escorted the Hell's Angel down the hall.

"It looks like Jenna has things well in hand, and I'm starving," Nana Jo said. She looked at her watch. "Let's go meet the girls so we can update them."

We headed out to the car, and I sent my sister a text letting her know our plans.

Nana Jo was uncharacteristically quiet for the entire ride from the courthouse to the bookshop. When I pulled into the garage, she was so lost in thought, I had to shake her.

"You're a million miles away," I said.

"I've been thinking about something. After what happened at The Avenue on Sunday, why do you suppose they chose Stinky Pitt to arrest Cloverton?"

I thought for a moment, but nothing came to mind. "I don't know."

"I mean, there was obviously bad blood between the two men. Why not send some other detective to arrest him?"

"Maybe he volunteered? Maybe there was no one else?"

"Seems fishy to me. I mean, if I were the chief of police, I would have wanted to avoid any more negative publicity. I'd have sent anyone else other than Bradley Pitt, unless . . ."

"Unless you wanted to implicate him further."

"Exactly."

We sat for several minutes. No matter which way we turned it in our minds, we still came up with the same thing: Bradley Pitt was deliberately sent to arrest John Cloverton to set him up to take the fall.

"If that's true, then you realize what that means, right?" Nana Jo said.

"It means that John Cloverton's murder was premeditated. Someone wanted him dead."

"They not only wanted him dead, but they wanted Pitt blamed for it."

# Chapter 13

Things at the bookshop were running smoothly. So, Nana Jo and I headed down to Frank's to meet the girls.

We went upstairs. Everyone took their same seats. We ordered drinks and waited until Jenna arrived.

Fifteen minutes later, she rushed upstairs. "Sorry I'm late."

Everyone stood up and applauded.

She looked confused. "What's that for?"

"Josephine told us what a wonderful job you did in court today," Dorothy said.

Jenna blushed. "Just doing my job."

When the applause died down, Nana Jo pulled out her iPad. "Let's get started. If there are no objections, I think Jenna should go first. She has some additional information that everyone needs to hear."

Jenna filled everyone in on the reports from ballistics and the coroner, and she finished by letting us know that Detective Pitt was going home to rest but that she would be in touch with him tomorrow. He wanted to help with the investigation.

"Do you think that's a good idea?" I asked.

"Absolutely not, but clients always want to help with their defense. I suspect he's going to need a handler. He's going to need someone who can keep an eye on him and keep him out of trouble." She glanced at Nana Jo. "I was hoping you could enlist Freddie for that."

Nana Jo nodded. "He'll do it." She made a note. "Now, who's next?"

Ruby Mae raised her hand. "I had a good long talk with my cousin Abigail last night. She's Chief Davis's secretary, and she gave me an earful." Ruby Mae pulled out her knitting as she talked. "Apparently, Chief of Police Zachary Davis has been in a fit ever since those newspaper articles first started hitting the papers. According to Abigail, he's been more stressed out than a cat in a room full of rocking chairs."

"There usually isn't smoke without fire," Nana Jo said.

"That's what I think too. Abigail knows the chief has taken a lot of *business* trips over the past few years." She used air quotes around "business." "He's also had her coding some of his expenses in different categories than what she thinks they should be."

"Like what?" I asked.

She finished the row she was knitting before continuing. "He'll go out to lunch at a pricey restaurant, and when the bill comes in, instead of coding it for something logical like Employee Meal, he'll tell her to code it for Department Function." She looked down her nose and raised an eyebrow. "Abigail says that's suspicious because if she coded it as Employee Meal, then she has to list all of the employees present, and there's a per diem amount allotted for each employee. If she codes it as Department Function, then she doesn't have to list names and—"

"And there's no per diem amount."

"Exactly."

Irma said, "Why, that dirty, cheating son of a b—"

132     V. M. Burns

"Irma!"

Irma broke into a coughing fit. "Sorry, but that burns my butt to think of our tax dollars being wasted."

"Wouldn't he still need to provide a receipt?" I asked.

"I'm betting he uses the credit card total instead of the itemized receipt that lists specifically what was ordered," Frank said. "You know, when you use a credit card, the first receipt will list each item ordered. You give the server your credit card, and what's brought back is a receipt to be signed and a brief summary with the final total, but none of the itemizations."

I thought back to the last time I'd used a credit card to pay for a meal and realized he was right.

Ruby Mae continued knitting. "Abigail says that's just the tip of the iceberg. He has a small petty fund account that isn't really monitored. He can spend about five thousand dollars per month for things like paying informants. Every month, he has her transfer five thousand dollars into that fund, and every month the fund is drained." She completed a complicated stitch before continuing. "Now, the police do use money from that fund, but she said the previous chief of police never exhausted all of the money every month. In fact, she said it was rare if he ever used all of that money. He might use five to ten thousand dollars per year, but not Chief Davis. He's using all five thousand dollars each and every month."

"Does he have to keep records?" Harold asked. "Receipts? Anything? Surely, he has some form of record keeping or accountability?"

Ruby Mae shook her head. "Not this chief." She leaned forward. "Abigail also said that he's been sweating bullets, afraid that John Cloverton would demand an audit of the books. Now that Cloverton's dead, he's back to business as usual."

We took a few minutes and mulled over the information

Ruby Mae had gathered. When the outrage died down, Nana Jo glanced around for volunteers.

Harold raised a hand. "Grace and I did get to the golf club yesterday. I didn't get a chance to talk to the mayor, but I'm going to try again this afternoon. He has a standing tee time at three." He glanced at his watch. "I have it on good authority that his fourth won't be able to make it." He smiled. "They'll add me in his place."

"That's great. Maybe you can find out if he knows anything helpful." Nana Jo was about to move on when Harold coughed to get her attention.

"I wasn't able to talk to the mayor, but Grace fared much better." Harold gave Mom a loving glance. "You should tell them what you found out."

"Well, I'm not nearly as clever as Harold, but it did occur to me that if Mayor Carpenter was involved in something underhanded, Mrs. Carpenter might know something about it."

"His wife?" I asked.

"Oh, no. Not his wife. Sharon Carpenter is an arrogant, harsh woman. She's hard-hearted, tightfisted, and downright cruel. Do you know that she didn't even give her maid a Christmas present? Well, I can tell you that didn't go over well, and Leslie gave her notice immediately. They can't keep servants, and I can't say that I blame any of those poor women."

"If you didn't talk to his wife, then who—"

"I talked to Charmaine Carpenter . . . the mayor's mother. Charmaine told me that Sharon is a downright shrew. She bullies poor Nelson within an inch of his life. She forced the poor man into running for mayor. He really didn't want to hold public office, but when Adele Forrester's husband ran for state representative, Nelson had to run for a higher office. Adele really did put on airs, but Nelson isn't cut out for being a politician."

"Who's Adele?" I asked.

Mother sighed. "Really, dear, weren't you paying attention? I told you she's married to Robert Forrester. Anyway, Charmaine said she noticed that some of the antiques had started to disappear. Nothing big, just small items." Mom reached into her purse and fished around until she found a small slip of paper. She pulled it out and started to read. "'A small silver lighter that belonged to Nelson's great-grandfather, a glass dish from Tiffany's, a cameo and pearl brooch, a silver tea service, and a pair of emerald earrings.'" She folded the paper and looked up.

No one commented. Eventually, Frank said, "Your friend Charmaine believes these items are somehow tied to the murder?"

Mom nodded. "Charmaine believes they may be the motive for the murder."

Jenna waved her hands. "Wait. I'm confused. How does a silver tea service and a pair of emerald earrings tie into the murder? Is she saying John Cloverton stole them?"

"Of course not."

Harold patted Mom's hand. "I think you forgot to mention the gambling, dear."

"You sure as heck forgot something," Nana Jo said. "Now perhaps you should start over again."

Mom took a deep breath. "About a year ago, Charmaine noticed that a few small items that had been in their family for years had disappeared. When she asked Sharon about it, she practically snapped her head off. When more things started disappearing, Charmaine wanted to call the police, but Sharon wouldn't have it. She accused one of the servants and fired the girl."

"Leslie?" I asked.

"No, couldn't be Leslie," Jenna said. "She quit when she didn't get a Christmas present, remember?"

"Oh, yeah. Sorry."

"I believe the girl's name was Marla," Mom said.

Nana Jo and I exchanged glances.

"Marla?" Nana Jo said. "Young, skinny girl with lots of attitude? Likes to flirt?"

Mom shrugged. "I honestly couldn't say. I've never seen her, but Charmaine did say she was a terrible flirt, which is why she didn't object when Sharon fired her. Charmaine didn't believe the girl was a thief, but the flirting had gotten to be a problem." Mom shook her head. "Now, where was I? Yes, so these things disappeared, but even after Marla was gone, things went missing. One day, Charmaine was out having tea and she saw her daughter-in-law meeting with another woman. She seemed upset, which is the only reason that Charmaine thought she should listen to the conversation." Mom gave us an innocent look. "Just in case Sharon needed assistance."

"Yeah, sure," Nana Jo said. "We get it."

"Charmaine was shocked because Sharon was telling her things about the chief of police, and she even said a few things that might have incriminated poor Nelson. Then she saw Sharon reach in her purse and take out a handkerchief. This woman opened it, and there was a ring that belonged to Charmaine's great-grandmother and a diamond and gold tie clip and cuff links that belonged to Nelson's father." She looked around. "Charmaine was shocked, I can tell you."

"Did Charmaine know who the woman was?" Nana Jo asked.

"Not at first, but a few days later she saw the woman on the news. She was standing right there next to John Cloverton. She asked Nelson who the woman was, and he said her name was Mildred Cloverton."

"The mayor's wife is the one who's been leaking information to the media?" I asked.

Mom nodded.

"But why? If she was the force behind him running for office, why would she deliberately sabotage him?"

Dorothy raised a hand. "I think I might be able to help with that." She turned to Mom. "That is, if you're finished?"

"Yes, that's all the information I was able to find out."

"Your information was surprisingly very helpful," Nana Jo said. "Well done, Grace."

Harold beamed proudly. "You did wonderful, my dear."

Dorothy had pulled out her phone while Mom was talking, and was frantically swiping and looking for something. "I didn't connect things until I heard Grace's information, but you know how when we go to the casino I usually go into the high-limits room?"

We all nodded.

"There's a woman that I've noticed quite often. I thought she looked familiar, but I never really put two and two together until now." She held up her phone and passed it around. "That's a picture of Mayor Carpenter and his wife at the Blossom Festival last year, and that's also the woman that I've seen in the high-limits room at the casino. And she has not been having very good luck, at least not while I was there."

We all looked at the picture of Sharon Carpenter smiling. While Mayor Carpenter was short and fat, Sharon Carpenter was tall and thin. She had a long, thin face and jet-black hair, which she wore teased in the front and pulled into a French roll with pin curls along the sides.

"We know that John Cloverton is a member of the Pontolomas," Dorothy said. "If Sharon Carpenter had lost a great deal of money, she might have made a deal to eliminate her debt."

"Could he do that?" I asked.

Dorothy shrugged. "I can ask my friend who works there, but I think the tribe's council members can do just about anything they want."

"Let's play this out," Nana Jo said, taking notes as she talked. "Sharon Carpenter has been going to the casino and losing a lot of money. Maybe she's in over her head. Cloverton recognizes her."

"Or Mildred," I suggested.

"Right, if Mildred recognized her, she might suggest a way that she can make all of her troubles go away."

"But if she's selling information, why is she also handing over her valuables?" Ruby Mae asked.

"Maybe the information wasn't enough?" Nana Jo said.

"Or maybe the information she sold was enough to cover her debts, but the jewelry was to keep Mildred from telling the mayor and to keep Sharon's name out of the paper?"

"Blackmail?" Jenna asked.

"Possibly," Nana Jo said. She turned to Dorothy. "Do you think your friend could look and see how much Sharon Carpenter owed?"

"I'm not sure, but I can ask."

Nana Jo looked about to move on when Dorothy stopped her. "Actually, I have more. My assignment was to check with my friend Lucas Banner. He's in public relations. Lucas and John Cloverton used to be in business together. They started a public relations company. When Cloverton married Mildred, he got bit by the politics bug. He lost interest in helping his clients and the business. Eventually, he sold his half of the business to Lucas and began pushing his own agenda. Lucas said John was always ambitious, but Mildred was even more so. John had the intelligence and the drive, but he had a problem keeping his pants zipped. He would go after just about anything in a skirt."

Irma patted her hair. "Nothing wrong with that."

"Not unless you're married and your wife is extremely jealous."

"Was Mildred jealous?" I asked.

"Extremely. Lucas said she would go into these mad rages if she thought John was even looking at another woman, let alone . . . well, you know. Anyway, that's all I was able to find out."

"That was quite useful in helping to understand John Cloverton's character, as well as Mildred's," I said. "Thank you."

Dorothy smiled. "I'll work on my friend in the high-limits room next and see what he can find out."

Irma raised her hand. "I talked to my friend who works in security at the casino. I asked him about John Cloverton. I didn't know about the mayor's wife, but it'll give me a reason to go back and work on him further."

Nana Jo rolled her eyes. "Get on with what you've found out."

"He said John has a suite at the casino's hotel where he can . . . entertain his lady friends. He was sure that Mildred didn't know anything about it, and the Pontolomas would never tell. According to Davy, John is there at least two nights every week. Lately, he's had a young girl with wavy hair with him."

"That must be Chastity Drummond, his assistant," I said.

"He didn't know the woman's name, but he did say that any cameras that might have picked up anything incriminating against the members of the tribal council would be erased before anyone could subpoena them. The guards were instructed to look through them nightly and flag the ones that they thought could be harmful. So, there won't be any records that could prove that John Cloverton was unfaithful if Mildred wanted to sue him for divorce."

Jenna muttered an oath.

Mom looked shocked. "Jenna Renee Rutherford, watch your mouth."

"Sorry."

Emma had been so quiet at the end of the table that I'd practically forgotten she was there until she raised her hand. "I heard a lot of gossip about Chastity." She was so excited, she practically bounced in her seat. "Before John Cloverton started adjunct teaching on campus, Chastity Drummond used to date this guy named Adam Harmon. Adam dumped her for a cheerleader, Stephanie Littleton. Well, Chastity didn't take getting dumped very well. In fact, she completely freaked out."

"Freaked out how?" Jenna asked.

"Screaming, throwing stuff. She tried to run him over with her car. He had to get a restraining order against her."

Jenna pulled out a notepad. "I'll look into the restraining order. It sounds like Chastity Drummond has quite the temper."

Something in my mind flipped on. "Can you describe Adam Harmon?"

Based on the description that Emma provided, I had a strong feeling that Adam Harmon was the rude quiet guy in the social media class. "What happened?"

"Stephanie dumped Adam for a guy on the soccer team," Emma said, "and last I heard, Adam was trying to get back with Chastity, but she's moved on. Was any of that helpful?"

"Definitely. We've learned that Chastity Drummond has quite the temper. If she tried to murder one of her former boyfriends who dumped her, she might have succeeded with another."

Emma fished through her backpack and pulled out a flyer. "I almost forgot. MISU is having a memorial for John Cloverton this evening. I thought maybe you guys might want to come."

"Absolutely, thank you," Nana Jo said. "Well done."

Frank cleared his throat. "My military contacts were able

to find out a bit about John Cloverton's military service. Turns out, he served in the same division with another prominent North Harbor resident. Any guesses?"

"Chief of Police Zachary Davis?" Jenna said.

Frank smiled. "Bingo. John Cloverton and Zachary Davis were friends. Cloverton's record was fairly clean, apart from complaints from some of the local men that Cloverton had . . . ah, deflowered their daughters, which can be a major problem depending on which part of the world you're deployed in."

"You're saying one of these fathers might have come seeking vengeance against Cloverton?" Nana Jo asked.

"Honestly, I doubt it, but it goes with what we learned from Dorothy's friend. John Cloverton was a playboy. If he cheated before, he was probably still cheating. Chastity Drummond may have been the latest flavor of the day, but it doesn't sound like any of them lasted very long."

"None, except for Mildred," I said. "I wonder why?"

"Zachary Davis was dishonorably discharged when he was caught selling military supplies on the black market."

"Why, that dirty little bas—"

"Irma!"

Irma burst into a coughing fit. This time, she reached into her purse and pulled out a flask. She took a swig and then returned the flask to her bag.

Nana Jo looked around. "Is that everyone?"

"I haven't had a chance to talk to Mildred Cloverton," I said, "but I'm going to swing by later today." I gave Frank a puppy dog stare. "I was hoping I could take over one of your delicious cakes."

"I have a lemon cake that has been very popular. Please, include my condolences."

"Of course." He really was a good man. Why was I hesitating? A good man who likes to cook is golden. Life with him would be spent with corn chowder soup, bacon sandwiches, and lemon cake. What more could any woman ask?

Nana Jo put down her iPad and cleared her throat. "I talked to my friend who's a research librarian. He looked through his archived newspapers and found a curious article." She seemed reluctant to talk, but she took a deep breath and came out with it. "It seems that when Detective Pitt was in high school, he was trying to break up a fight between a couple of boys. Well, things got very heated, and the bigger boys turned on him. They beat him to a pulp. He was hospitalized with two broken ribs and a broken leg."

Jenna put her head in her hands. "Please don't tell me one of the boys was John Cloverton."

Nana Jo nodded. "I vaguely remembered it when it happened, but the problem was the incident took place on tribal land."

"Which is considered a separate nation and not subject to the laws of the United States," Jenna said.

"Wait, I don't understand," Mom said. "What do you mean?"

"American Indians and Alaska Natives are United States citizens and therefore are subject to federal, tribal, and state laws. However, for crimes committed on federal Indian reservations, only federal laws apply. Even still, not all federal offenses are prosecuted. It's a big contention between Native Americans and the Justice Department. I just read an article about it. Crime on federal reservations is two and a half times higher than virtually anywhere else in the country. The statistics for crimes against Indian women are shocking, and they are ten times more likely to be murdered and four times more likely to be raped or sexually assaulted than the national average."

"Good God," Nana Jo said. "What's going on? Haven't those people suffered enough? I mean, they had their land

142 V. M. Burns

taken from them. They were murdered. They were lied to and given promises which we failed to keep."

"Why isn't anyone reporting about that?" I asked. "Why is it I can pick up a newspaper like the *North Harbor Herald* and read about rumors and accusations, but this is happening right under our noses and no one is doing anything?"

"Don't shoot the messenger," Jenna said. "I have no idea. The Justice Department claims there's a lack of evidence, but who knows the truth."

We sat in shocked silence for several moments. Eventually, Jenna stood up. "I've got to go track down my client and find out when he planned to tell me that he and the man he is accused of murdering had a history." She sighed. "This explains why the district attorney was so cocky in court." She walked toward the stairs but turned before she went down. "I sure hope you all can figure out who murdered John Cloverton, because otherwise, Detective Bradley Pitt will have about as much chance of beating this as a snowball in . . ." She glanced at our mom. "Well, you know where."

# Chapter 14

Christopher, Zaq, and Emma agreed to hold down the fort at the bookstore while I took the cake that Frank had packed up for me to Mildred Cloverton's home.

Mildred Cloverton lived in the same area as my sister, Jenna. It was a street known as the historic district. During North Harbor's thriving past, this was the place Southwestern Michigan's wealthy manufacturing titans called home. There were large Victorian and Georgian homes, cobblestoned streets, and yards with wrought-iron fences. Unfortunately, when the automobile-manufacturing jobs left town, many of the area's wealthy families followed suit. The large homes fell into disrepair. The people who remained broke up the big older homes and converted many of them into rentals. In the last decade, there was a movement to save the area and the homes that were vacant were bought by the city and sold for a dollar each to individuals willing to rehab the homes, convert them back into single-family residences, and live in the area. Jenna and Tony were among some of the first to snag one of the Harbor's painted ladies.

John and Mildred Cloverton's home was a large Victorian that had been renovated to the max. I'd passed the house many times over the years and often commented about the extent of the renovations. There was too much of what Nana Jo called gingerbread for my liking. Between the embellished millwork that surrounded the wraparound porch, the turned posts, turrets, and stained-glass windows, the bubble-gum pink and white-trimmed house reminded me of a wedding cake topper or a dollhouse. No detail was left undone. Wherever an embellishment could be placed, it was.

I pulled up to the front, and Nana Jo and I stared.

"All that gingerbread and sweetness makes my teeth ache," Nana Jo said. She opened her door. "Come on. Let's get this over."

We walked up the front porch and rang the doorbell.

Mildred Cloverton opened the door and stared as though she knew our faces but couldn't remember our names.

"Mrs. Cloverton, my name is Samantha Washington, and this is my grandmother, Josephine Thomas. We're in your class."

"Oh, yes, now I remember."

"We heard about what happened, and we wanted to come by and give you our condolences," Nana Jo said. "We are both very sorry for your loss."

"My loss?" Her eyes glazed over as though she had no idea what loss we were referring to. Within moments, she was back and forced a smile. "I'm dreadfully sorry. Please, won't you come in?"

She held the door open, and we stepped inside. I'd often wondered if the inside was as hideous as the outside. It was. The house was crammed full of Victorian furniture and covered with lace doilies. The hardwood floor peeked out from under the large rugs that covered practically every inch.

"My boyfriend owns the North Harbor Café downtown,

and the food is wonderful, but the cakes are fantastic." I held out the white box. "He sent this along with his condolences."

"How kind." She took the box and then stood awkwardly as though she had no idea what to do with it.

Situations like this were where Nana Jo shone. She put an arm around Mildred and gazed into her eyes. "How are you holding up? Have you eaten today?"

"Eaten?" She thought. "I don't know . . . I don't think I have, but I honestly can't remember."

Nana Jo patted her arm. "That's okay. You're probably in shock, but you must eat." She turned to me. "Sam, take that cake in the kitchen." She turned back to Mrs. Cloverton. "You don't mind if I call you Mildred, do you?"

Mildred shook her head.

"Good, and you must call me Josephine."

Hearing no opposition from our host, I wandered around a corner where I assumed the kitchen was located. I was right. The kitchen was small, with avocado-green appliances. I put the box on the counter. Nana Jo joined me. "I think the woman is in shock. You go in there and stay with her. I'm going to make her some scrambled eggs and hot tea."

Mildred was sitting on the Victorian settee in the living room. I sat next to her, expecting to sink into the cushion, but I nearly bounced up again when my rear hit the hard cushion covered in velvet upholstery.

"You look familiar," she said.

Considering we'd just told her who we were, I wondered if she was suffering from more than just shock. Nana Jo was the one with the nursing experience. She should be here. I could certainly scramble eggs. I patted Mildred's hand and tried to think of something to say or do. "You saw us at the social media class. I'm an author, and my publisher wants me to build my social media platform."

"Have you written anything I might have read?"

Boy, how I hated that question. "No, my book hasn't been published yet, but I write British historic cozy mysteries set between World War One and World War Two. I used to teach English at North Harbor High School, but when my husband died I opened a mystery bookshop."

"Your husband died too? Was he poisoned?"

"Ah, no. He died from cancer."

Nana Jo came out with a tray. There was a steaming-hot cup of tea and a plate with scrambled eggs and toast. She also had a slice of Frank's lemon cake. "Now, you need to eat, and I'm going to sit here and see that you do."

Mildred Cloverton must have recognized the authority in Nana Jo's voice, because she ate most of the eggs, half of the toast, and none of the cake. She did drink the tea. I wondered if she was afraid that we had poisoned the cake. I was tempted to pick up the fork and take a bite to prove to her the cake was safe to eat. Well, partly to prove to her the cake was safe and partly because Frank's cakes were moist and delicious and I was looking forward to eating it. Normally, when you bring a cake to a grieving widow she offers you a slice. Mildred must have missed that lesson in the grieving-widows handbook.

When Mildred finished her tea, she turned to Nana Jo. "Thank you. That was delicious, and I have to say, I feel better already, but you mustn't wait on me. You're guests. I should be the one serving you." She rose to stand.

"Oh, no, you don't," Nana Jo said. "You're still suffering from shock. There'll be no waiting on us today."

"But there's no way I can possibly eat an entire cake by myself—" Her voice caught, but she recovered. "Please, it's much more enjoyable to eat when someone else is eating too."

I hopped up. "You're absolutely right. I'll just go cut slices for Nana Jo and myself, and we'll all sit here and eat cake together." I walked back into the kitchen. I rummaged around until I found two more plates and cut hefty slices of cake for both of us. Then I grabbed two forks and went back into the living room. I handed one plate and fork to Nana Jo and then took mine and moved back to the concrete slab that was masquerading as a settee. This time I was careful to sit lightly.

I took a large bite of the cake and allowed it to dissolve on my tongue. "Hmmm. It's delicious; really you should try it."

Mildred took a small bite. Her eyes grew big, and she stared. "That was wonderful."

I mumbled around my second or third forkful of cake, "See, I told you."

In record time, those slices of cake were done and we were left licking our forks in a comfortable sugar haze.

"Thank you," Mildred said. "That really was the best cake I've ever had."

I put down my fork. "I'll be sure to tell Frank you enjoyed it."

"Is there anything that you need?" Nana Jo asked. "Anything we can help you with?"

She hung her head. "No. The police haven't released his body yet, so I can't make funeral arrangements, but the university is having a memorial service for him later today." She turned to us. "Will you two be able to attend?"

"We're planning to come," I said.

Nana Jo grabbed her hand. "Mrs. Cloverton, I'm sure you know the police believe that your ex-husband, Detective Pitt, is responsible for your husband's death."

Mildred Cloverton looked down. "Yes, I know."

"Well, I taught Detective Pitt when he was in second grade, and over the past couple of years our paths have crossed many times, and I want to tell you that I don't believe he had anything to do with your husband's murder."

"You don't?" Mildred stared. After a few moments, she sighed. "I'm so relieved. I thought I was the only one."

"You don't think he did it either?" I asked.

"Not at first, but he did hit John at the restaurant. He's always been . . . self-conscious about . . . well, you know." She looked away. "Plus, it was his gun, but . . . I just don't know."

"Well, we're going to find out who really killed your husband if it's the last thing we do," I said.

# Chapter 15

"Well, what did you think?" Nana Jo asked when we were alone in the car.

"She definitely seems to be dazed or in shock. Although I'm sure I was much the same way after Leon died, and he wasn't murdered."

"She seemed a bit . . . odd to me. I can't really put my finger on it, but there was something not right. Did you notice how she kept tearing her napkin?"

"Nerves?"

"Maybe. I'm sure she must be under a great deal of strain, but there's something she's not telling us."

"Understandable; she barely knows us."

"True. Well, anyway. We've done our Christian duty, and I'm sure once we find out who really killed her husband, that should give her some form of peace."

I wondered. If someone had murdered Leon, I'm not sure I'd be at peace. I'd want revenge. I'd want to see them suffer a painful end, but then maybe Mildred Cloverton was more Christlike than me.

Back at the bookshop, Jillian and Dawson had joined the crew, and given the jovial mood, I guessed things had gone well for both of them.

Dawson was all smiles. "I passed. I can't believe it."

Nana Jo and I took turns hugging him and congratulating him.

Jillian had the biggest smile. "He didn't just pass. He aced it."

We complimented him until he blushed with embarrassment. He turned to Jillian. "Tell them about your audition."

I gazed into her face, and you didn't need to be a mind reader to see that she was pleased.

"The audition was amazing. I was so nervous up until time to dance. Then I just felt a flood of peace wash over me. It was amazing. The music started, and I felt so calm." She turned to me. "Regardless of what decision they make, I have no regrets."

I hugged her. "That's wonderful. I'm so happy for you."

"This calls for a celebration," Nana Jo said. She sent Zaq down to Frank's to buy another lemon cake and a bottle of champagne.

I rushed upstairs and got glasses, plates, and silverware and brought them down. Thankfully, there weren't many people in the store, and we were able to toast to the promise of new opportunities and success.

Nana Jo and I took over the reins of the bookshop and kicked the young folks out to celebrate in their own way. When the last customer left, we cleaned up and prepared for the next day. We still had an hour before the memorial was scheduled to start for John Cloverton, so I took the opportunity to get a bit more writing done.

"Peter!" was all the warning Detective Inspector Covington got before Lady Clara hurled herself into his arms.

Stunned, he pushed her away so he could stare into her eyes. "Clara? What are you doing here?"

She poked out her lip. "That's a fine welcome, and I come all the way—"

He pulled her into his arms and kissed her. When he came up for air, he looked around. He noticed James, and a slight flush rose up his neck. He pushed Lady Clara an arm's length away. "James . . . ah, Lord Browning." He extended his hand to shake.

"You had it right the first time." The duke smiled. "Please call me James. After all, you're practically family."

The color deepened, and Peter looked confused. "I'm happy to see you both, but . . . what are you doing here?"

"We're about to grab lunch. Would you care to join us?" James caught the eye of the owner, who hurried over and bowed.

"What can I do for Your Grace?"

"Do you have a private area where my friends and I can have a few pints and a bite to eat?"

The red-faced publican directed the group to an alcove set off from the rest of the pub. James ordered pints for the three of them, and their host hurried to get their drinks, promising to take care of them personally.

Clara nestled next to Peter and seemed reluctant to let him out of her sight.

Once the drinks were served, James raised his tankard. "To old friends."

"Old friends."

They drank.

"Are you two going to tell me what you're doing here?" Covington said.

"Daphne and I are staying at Chequers."

Covington frowned. "Isn't that the prime minister's retreat?"

James nodded. "It is, but the duties of the empire won't allow him to get away, so he asked if Daphne and I would come and help nurse a sick friend."

Covington turned to Clara. "Are you nursing this friend also?"

"No. I'm going to be working at Bletchley Park, tending to ailing government workers."

"Bletchley Park! Are you out of your mind?"

"No, I'll be working there, not installed as a patient."

"But you can't work there. I won't allow it. It's . . . not safe."

Lady Clara unwrapped her arm from the detective's. "You won't allow it? I don't recall asking for your permission."

Peter Covington turned from Clara to his friend. "James, please talk to her. I've only been here a few days, but there are some strange things going on at that place." He leaned across the table. "Very strange things are happening, and none of the locals seem to have the slightest idea what's going on."

James's face looked serious, although if Peter Covington hadn't been so intent on convincing his friend of his point, he might have noticed the duke's eyes held a playful light. "Whatever do you mean?"

The detective glanced around to make sure they couldn't be overheard. "Well, they've hired a lot of young people, men and women. The women all appear to be mostly members of the aristocracy. They rent rooms with local families and travel to Bletchley Park during the day."

"There doesn't seem to be anything sinister in that. Even debutantes need to eat these days. Long gone are the days when well-bred women spent their days embroidering cushions, learning French, and waiting to be introduced to a wealthy suitor so they could marry well."

Peter Covington ignored the remark. "The men are all educated college students who go around speaking Greek and Latin."

"I'm glad some of the dead languages are being spoken again, but I can't see how any of this poses a danger for Clara."

Lady Clara was seething. "Thank you!"

The detective looked from Lady Clara to James. Something in the duke's manner made him pause. "You know, don't you?"

"My good man. I have no idea what you're referring to. However, I can assure you that Bletchley Park is perfectly safe." He glanced at Clara. "Rest assured. I would never deliberately place Clara in harm's way." He took a sip. "In fact, I may be making more trips here myself."

Peter Covington stared at his friend and leaned back. "Does whatever is happening at Bletchley Park have anything to do with why I was reassigned, why I keep running into the blokes from the American Embassy, and all the bizarre things that seem to be happening?"

James glanced around and saw the proprietor hoovering nearby. "I couldn't possibly say. Why don't you join us for dinner at Chequers tonight? I'm sure Daphne, Lady Elizabeth, and Lord William will love to see you. We can talk more then, and maybe you can tell me more about the *bizarre* things." He smiled. "Now, I'm starving. Shall we eat?"

Nana Jo and I drove to Shady Acres and picked up Irma, Dorothy, and Ruby Mae and headed to MISU. The memorial service was held in a small chapel in the center of campus. It was quaint and picturesque and looked as though it would be a beautiful spot for a wedding. The white-steepled building had stained-glass windows, wooden pews, and a carved wooden altar. The vaulted ceiling and simple design gave the chapel a spiritual feel. I found myself imaging the ends of the pews decorated with English roses, Asiatic lilies, and lilacs.

"What a cute chapel," I whispered, even though the ceremony hadn't started.

"This was one of the first buildings built on campus," Emma said. "The monks who started the school built it over two hundred and fifty years ago. The trustees wanted to modernize the building, you know, add electricity and heat, but the student body protested."

Nana Jo fanned herself. "Air conditioning would be nice. It must be hotter than the devil in the summer."

"Not all of the windows are stained glass," Emma said, and I noticed that every other window was raised.

"I feel a breeze," I said.

"That's one of the benefits of being located on Lake Michigan. And history isn't the only reason we opposed modernizing the chapel. This is the only original building left. All of the others were modernized, and all of them caught fire and burned to the ground."

Nana Jo pointed to the candles that lined the area. "Well, candles in a two-hundred-fifty-year-old building can't be good either."

"You're right," Jillian said, "which is why the building isn't used often. Just occasional weddings and short memorial services like this."

We found seats that provided great views.

Mildred was escorted in by a priest and a woman I recognized as the university's president from the solicitation mailers I received. All of the students from our social media class came.

I glanced around. "I'm surprised Chastity didn't—"

Nana Jo poked me in the ribs and inclined her head toward the door.

Red-faced and tear-streaked, Chastity Drummond stumbled into the chapel. She plopped on the first available seat and sobbed quietly.

Nana Jo rose and walked to the back of the chapel. She sat next to Chastity, put her arm around her, and held her.

The priest started the service with a brief prayer. The service was traditional, with hymns, a Scripture reading, some words from the president, and a few reminiscences from other faculty members. In the end, Mildred stood and thanked everyone for coming.

"Is it just me or was that a bit . . . cold?" Emma whispered.

"Not just you."

Jillian glanced at her watch. "That entire service didn't last thirty minutes."

We rose and walked toward the front of the building to give condolences to the grieving widow.

Mildred's expression was stoic as she shook hands. While waiting for my turn in line, I couldn't help but notice that only half her attention seemed engaged with the fellow mourners sharing their condolences. Her gaze kept drifting to the back pew, where Chastity Drummond continued to sob.

The line progressed, and I once again expressed my condolences for Mildred's loss.

Mildred looked as though she didn't remember who I was. I was just about to remind her that we had shared a cake just a few hours ago when I saw the lightbulb go on in her head.

"Forgive me, Samantha. I'm just so overwhelmed. Moments like this . . . well, it makes everything real."

My mind flashed back to Leon's funeral. There was so much to do. I felt like I was running on autopilot. Nonstop parades of people from my work, his work, church, family, and friends came to express their sympathy. They wanted to let me know they were there to help when all I wanted was to be left alone so I could fall apart in the peace and comfort of my own home. On impulse, I reached out and hugged Mildred. At first, she stood there stiff and immovable, but eventually, I felt her relax.

When I released her, she pulled back and stared at me. "Thank you. Can I talk to you . . . when this is over?"

"Of course." I glanced back and remembered the line of people still waiting for their turn. "I'll wait for you outside."

Emma, Jillian, and I walked to the back pew. Nana Jo and Chastity were nowhere to be seen. Ruby Mae was seated on a nearby pew having a conversation with two students who looked like relatives. Irma was standing close to a small, thin man dressed in tweed with a bow tie. We filed outside and saw Nana Jo and Chastity standing under a nearby tree. Just as we headed toward them, Adam Harmon approached.

"Get away from me!" Chastity screamed.

"Come on, Chaz. I just want to talk."

"No. You stay away."

Adam extended his arm. Chastity screamed and lunged at him. She swung her arms like windmills, scratching his face and pummeling his chest with her fists.

He tried to protect himself, but he eventually reached out and grabbed her wrists.

We hurried to help. Emma and Jillian pulled Chastity away, while Nana Jo and Dorothy moved in between them.

"Chastity, come on," Adam Harmon said. "I just wanna talk."

Nana Jo pointed her finger in his chest. "Young man, listen to me." She narrowed her eyes and used her stern teacher voice. "It's clear that Chastity doesn't want to talk to you right now. I strongly encourage you to give her some space."

Adam Harmon looked for a brief moment as though he didn't intend to heed Nana Jo's warning. However, she and Dorothy not only were both taller than him but also each probably weighed a hundred pounds more. Despite his athletic build, my money was on the two martial arts experts.

Dorothy glared. "Son, I'd highly recommend you think about whether you want to get knocked on your butt by two old women in front of all of your friends."

Adam Harmon glanced around and noticed the crowd that Chastity's outburst had attracted. He turned and walked away.

Emma and Jillian had taken Chastity to a stone bench in the formal rose garden, which was situated at the end of a gravel path lined with miniature privet hedges and classic rosebushes.

Chastity slumped against Jillian, her energy spent. "I don't know why he won't leave me alone. He doesn't understand. No one understands. John was the only one who . . ."

"You loved him, didn't you?" Nana Jo asked.

She looked up. "John was wonderful. He treated me like a queen . . . like I was special." She gulped. 'We were going to be married."

"Liar!"

We were all so focused on Chastity, we hadn't noticed that Mildred Cloverton had arrived. "You little liar. You were nothing to him. Nothing!"

"That's not true," Chastity whimpered.

"You were just one more of his dalliances in a long string of silly young girls who thought they could come between us, but you're wrong. None of you meant anything to him."

Chastity mustered up her courage. "That's not true. John loved me. We were going to be married. He was going to divorce you and—"

Mildred laughed. "Divorce me? Is that what he told you? He couldn't divorce me and marry you even if he wanted to. John was Catholic. Didn't you know?"

Chastity's lip quivered, and she looked about ready to faint. "But . . . he was . . ."

Mildred laughed. Her laugh echoed with a ring of madness that sent a shiver down my spine.

"That's enough of that," Nana Jo said. She turned to Emma and Jillian. "Take Chastity back to her dorm."

They nodded and helped the trembling girl to move, half dragging her across campus.

We turned back to Mildred, who collapsed onto the ground and sobbed.

Dorothy and Nana Jo helped her onto the bench.

I handed her a handkerchief, and when her sobs slowed I said, "You knew that your husband was having an affair with Chastity?"

"Of course I knew. Wives always know." She sniffed. "Not that it mattered. John didn't try to hide the little tarts. Every month or so there would be a new one. Each one younger, thinner, prettier than the one before." She took several deep breaths. "Black, white, Asian, Hispanic . . . it didn't matter to him. John was addicted to women." She looked at me. "But it wasn't serious. None of them meant anything to him. They were just . . . like a drug to an addict." She waved her hand. "She was no different than any of the others. In fact, he was already starting to tire of her constant requests for more. That's one surefire way to get John to lose interest. Ask for more . . . ask for commitment."

I struggled to understand. I couldn't imagine this type of relationship.

"Did you and John have an open marriage?" Nana Jo asked.

Open marriage? What did my grandmother know about open marriages? If my grandfather had dared look at another woman with anything resembling lust, she would have pulled out her revolver and shot him.

Mildred sighed. "Open on his end? Yes. I didn't . . . I wasn't addicted to men."

"Did he tell you that he planned to end things with Chastity?" I asked.

"He didn't have to. I recognized the signs." She smirked. "Trust me, things had cooled off, at least on his side."

I glanced at Nana Jo, but she didn't seem to have any further questions. I turned to Mildred. "Was that what you wanted to talk to me about?"

"No, actually, I wanted to help."

"Help?"

"Earlier, you said you intended to find John's killer. Well, I want to help."

"So, you don't believe Detective Pitt is guilty either?" I asked.

"I was married to Brad for ten years. Frankly, I find it hard to believe him capable of that much emotion." She smiled.

"That's partly what ended our marriage. He was such a . . . cold fish." She glanced into the distance. "John was the complete opposite. He was so passionate and ambitious. He just swept me off my feet." She looked from Nana Jo to Dorothy and then back at me. "I suppose it's possible that Brad killed him. The police think so. I mean, John was killed with the gun Brad kept in his nightstand. Plus, he was furious with John, but . . . I believe in keeping an open mind. If there's the slightest chance that someone else killed him, then I want to see that justice is served. Please."

I shrugged. "Why not?"

She smiled. "Thank you. Now, where do we start?"

# Chapter 16

We started by sending Mildred home to rest. It was getting late, and I knew Dorothy had a date. Normally, I wouldn't have agreed to go to the Four Feathers twice in one week, but given the fact that both Dorothy's and Irma's sources worked there and the victim was a member of the tribe that ran it, I figured the casino might hold some useful clues.

The drive from MISU to the casino was short and uneventful. We continued our routine and started with dinner. As usual, by the time I had dropped off my passengers, parked, and made my way back to the restaurant, they were already seated. Over dinner, we talked about what we'd learned from Mildred.

"Who were you chatting with in the chapel?" I asked Ruby Mae.

"Two of my great-grandkids and a great-nephew. They confirmed that John Cloverton didn't believe in discrimination. He'd chase after anything in a skirt. My granddaughter and a friend met him when they volunteered to work on his campaign. They said he flirted with all of them . . . that is, whenever Chastity or his wife wasn't there. But he was on his best behavior whenever his wife or Chastity was around." She knitted. "According to the kids, both women had bad tempers."

"Well, we can confirm that firsthand," Dorothy said. "Plus, there's that ex-boyfriend, Adam Harmon. He might have killed Cloverton too. I thought I was going to need to flip him on his backside right there in front of the chapel."

Ruby Mae smiled. "I think you would have enjoyed flipping that boy."

Dorothy grinned. "I admit it."

Nana Jo turned to Irma. "What about you? Before I took Chastity outside, I saw you had cornered some old fogey."

"That was Professor Smith." Irma preened herself. "He's taking me to a poetry reading tomorrow night."

Nana Jo rolled her eyes. "You were supposed to be getting information to help Detective Pitt, not picking up strange men."

"Some of us are able to do both." Irma patted her hair. "Smithy was Chastity Drummond's mentor. According to him, she was obsessed with John Cloverton. She told him that Cloverton planned to leave Mildred and marry her."

"Did he say that Cloverton actually told her that he was leaving his wife?" I asked.

"No. In fact, he tried to tell her that married men rarely left their wives for their . . . paramours." Irma glanced around the table. "That means 'lovers.' I looked it up."

"We know what it means," Nana Jo said.

"How did she take it?" I asked.

"Smithy said she went completely ballistic. He was worried about her. She was just recovering from being dumped by that Harmon boy, and she'd nearly had a complete mental breakdown. Then she'd immediately jumped into this relationship with Cloverton. Well, I can tell you that he was very much concerned about what she might do."

We talked a bit longer and then followed the rest of our routine. Irma went to the bar to track down her security friend, while Dorothy headed to the high-limits room in search of hers. Ruby Mae was being showered with love, attention, and pastry by her relatives, and Nana Jo wandered out to the blackjack table.

Despite routine trips to the casino, I didn't consider myself a big gambler. However, I did find the slots surprisingly calming despite the flashing and blinking lights, music, entertaining graphics, games, and videos that interrupted play. I suspected it was the mindless routine of merely pushing a button or pulling a lever. I found the games practically did everything with a minimal amount of interaction from me. On occasion, I would be asked to make a selection, but those were few and far between. Most of my time was spent simply watching the wheels spin, which didn't require a lot of mental energy.

I found a penny slot that I'd played before called Sun and Moon. I knew from experience this game did practically all of the work. I inserted twenty dollars and selected a bet that would cost me one dollar and fifty cents. I pressed "spin" and was surprised to see that I got five moons. In addition to tripling my twenty-dollar investment, I was now awarded fifty spins. I sat back and allowed my mind to wander while the machine went through its paces.

John Cloverton was a predator. He was a Don Juan who preyed on young, vulnerable women like Chastity Drummond. Normally, I didn't have a lot of sympathy for women who dated married men, but Chastity was different. She had been dumped by her previous boyfriend. It sounded like she was on the verge of a nervous breakdown when John Cloverton came along. He was handsome, and she probably found his attention flattering, especially after a breakup. If Mildred Cloverton was right and John had tired of Chastity, she might have been capable of murder. Based on her interaction with Adam Harmon, she was certainly capable of violence.

I glanced at my machine. I must have gotten more suns and moons, because rather than decreasing, my number of free spins was now at eighty-seven.

Mildred said John Cloverton was addicted to women. Sharon Carpenter was also addicted, but her addiction appeared to be gambling. If she owed the casino money, how far would she have gone to have her debts eliminated? She shared secrets that might have gotten her husband ousted from office. Or did she? Charmaine Carpenter sounded like an overprotective mother-in-law. She might have embellished Sharon's faults to make her daughter-in-law look bad. I've certainly heard similar stories from friends through the years who've had mothers-in-law who were overbearing monsters-in-law. Leon's mother was the kindest person I'd ever met and never interfered in our lives. When she died, I mourned as much as Leon did. I wondered about Frank's mother. I knew she was alive, but he rarely talked about her.

I glanced at my machine. One hundred and twelve games. I must have retriggered the fifty spins.

What about the chief of police, Zachary Davis? If Ruby Mae's cousin was to be believed, he was misappropriating money from North Harbor's already small coffers. Would he have murdered John Cloverton to put an end to the negative publicity? Abigail had told Ruby Mae that Davis was fearful that Cloverton would demand an audit. What lengths would he go to in order to avoid an audit and potential jail time?

I watched the wheels spin, and something in my brain spun. There was some piece of information . . . some clue that was spinning like the wheels of a slot machine. Unfortunately, the clues kept slipping by. The harder I tried to stop the wheels spinning, the more frustrated I became. Experience had taught me that dwelling on this issue wouldn't produce the jackpot I desired. So, I forced myself to focus on the game and let the clues spin in the background. When the free spins finished, my twenty dollars had turned into three hundred. I cashed out my ticket—no point in pressing my luck.

I needed to think. Writing helped me sort through problems. So, I looked for my quiet corner near the hotel reception area, sat down, and pulled out my notepad.

"Peter, you're late." Lady Clara rose to greet the detective, but something in his face made her stop. "What's happened?"

"I'm afraid I can't stay. I only came by to give my apologies. There's been a murder at The Park."

Lady Clara halted. "Murder?"

"Dear God," James said. "Who?"

"Stop firing questions at the poor man," Lady Elizabeth said. "Peter, have a seat and tell us what happened." She turned to the butler, who had just entered. "Thompkins, please bring Peter a drink . . . brandy."

Peter opened his mouth to protest but changed his mind. He sat in a chair by the fireplace and turned to James. "I knew there was something wrong at that place. When the call came in that there'd been a murder, I was terrified that it was . . ."

Lady Clara hurried to his side. She dropped to her knees and grabbed his hand. "I'm sorry you were worried, but I'm fine."

Thompkins entered with a tray with a glass of brandy and offered it to the detective.

"Thank you." He took the drink. His hand shook

slightly. "That's why I didn't want you working there."

"Clara's perfectly fine," James said. "She wasn't scheduled to start working until tomorrow, but . . . who's been murdered?"

Peter took his hand from Lady Clara to get his notepad. He pulled it out of his pocket and flipped a few pages. "A young man named Philip Chester."

James released the breath he was holding, and his shoulders relaxed. "How?"

Peter moved to the edge of his seat. "That's the strange part. At four o'clock I was sent a note to come to Bletchley Park."

"From whom?" James asked.

Peter glanced at Clara. "I assumed it was from you."

"It wasn't me," she whispered.

"Why did you think the note was from Clara?" Lady Elizabeth asked.

Peter flushed. "It was . . .personal."

"What exactly did it say?" James asked.

"'Darling, meet me at The Park at five.'"

Lady Clara shook her head. "I didn't write it."

"Did you know this man . . . this Philip Chester?" James asked.

Peter shook his head. "Never heard of him before. I asked around, and he's some kind of maths genius." He stood up and paced. "When I got to The Park, there's Chester on the floor having convulsions and a box of chocolates lying nearby. The chocolates had my name on them."

Clara gasped. "Your name? But . . ." She stared hard. "Don't tell me I'm supposed to have sent them."

Peter Covington nodded. "The card read: *'To P.C. With all my love, T.'*"

"T?" Lord Browning asked.

"Trewellan-Harper," Peter explained.

The color drained from Lady Clara's face, and she swayed. Peter hurried to her side and helped her sit down.

"I'm fine. Really, but someone tried to kill you."

Peter rubbed the back of his neck. "I'm afraid it isn't the first time."

"What do you mean?" Clara asked.

Lady Elizabeth pushed the button to summon the butler. When Thompkins arrived, she said, "You'd better tell the cook we'll be eating late, and I think we may need more brandy."

"Yes, m'lady."

Thompkins returned with a tray and five glasses. He poured the amber liquid into each and distributed them around. When he was finished, he turned to leave.

"Thompkins, perhaps you'd stay," Lady Elizabeth said. "I suspect we might need your assistance."

Thompkins bowed and stood silently in the corner.

"Now, James, I think it's time you told us the truth about what's really going on at Bletchley Park, so we can figure out who killed that poor man and prevent them from succeeding in killing Peter."

# Chapter 17

Part of our routine involved meeting in the lobby around midnight. So, I put away my notepad and prepared to head down to the lobby. Along the way, I passed a sculpture I'd noticed on previous visits but never stopped to examine in detail. Tonight, I stopped. The sculpture was a wood-carved figure of an eagle. The wings were extended, and the span appeared more than six feet from tip to tip. The feathers were intricately carved, as were all the bird's features. I was particularly in awe of the feet, which had sharp talons that looked as though they could easily rip a person to shreds.

"The eagle is sacred to my people."

I jumped at the unexpected voice. "Oh, I didn't hear you." I patted my heart.

"Sorry, I didn't mean to scare you."

An older man with tanned skin that was so wrinkled it looked like leather stood beside me. He had a head full of thick white hair and sharp eyes. His nose was prominent, and he wore an amulet around his neck that bore the symbols of the Four Feathers.

"This sculpture is amazing. There's so much detail."

He smiled. "Thank you."

"You did that? You're the artist?" I turned and stared at the metal plate with the artist's name and bio.

He chuckled. "Guilty as charged."

"That's beautiful. It looks so realistic. It looks like that eagle could just take off."

He placed his hand over his heart. "Thank you. That is the best compliment you could have given me. My people believe that all living things have souls. Trees have souls—water, earth, and air. When I take a piece of wood that has died from the ground and carve the wood into an eagle, it allows the wood's soul to return. The wood's soul combines with the soul of the carved creature, and both of them live as one."

I was mesmerized by his words. "That's beautiful."

"You are a very kind and . . . smart woman. You understand what it means to bring something that is dead back to life."

I paused. "I write books, and sometimes when I'm writing, it feels like I'm taking something that's dead. Words, just plain black letters, and by arranging them on the page, I'm able to pull things from my mind that don't exist—things that aren't real—and breathe life into them. I'm able to create people who feel real to me." I stopped and sighed. "It's silly, I know."

He held up his hand. "No, it's not silly. You, too, are an artist, just like me. My medium is wood, but yours is paper and words."

"I guess so. Well, I'd better go. My grandmother is waiting for me." I started to walk away, but when I turned back to thank him he was gone.

I got a shiver down my spine but shook it off. *There are probably hidden doors all over this place.*

Nana Jo and the girls were all waiting in the lobby for me. When we settled up at the end of the night, I wasn't the only one who had managed to come out ahead. Everyone, including Irma and Ruby Mae, had been successful, but the biggest winner was Dorothy. Thanks to her good luck, we all walked out fifteen hundred dollars richer. The winnings from the high-limits room were always impressive.

I brought the car around, and everyone piled in. I was barely off the premises before Dorothy started sharing what she'd learned.

"Emile wasn't working, and I was bummed out until I looked up and saw Sharon Carpenter walk in."

"Was she alone?" I asked. "Did you talk to her?"

"Hold your horses and I'll tell you." Dorothy took a deep breath, which I suspected was more for dramatic effect than out of a need for oxygen. "So, I was playing blackjack when she walked in and sat down right next to me. I couldn't believe my luck. We just started talking. You know, nothing serious, just the usual *'Have you been here long? Found anything that's paying?'* The normal stuff. She said she'd been there most of the day and had just about lost her shirt, but she refused to leave. She just had to win her money back."

"That's never good," Nana Jo said. "I've seen people like that. It never works out the way they want, and they just keep throwing good money after bad. Before they know it, they're head over hills in the hole."

From the rearview mirror, I saw Dorothy nodding. "That's exactly what seemed to happen to her. She panicked, and the more she lost, the more panicked she became. It was awful. I tried to help her, but she just kept making more and more reckless bets, and then she had a complete meltdown."

"Poor woman," Ruby Mae said. "The casino shouldn't be allowed to do that. It seems like they ought to be able to ban her from the premises."

"They do have a program for people who are addicted, but it's a self-reporting program," Dorothy said. "The person turns their name into the casino, and they aren't allowed to gamble, but . . . it's hard to enforce."

"I'm sure it is," I said. "That building is massive." I thought of how my artist friend had disappeared so suddenly.

We talked about the dangers of gambling, but as we got closer to home Dorothy continued to fill us in.

"It didn't take long for her money to run out. She went to the ATM a couple of times but hit her daily limit for withdrawals. Then she went to the cashiers and tried to cash a check, but they wouldn't take it. Her last one bounced."

"That fits in with the papers I found on Mayor Carpenter's desk," Nana Jo said. "I finally got a good look at the photographs I took. I thought the mayor was taking money from city accounts, but they were his personal accounts. I'll bet he's been moving money out of accounts that his wife has access to and into other accounts for her own good. There was also a brochure for a retreat and plane tickets to Portugal. I thought he was moving his money around because he was planning to skip town." She turned on her visor light and swiped her phone. "The retreat is for gambling addiction."

"Glad to hear he's aware of the problem and trying to get her some help," I said.

"When she couldn't get any more money, I found her crying in the bathroom," Dorothy said. "I got her pulled together and took her into the bar."

"That's why you were on my turf," Irma said.

Even with the dim light in the car, I knew Nana Jo had just rolled her eyes.

"I bought her a drink, and she shared that she'd gone through a lot of money," Dorothy said. "She owed money to the casino. John Cloverton had extended her a *lot* of credit, and she couldn't pay it back fast enough. She said Mildred was helping her pawn small things to help pay down the debt."

"That's why she was taking family heirlooms and passing them along to Mildred," I said.

"She was afraid someone would recognize her if she tried to pawn the items herself. She took a few small things that she didn't think would be missed and passed them along. Mildred would pawn them, and then Sharon's credit at the casino would be reinstated."

"That poor woman," Ruby Mae said. "My husband was addicted to alcohol. He tried to stop many times, but he just couldn't. I don't know what was worse, seeing him drunk out of his mind or seeing him trying to quit. It was almost a blessing when he walked out."

That was the most I'd ever heard Ruby Mae talk about her husband. I knew he'd walked out on her, leaving her to raise their nine children alone, but I didn't even know if he was alive or dead or whether they'd ever gotten divorced.

I pulled up to Shady Acres, and we sat in the car talking.

"That's everything," Dorothy said. "I hope Mayor Carpenter is able to get her some help. That poor woman is miserable."

Irma's security connection wasn't available, so she was forced to hang out in the bar. She had made dates with two different men within the next week, so she hadn't suffered too badly.

We made arrangements to meet tomorrow for lunch before I pulled off. I drove home and thought about all of the changes getting married would bring to my routine. I enjoyed spending time with Frank, but I also enjoyed the time I spent with Nana Jo and the girls. They had become my family.

I pulled into the garage.

"Samantha, your mind is a million miles away," Nana Jo said. "Have you figured out this case?"

"I'm sorry, but I was thinking about something else."

She waited for me to elaborate. "I was just thinking about

how many things would change if Frank and I got married. Don't get me wrong; I'm sure many of the changes will be for the better. I do care about him. It's just that I enjoy spending time with you and the girls, and he might not want me to go out as much."

Nana Jo patted my hand. "Frank has never struck me as particularly possessive or emotionally needy, but you know him better than I do."

"He's very independent and has allowed me to be too, but when Leon and I first got married we spent a lot of time together. I think that's why Mom started having our Sunday time, which was just the two of us."

"You and Leon were both young. I think that's normal. Frank's older and very independent. He has his restaurant, which takes up a lot of his time. I really don't know how things would change, but you should talk to him."

We got out of the car, and I noticed a light on upstairs in the building, which indicated that Dawson was there.

When we got upstairs, I was right. He was studying with papers strewn all over the dining room table. There was also the most amazing smell of oatmeal, sugar, and raisins.

Nana Jo sniffed. "What is that wonderful aroma?"

Dawson gathered his papers. "I'm sorry; I didn't realize how late it was."

Nana Jo sat down at one of the empty chairs. "Sit down and pass that plate of whatever you've been baking over here."

Dawson pulled his backpack out of the chair so I could sit. "Brown butter oatmeal raisin cookies."

Nana Jo took a bite. "These are delicious. There's just one thing missing." She chewed.

Dawson stared, anxious to hear what was missing.

"Milk. I'm going to need a glass of milk or a cup of coffee."

"Coffee," I said. "They are moist and delicious, but I

agree. They would be even better with a cup of coffee." I swallowed, got up, and made coffee for both Nana Jo and me.

Nana Jo looked at her watch. "Are you sure you want coffee this late at night?"

"I may not sleep, but I absolutely want a coffee." I sat down and drank my coffee and ate three more cookies.

"What are you studying?" Nana Jo said. She stopped munching cookies long enough to glance through the papers.

"Spanish." He ran his hand through his hair, which was already standing on end from previous gestures. "I shouldn't have waited so late to complete my language requirement, but I've never been great at languages. Heck, I can barely speak English."

"Maybe I can help," I said. "What are you trying to do?"

"I have to write an essay in Spanish." He held up his Spanish dictionary. "But it's slow going."

I had taken seven years of Spanish prior to college and then another two years while at the university. At one time, I had been very good. Unfortunately, that was close to twenty years ago. "What can I help with?"

Dawson had a few sentences, but it was clear he had a long way to go. He tossed his pen down. "I just can't think in Spanish, and it takes me a long time to think up the right words."

"You're not going to think in Spanish after one year of basic Spanish. Stop beating yourself up for that. I recommend you figure out what you want to write and just write it in English. Then, once you have that down in English, translate it. It should be faster than plodding along and trying to write it in Spanish."

Dawson stared at me as though I'd just given him the meaning of life. "I should have thought of that."

Nana Jo took another cookie. "Your brain is addled right now. You were so nervous about getting this right that you weren't thinking straight. Now, why don't you try writing it in English and then translate it, and Sam can look it over for you in the morning."

Reinvigorated, Dawson pulled out his notebook and started writing. "I do better on paper. If I type it, then I'll be tempted to use Google Translate, and my professor has already said she is a master at detecting papers that have been translated by Google."

Nana Jo and I each grabbed a cookie and headed to our rooms to allow him to write in peace. Dawson promised to look after the poodles. Snickers was asleep in his lap, while Oreo was curled up in a ball at his feet. So, I wandered off to take care of my nightly preparations.

The coffee had smelled great and tasted even better, especially when washing down those oatmeal cookies. However, the caffeine kicked in when I tried to sleep, and I found myself tossing and turning. Eventually, I stopped fighting. I got up and flipped on my computer. Writing helped me sort through my problems just as baking helped Dawson. Perhaps a little writing would help me make sense of all the information we'd collected and figure out who'd killed John Cloverton.

⁓

Lord James Browning sat in an armchair near the fireplace. He thought for several moments and then tossed back his brandy. "This is highly confidential and can't leave this room."

Each person nodded their consent.

"War with Germany is coming. Despite everyone's best efforts, it's going to happen. Even the prime minister has realized there's no other way."

Clara gasped and clutched Peter Covington's hand.

176 V. M. Burns

Lord William filled his pipe and huffed, mumbling, "Bloody business, this. Bloody business."

James took a deep breath. "This war will be different than previous wars. We have so much technology now. Between the wireless, telephones, and telegraphs, we have to provide a way to stay on top of the enemy. Sir Hugh has been tasked with establishing a place for military intelligence. A few years back, he was integral in establishing the Secret Intelligence Service, S.I.S. Unfortunately, we have excellent reason to believe that S.I.S. has been compromised. There's no way to know how deep the infiltration goes, but with another war looming, we have to be ready. Rather than combining with the old organization, Sir Hugh decided to set up something completely separate. Using his own money, he purchased the Bletchley mansion and fifty-eight acres of land."

Lord William puffed on his pipe. "Good job, that. No way to keep anything secret if you have to go and ask Parliament for the money to fund your top-secret department."

"Exactly," James said. "This way, very few people know the truth about what goes on at Bletchley Park."

Lady Elizabeth stopped knitting and looked up. "That's all good and well, but what is going on at Bletchley?"

"It's the headquarters for the wartime intelligence station," James said.

Peter Covington frowned. "But what will they do? Why all the young debutantes and college students?"

James stood up. "Its primary mission is sabotage, but Sir Hugh's vision is that it will be the secret headquarters for Britain's brightest men and women to work on ways to stop Hitler in his tracks. We know the Germans have some very sophisticated encryption devices. Our hope is that we can figure out ways to crack those so we can stay one step ahead of the Nazis. Bletchley is where the government codes and cyphers will be taught, so being close to the university helps with identifying people. We've enlisted mathematicians, scientists." He glanced at Lady Clara. "People who are good at languages and can help with translations to help the war effort."

"I see," Lady Clara said. "That's why you've recruited debutantes. Most of us have spent years learning French and Latin, as well as German."

"Plus, we believe the young members of aristocratic families are vested in Britain's success. Most of them come from monied families and won't be easily enticed by money or power."

Peter Covington gawked. "You mean all of those people are working for the government?"

"All of them," Lord Browning said. "They've all been sworn to secrecy. They must all sign a document stating that they won't talk about what happens at Bletchley Park to anyone; not even their family members will know what they've done."

"I'll be glad to sign up to do my part for England," Lady Clara said. "I'll admit I'm not the sharpest when it comes to maths, but I enjoy puzzles and am pretty good at them, and I speak French, German, and Italian fluently."

"That's why I thought of you," James said.

"Look here," Peter Covington said. "Is this dangerous?"

"Less dangerous than joining the Women's Royal Naval Service," James said, "but I'm not sure any place in Britain will be safe once the war starts." He paced. "Reports coming from Austria and Czechoslovakia indicate that the German forces have been ruthless toward women and children."

"Dashed unsportsmanlike," Lord William said.

Lady Elizabeth took a deep breath and set aside her knitting. "Women have always done our part. We may not be able to fight side by side with our men in the trenches to protect our homeland, but I can assure you, when the time comes, we will do what we can." She turned her full attention to Lord Browning. "Now, James, I take it that Philip Chester was one of these maths experts who was enlisted to help decode messages."

"Yes, I didn't know him personally, but he was supposed to be practically a genius. He and a fellow named Turing . . . Alan Turing . . . both signed up together. I gathered that they were really close. I just hope this doesn't mean Turing will back out. The fellow is a genius, and he's the one we really need."

She turned to Peter Covington. "Now, what do you mean this wasn't the first time?"

"Ever since I got here, there have been . . . accidents," Covington said. "First, the brakes went out on my car. I ended up driving off in a field and nearly took out a cow."

"Could it have been an accident?" Lady Daphne asked.

"I had the car checked before I left London. The brakes were fine. When I took it to the garage here, the brake line had been cut in two." He looked around. "Then there was a car that nearly ran me off the road while I was bicycling. I tried to chalk it up to some fellows who'd had too much to drink, but the more I think about it . . . that car had to have been following me. Now, the poisoned chocolates."

Lady Clara hopped up. "That just makes me angry that someone would use me . . . well, my name to get to you."

Lady Elizabeth smiled. "Whoever's involved in this has obviously been following you. They know about you and Clara."

"We've hardly kept our relationship secret," Lady Clara said. "We've gone to dinners and parties all over London, but . . . who would know about us here in Buckinghamshire?"

"Of course, it's possible that the attempts don't have anything to do with Clara. I'm a policeman. I've arrested a lot of men who would love nothing better than to take out a member of Scotland Yard. It comes with the territory."

"True, but there's something suspicious about this . . . something that goes beyond your being a detective," Lady Elizabeth said, picking up her knitting. "I think it's time we figure out who murdered Philip Chester and who's been trying to kill Peter, and quickly."

"Why the urgency?" Lady Daphne asked. "I mean, of course we want to make sure that Peter's safe, but . . . oh, I see."

Clara glanced from Daphne to Lady Elizabeth. "Well, I wish someone would explain it to me."

"How did Chester end up eating the poisoned chocolates?" Lady Daphne said. "He was supposed to be on a top-secret mission. If the chocolates were intended for Peter, then how did he get them?"

"You mean whoever killed him may have known what was going on at Bletchley?" Lady Clara asked.

James and Daphne exchanged a long look.

Lady Elizabeth knitted. "If that's true, this is more than just a case of murder or mistaken identity."

James sighed. "In fact, all of England could be in grave jeopardy."

# Chapter 18

Unlike many of my previous bouts of late-night writing, this time I not only saved my manuscript, but I also actually got into bed. The next morning, after I showered and dressed, I found Dawson, Snickers, and Oreo curled up on the sofa.

I was just about to wake Dawson when Snickers woke up and took care of the task for me. Dawson made the unfortunate mistake of sleeping with his mouth open. Snickers took advantage of the opportunity and stuck her tongue in his mouth.

He jumped and looked around, trying to get his bearings. When he realized what had happened, he used his sweatshirt to wipe his mouth.

Snickers wasn't impressed. She stretched and then jumped down.

"You'd better grab a shower," I said. "I'll make breakfast, and then we'll start on your paper." I headed for the stairs, but he stopped me.

"I might as well take them down to go potty. I've got to go down anyway." He stretched. "Give me fifteen minutes."

After several minutes, Snickers and Oreo trotted upstairs,

and I knew Dawson wouldn't be far behind, so I started the eggs and pushed the lever to drop the toast into the toaster. Dawson often made delicious cinnamon rolls, lemon bread, and other pastries, but I tended to stick to traditional breakfasts of bacon, eggs, toast, and coffee. On occasion, I varied my routine and toasted a bagel or English muffin, but that was about as much diversity as I added where breakfast was concerned.

The aroma of bacon drew Nana Jo into the kitchen, and I handed her a hot cup of coffee and a plate. She grunted her thanks, chugged down half the coffee, and sat down to eat and read her newspaper.

I gave Dawson a plate that was piled high with almost double the amount that was on Nana Jo's and mine. When he started playing football at MISU, his coach wanted him to "bulk up." So, Dawson had gained over fifty pounds in two years, although he still looked slender. I watched as he scarfed down nearly a half pound of bacon, six eggs, four slices of toast, and a bowl of cereal. I looked down at my two slices of bacon and a half slice of bread and could feel five extra pounds adhering to my hips. Only in my fantasy world would someone ever tell me to *bulk up*.

After breakfast, Nana Jo went down and opened the store, while Dawson and I worked on translating his essay. It had been a long time since I'd actually written or read anything in Spanish, but it was a bit like riding a bike, and as I continued, it came back to me. I suggested he keep things simple and only use words that were in his small vocabulary. Not surprisingly, his biggest challenge came with conjugating verbs. Present perfect and simple past tenses were common areas of confusion.

"I just don't understand the difference," he said. "Both of them happened in the past, so why are there two?"

"Well, there are always going to be exceptions, but I find

it easier to think of *present perfect* to describe what someone has done and is still doing. You're going to be using the verb *haber*, which is '*to have.*' This is usually something that started in the past and is still true now." He looked puzzled, so I pointed to a sentence in his paper. "Here, you wrote: '*George lived in London for two years.*'" I looked up at him. "Does George still live in London?" He nodded. "Then you'd use the present perfect tense. *George had lived.*" I scanned the paper for another sentence. "Okay, here you wrote: '*I baked a cake.*' You're not still baking that cake. You did it. It's over and done. So, that's simple past tense." I watched the lightbulb go off. He grabbed his paper and quickly made changes to the verb tenses and passed it back. I looked it over and smiled. "Looks good."

"Whew." He wiped imaginary sweat from his forehead. "I think I got it, at least for the next five minutes. I'm going to make the other corrections and type it up." He tilted his head, and his eyes pleaded. "Would you have time to look it over one more time before I turn it in?"

"Of course."

He hugged me. "Great. I'm going to get busy typing."

I went downstairs and helped Nana Jo with the store, primarily to give Dawson some quiet time. The morning traffic in the store was certainly not going to be overwhelming.

Nana Jo and I worked together well. She handled customers while I stocked shelves and managed inventory. I was contemplating where to put a box of children's mysteries when I heard Nana Jo say, "It's great to see you. How are you doing?"

"Good . . . I mean, fine. Not bad. I just thought I'd stop by and . . . see how things were going. I mean, you know."

I recognized the voice and peeked around a bookshelf. "Detective Pitt, it's good to see you."

"Good to see . . . good to be here." He rocked awkwardly

on the balls of his feet, his hands shoved down into his pockets. His glance moved around the store.

"Are you looking for a book, or do you have time to sit and have some coffee?" I said. "Dawson made oatmeal cookies that are delicious."

"I guess I have time to sit for just a minute." He moved to the back and plopped down at one of the bistro tables.

I went behind the counter and placed a half-dozen cookies on a small plate. "Would you like tea or coffee?"

Detective Pitt had shoved a cookie into his mouth, so I waited while he chewed and swallowed. "Coffee."

I used the single-cup coffee brewer to make coffee for both of us. I placed his mug on the table and sat across from the detective. We sat in awkward silence for several moments while Detective Pitt munched on cookies and washed them down with steaming coffee. I tried to ignore the crumbs that tumbled out of his mouth onto his chin, shirt, and lap.

"Your sister tells me that you and your nosy seniors have been doing some investigating," he said.

Despite the word choice, his tone was more inquisitive than harsh.

"We have," I said. "It turns out you aren't the only person with a motive to kill John Cloverton."

"Motive? What motive would I have for wanting to kill him?"

"Jealousy. After all, he did have an affair with your wife, which ended your marriage and—"

He snorted. "That's not a motive for murder. If anything, I was grateful to the poor clod for taking her off my hands."

"You weren't angry because he took Mildred away?"

"Hardly. Mildred was nuts. I was happy to see the back of her, and if John Cloverton was crazy enough to want her, then all I could say was good luck and thank heaven."

I stared in his eyes to see if his cavalier attitude was merely male bravado in an attempt to save face or whether he truly meant what he said. I wasn't a personality expert, but he looked sincere. "Are you telling me you didn't harbor any bad feelings toward John Cloverton?"

He shook his head. "Absolutely none."

"Then why'd you punch him?"

He colored. "I already told you. He insulted my . . . manhood, and I lost my temper. That's all. I haven't spent the last years of my life pining after my ex-wife. At the time, sure, I was upset. I'll admit it. Who wouldn't be? If you found out your spouse had been cheating, you'd be upset too. But after she left, and the divorce was final . . . I realized it was all for the best. Millie always did have a problem with jealousy and anger. She was ambitious. She wanted me to rise to the top of the force and then run for some public office." He shook his head. "I'm a cop, not a politician. She wanted more than I was able or willing to give. She found another sap who she could push, and that was fine with me. Like I said, she was obsessed and cuckoo." He circled his finger on the side of his head. "It's been worth every dime I had to pay in alimony to get free."

"Alimony? I didn't realize you had children, and considering she was the one who cheated, I would have thought you wouldn't have had to pay alimony."

He shook his head. "Nah, no kids. Alimony was the price of freedom, and it was money well spent."

"Where'd you go after John Cloverton left the police station?"

"I left the station and drove home. There's a bar about two doors down from my house, so I walked there and had a couple of drinks." He looked in my direction as though checking to see if I was judging. "I walked home and went upstairs. I got into bed . . . *alone* and went to sleep. I stayed there until the next morning, when I was awakened by a telephone call telling me that Cloverton was dead." He rubbed his neck. "I've gone over this a hundred times in my head, so I could recite it in my sleep."

"When's the last time you remember seeing that gun?"

"I don't know. I don't open that drawer often. I just know it's there. Maybe a couple of weeks ago."

I was working through how to phrase my next question in a manner that wouldn't be offensive when Detective Pitt surprised me. "If you're trying to find politically correct words, don't waste your time. Just spit it out."

"Who would have access to the murder weapon?"

"No one."

# Chapter 19

"That's impossible. If you didn't kill him, then somebody else did. Somebody had to have been able to—"

He shook his head. "No one. Nobody connected to this case had access to that gun."

"How much of a pain was John Cloverton to the North Harbor police and the mayor, really?"

He scratched his head and held my gaze as though he was deciding whether to trust me. He must have made up his mind, because he looked around to make sure no one was listening and then whispered, "This stays between us, right?"

"As long as Jenna doesn't need it for your defense."

"No. This is just between you and me."

Eventually, I nodded. "Okay."

He leaned forward, and I could smell the oatmeal raisin cookie, coffee-flavored breath as it hit my face. "Most of the officers in the department suspected there was something not quite on the up-and-up with Chief Davis's accounting. Cops don't make enough money to afford expensive suits, silk ties, and handmade shirts." He pointed to his polyester shirt. "Schoolteachers in this town make more than cops."

"They can't make that little and survive."

"Barely more than minimum wage. That's why most of us work a part-time job doing security at churches or for college football games, or we sign up for as much overtime as possible. Yet Chief Davis drives a brand-new Italian sports car. Me? I drive a thirty-year-old rust bucket with bald tires and no heat. Where is he getting that kind of money?"

"Maybe his family has money?"

He was shaking his head before the words were out of my mouth. "Nope. He's got one brother who barely has a pot to . . . well, you-know-what in. His wife's family was okay, but they weren't Italian sports car wealthy. Mostly just working-class folks. His wife was a waitress before she married the chief. They have two kids, both in expensive private schools." He gave me a knowing look and then named the most expensive private school in the area. "Tuition for that school costs more than I make in a year."

"Maybe they got scholarships."

"Are you kidding? Junior is dumber than a bag of hammers, and the girl . . . well, she's got her mother's looks, but I'm not sure her elevator goes all the way to the top floor, if you know what I mean."

"If you think he has been stealing money, then why didn't you do something? Why didn't you say something?"

He stared at me as though I'd suddenly lost all my marbles. "I never said he stole money. I don't have any proof that he's stolen anything. All I said was that it seems suspicious to me. That's all." He held up his hands innocently. Then he leaned forward. "Inquiring minds want to know, where did the money come from? If John Cloverton had some evidence or . . . forget evidence. Cloverton implied out loud that something was going on. He was making a lot of noise with all those articles in the paper. Sooner or later, the public was going to want an investigation." He glared. "If you wanna know who set me up, who would know when I left the station? Who would have the guts to come into my home and take my gun? Who would use it to murder Cloverton and then replace it? Davis has hated me ever since he became chief of police."

"Why?"

"He resents the fact that I made detective. He thinks I only got promoted because the previous chief was my cousin, but that's not true. I earned my rank." He bit into the last cookie but started talking before he finished chewing. "I should have known he was setting me up when he ordered me to that hotel on Sunday. He must have *known* Cloverton was coming. He knew Cloverton would say something that would get me riled up. Heck, he may have even arranged for Cloverton to be there." He shoved the rest of the cookie in his mouth. "If you wanna know who murdered John Cloverton, then twenty bucks says it's Chief Zachary Davis. You mark my words."

# Chapter 20

After finishing off the cookies and his coffee, Detective Pitt left me sitting at the bistro table, pondering this dilemma. I'd promised to keep what he told me confidential, but did that mean I couldn't share it with anyone? Or could I use the information but not divulge where it came from? Surely, he wouldn't exclude his attorney from this information.

"Sam, wake up."

I looked up, and Jenna was standing in front of me. I nearly fell out of my chair. Was this a sign from God?

"Look, I don't have much time. The twins want to throw Mom and Harold a bon voyage party. What do you think?"

"What? Oh, yeah. With everything going on, I forgot they're leaving for Australia in just a few short days."

"I think Mom would like a send-off, but I don't have the time to do anything elaborate. Do you think Frank would let us use his upstairs?"

"I'm pretty sure he will . . . if it's free. I can ask. We're going out to dinner tonight, but I'll send him a text." I pulled out my phone and sent the message while it was at the front of my mind.

"Great. Maybe Dawson can provide some dessert, or we can buy the food from Frank. I don't know or care, but I know Dawson has finals."

"I'm sure he'll want to bake something. He's so grateful for the money that Harold put in trust for him and the twins. Plus, he baked their wedding cake, and I think it would be nice to have something reminding them of that time."

She looked at the empty plate of cookies. "What's this?"

"It was a plate of oatmeal cookies, but Stinky Pitt finished them off."

She must have noticed something in my face, because she asked, "What's wrong?"

"Nothing. Why do you ask?"

"Because you're my sister and I know you. Plus, you're a terrible liar." She made herself a cup of tea and then sat down. "You might as well tell me."

I used the time she spent getting her tea to make up my mind. I shared the information that Detective Pitt had told me, emphasizing that he had told me in confidence.

She sipped her tea. "I think it'll be easy enough to check. Now that I have a trust fund, I can afford to hire an investigator to look into Chief Davis's finances. I can also ask around to see if anyone has heard rumors about the chief's accounting. Plus, there's Ruby Mae's cousin Abigail. She might be able to help us. I think we can confirm his suspicions without involving Detective Pitt." She squinted and shook her head. "Although I'll never understand why he would confide in you. I'm his attorney and the only one required to keep his conversations confidential."

"Maybe he wasn't confident that the pit bull would be able to stop herself from using any information she found, regardless of her client's wishes."

"Whatever." She shrugged and finished her tea.

My phone dinged, and it was from Frank. "He said yes."

There was more to the message, but it was personal. However, I could feel the heat rise up my neck as I read it.

"Great." Jenna stood. "I'll confirm the date and time with the twins and send it to you." She walked out, mumbling that not only was I a poor liar, but I also had a horrible poker face.

Nana Jo had kept the bookstore running all morning, practically single-handed. So, I took over for the afternoon so she could get a break.

The traffic was relatively light and nothing that I couldn't handle. By late afternoon, Dawson came down, and I read through his paper. It was much better. I suggested a minor change, but it looked good.

He was insulted that we would even consider anyone else to make Mom and Harold's cake and promised it would not interfere with his exams. He only had one left, and he felt well prepared.

By the end of the day, I was tired, but it was a good tired. I loved talking to the regulars who came in looking for new books and new authors—such a great feeling. I was excited that one day these same people might even purchase my book.

I watched Snickers and Oreo as they unfurled themselves and stretched after their naps. I took them outside. I couldn't help but notice that Snickers was moving a lot slower and her muzzle was lighter and full of gray hair. When I first brought her home, she'd been classified as a "chocolate" poodle. Her coat had been the color of an espresso. Now, with all of the gray sprinkled in, her coat looked more café au lait. I picked her up and gave her a squeeze. She gave my nose a lick and yawned. I made a mental note to pick up more dental-cleaning treats. Because of her age and heart condition, the vet no longer did dental cleanings for her. At fourteen, she wouldn't have a lot more time, and I couldn't contemplate my life without her. So, I held my breath and squeezed her tight.

When I put her down, I called for Oreo. He was playing fetch by tossing a stick in the yard and then running to get it. Part of me felt slightly guilty, but experience had taught me if I threw the stick for him he'd get it and then run away, expecting me to chase him. That wasn't going to happen. He bounded toward the house. I tried to remember if I'd seen him potty but was glad when he stopped and hiked his leg before running inside. We went upstairs.

I decided to put forth a little more effort in getting ready for my date with Frank, and I showered and changed into one of my favorite dresses. It was a blue and white A-line dress that reminded me of a blue willow china set Nana Jo inherited from her mom. Something about that dress sparked something in my memory. However, before I could focus on what it was, it was gone. I tried for a few moments to retrigger the memory like the bonus games on a slot machine, but time was wasting and Frank would be here soon.

I gave myself one last glance in the mirror and then headed out.

Nana Jo and Dawson were in the dining room making plans for Mom's party when I heard the doorbell. Dawson offered to go and open the door, but I told him not to worry about it and I went downstairs.

When I got to the door, Frank's reaction was all that I could have wished. He helped me into his car, and we were off.

Frank drove a black Porsche Cayenne. It was as luxurious as the name implied. The leather seats were as soft as a baby's bottom. As a foodie, Frank loved trying new restaurants, and a new one had recently opened in the nearby town of Coloma, Michigan. We pulled up to the Blackbird Waterhouse, a historic resort building built in 1931. Over the years, it had been home to everything from an inn to various restaurants and pubs. Its location on a busy road, well, busy for a town of about twelve hundred people, and its proximity to Lake Michigan meant that during the tourist season it received a good number of visitors.

Inside, the sprawling building had a large pub area where locals liked to hang out, drink beer, and watch sports. The low ceiling made the room feel like part of the original building, but it was just one of many additions made over the years. We passed through the bar to the host station, which was part of the original building and was highlighted by a massive stone fireplace. Frank had made reservations, so we were shown to our table and seated.

I looked around. "I remember this place from years ago, but it didn't look anything like this."

"It has new owners who've invested quite a bit of money into improving the restaurant, and they've hired a first-rate chef. I've been anxious to try this place for months, but just never made it up here."

We ordered a cocktail, and Frank asked for the wine list. I wasn't much of a wine drinker, despite his best efforts.

The menu was a combination of high-end pub food and fine dining, which seemed smart to me, something for everyone. I was tempted to order the Blackbird burger but decided on the teriyaki-glazed Scottish Salmon instead, while Frank chose the Seafood Paella.

"You look beautiful tonight."

I smiled. "You're looking rather snazzy yourself."

Our conversation felt comfortable. I enjoyed spending time with Frank. He was thoughtful and easy to talk to. I found myself sharing the things I'd learned over the past twenty-four hours, including everything I'd heard from Detective Pitt.

"Do you think he's right?"

I thought about it. "I hadn't really noticed the quality of Chief Davis's clothes until Stinky—I mean, Detective Pitt mentioned it."

Frank laughed. "I noticed you've been trying not to call him Stinky Pitt."

"It's hard to break old habits, but I'm determined to stop. Nana Jo never did it around other policemen, but it slipped out when he came to MISU to arrest John Cloverton. Of course Cloverton heard it and probably taunted him all the way back to the station."

"Did you ever find out why they sent him to arrest Cloverton?"

"Detective Pitt thinks it was part of the setup."

"What do you think?"

I took a bite of my salmon, which was moist, flaky, and perfectly cooked. "I don't know."

"How is it?"

I smiled and slid my plate closer so he could take a bite.

He tasted the rice and the grilled veggies and offered me to taste his, which was served with saffron rice, but I declined. I wasn't quite as adventurous as Frank. Besides, I was quite content.

Frank hadn't asked me about my answer and I wasn't prepared to provide a response, but I did have questions. "If we were to get married, where would we live?"

"Where do you want to live?"

"I don't know. I love my commute to work."

"How would you feel if I were to move in?"

"There are only two bedrooms."

"I rather assumed that I'd be sharing the master bedroom with you." He smiled.

I rolled my eyes. "I know, but . . . Nana Jo."

"I love your grandmother. I wouldn't expect her to move out if I moved in. Your space is over two thousand square feet."

"You'd be okay with her staying?"

"Of course." He reached out and took my hand. "I don't

want to change or restrict your life. I fell in love with you, and I don't want to change that. I don't need one hundred percent of your time, but I would like to share more of it."

"So, the trips to the casino with the girls and our . . . sleuthing expeditions?"

"I wouldn't try to change that, even if I could." He chuckled. "Although I would prefer it if you didn't spend so much time chasing down killers and putting your life in danger, but maybe if I'm a bit closer, you'll let me help protect you."

I laughed. "I don't know. So far, that's been Nana Jo's job."

"She's done a fine job too. The last thing I want to do is make your gun-toting grandmother angry. I don't want her shooting up my restaurant."

I laughed. "Good thing she likes you."

After dinner, Frank drove to the beach and we sat on a large boulder and listened to the waves. It was a wonderful way to end a lovely evening.

When he drove me home, we took our time saying good-bye. Just when things were getting passionate, his phone rang. He swore until he saw who the call was from. But then he turned on the screen so I could see. "Buonasera."

Frank was fluent in multiple languages, so he was able to talk to Lexi and Angelo in Italian for several moments before he switched to English. I could tell from the way Angelo giggled that whatever they'd talked about made him very happy.

Five more minutes spent talking with Angelo and Lexi warmed my heart, but it was over too quickly. Angelo said something in Italian before Lexi poked him, and Frank gave him a signal to be quiet. Normally, I would have pumped Frank to find out what they were up to, but I missed those two so much, I couldn't summon the energy to do anything more than cry.

Frank held me while I wept. When I was done, I felt silly. "I'm sorry. They're with their family. They're happy, and I'm happy for them."

He kissed my tear-streaked face. "I know you're happy for them, but it's okay to miss them too."

I pulled myself together and climbed upstairs. Nana Jo was curled up on the sofa with Snickers and Oreo. I watched them for a few moments and then quietly made my way to my room. I finished my nightly preparations and got ready for bed, but my brain wouldn't turn off. So, I gave up trying. I went to my laptop and tried to sort through everything running through my head by getting lost in the British country-side.

Lady Daphne turned to her aunt. "What are we going to do?"

"This may be difficult since we're unfamiliar with the area," Lady Elizabeth said, looking up from her knitting, "but I'd like Thompkins to talk to the servants. They're all local, aren't they?"

The butler stepped forward. "Yes, m'lady."

"They'll know about newcomers and probably anyone who is behaving . . . unusually."

The butler gave a stiff bow.

"William, I think it's imperative that we find out if the truth of Bletchley Park has been leaked," Lady Elizabeth said. "I was hoping you might reach out to your friend Nigel Greyson at the Home Office. He may be able to offer some insight into this business." She turned to James. "Would that be okay?"

Lord Browning nodded. "Yes, of course. Greyson was heavily involved in GC and CS during the Great War, and he's still in the loop on things."

"What's GC and CS?" Lady Clara asked.

"Government code and cypher school," James said.

Lady Elizabeth turned her attention to her cousin. "Clara, given what you know now, do you still want to work at Bletchley?"

Lady Clara stuck out her chin. "Absolutely. Knowing that I'll be helping the war effort makes it even better. Now I won't have to quit to join the Wrens."

Detective Inspector Covington started to object, but one look at Clara's face made it clear her mind was made up. He sighed. "You will at least *try* to be careful, won't you?"

She smiled. "I will if you will."

"I knew you'd feel that way," Lady Elizabeth said. "You'll be on the inside and able to talk to some of the workers, especially the women. I don't think they'll be likely to talk as freely to the police. People from that circle tend to believe the police are beneath their notice."

Covington nodded an acknowledgment. "I have noticed that."

"Now, Daphne. I can help Clara in talking to the debutantes. I'm sure I know most, if not all, of their families well, and should be able to get them in one place. I was thinking about a tea, but I want to clear it with you first, of course."

"I think that's a great idea," Lady Daphne said. "Please don't stand on ceremony. I'm rather new to hosting." She blushed. "So, it would be wonderful if you would get things started."

Lady Elizabeth smiled. "Of course, dear. I'd also like you to talk to some of the locals. You're new to the area, and they'll be curious. Tea with the vicar and prominent members of society should easily identify the village gossip."

"I've already gotten invitations to tea from several households. This will help me fulfill my social obligations and allow me to help with the investigation at the same time."

"Peter, I'm sure you'll be following your own lines of inquiry regarding the murder."

"I will, but I suspect I'll be facing a bit of opposition. I'm not in the inner circle of Bletchley, so I'm afraid this murder is going to be categorized as another unfortunate accident and closed."

"I'm sure you're right," Lord Browning said. "We can't risk a lot of outsiders figuring out what's going on up there. I know this is going to sound bloody cold, but keeping Bletchley Park's secrets is far more important than the life of any one person."

"I'm not happy about it, but I do understand."

"Good, then perhaps you can see if there is anyone who would have wanted Chester dead and if there is any connection between Philip Chester and your friend who was murdered at the American Embassy."

"You think the two deaths are connected?"

Lady Elizabeth resumed knitting. "It seems likely that your friend's murder is what set things in motion. He either knew something or saw something that made him dangerous, so the killer strikes. You're transferred to prevent you from finding out what happened. The killer may or may not have realized what's going on at Bletchley Park, or . . ." She glanced up from her knitting to stare at the detective. "I hate to say it, but the killer may have followed you here to try and finish the job."

Clara gasped.

"It's also possible the killer may have come here on their own for whatever reason. The two murders may not be connected at all. There's a chance that Philip Chester was the intended victim, but . . ."

"But you don't believe it," James said.

"Let's just say that I don't believe in coincidences. I'm going to talk to my cousin to see what information he can shed on this situation."

The air crackled with static.

"Your cousin King George?" Covington asked.

"No, my cousin Winston Churchill. He's been in Parliament for years, and if anyone knows about a connection between Bletchley and those invited to dinner at the American Embassy, it'll be him."

Lady Clara appeared to be a million miles away. She chewed her lower lip and gazed into the distance.

"Clara, is something bothering you?"

"I was thinking there may be one other person I could talk to." She paused for a few moments and then made up her mind and hurried on. "Marguerite Evans is a dear friend. She was at the embassy when Oliver Martin was killed. They seemed to hit it off well. I've just been wondering if . . . well, if he might not have said something to her that might help us figure out who killed him and why."

"Wouldn't she have mentioned it when I questioned everyone?" Covington said.

Lady Clara shook her head. "Not if it was . . . confidential, like Bletchley Park. If she'd been sworn to secrecy, then she might not have felt like she could tell anyone."

Lady Elizabeth stared at her young cousin. "I think that's a great idea. She might speak to a friend when she didn't feel that she could tell anyone else." She looked around. "I think that's everyone."

James coughed. "I believe you missed me. What's my assignment?"

"Actually, I have a critical assignment for you, but I think we should discuss it privately."

# Chapter 21

"Planning a going-away party in forty-eight hours is crazy," I said to Nana Jo as I flipped through websites on my phone looking for gifts. "And I don't know who these people are on the Internet who think they have the *perfect gift* for someone moving to Australia, but they obviously have never met my mother."

"Planning a going-away party in two days is no crazier than planning a wedding in two weeks, and we pulled that off."

"Aren't you the least bit stressed?"

"Nope."

"Why not?"

"Because Grace is my daughter, not my mother. I'm not burdened with the same feelings of trying to please her that you and Jenna have."

"I doubt that Jenna is worried about pleasing her either."

"Your mother may be scatty, but she loves you. Whatever you give her, she'll love it because it came from you."

"Yeah, right." I flipped through the websites faster than before. "Have you ever met my mother?"

"Long before you did."

I got a text from Jenna and stopped my frantic web search long enough to read it. "Listen to this: *'I've got court tomorrow. Can you pick up decorations? Thanks, J.'*" I stared at Nana Jo. "Can you believe that? She's dumping the decorations off on me just because she has to go to court."

"How hard is it to pick up a few balloons and streamers? I can swing by the party store tomorrow if that'll help."

The guilt descended like a cloud. "No. I'll do it. I just get frustrated that she treats me like my work isn't as important as hers. She's done that my entire life."

Nana Jo put down the book she was reading. "What's really bothering you?"

"What do you mean?"

"You've been swiping that phone as if your life depended on it. Your mother is not a horrible person, and she will not bite your head off if you don't find the *perfect gift*." She accented it with air quotes. "And, whenever Jenna doesn't want to do something, she dumps it in your lap. She's done it since you were five years old. You're an adult. If you don't want to get the decorations, just tell her you're busy running a bookstore, solving a murder investigation, and living your life. She'll respond with a sharp retort and send Tony or one of the twins to do it. Now, what's really bothering you?"

"I don't know. I guess I'm just . . . confused. Everything is changing, and I don't like change. Mom and Harold are moving to Australia. The twins are graduating and will be moving away. Emma will be leaving for medical school, and Jillian will be off to Chicago, New York, or Moscow touring the world and dancing. Dawson still has one more year of college, but before long, he'll be gone too. Frank wants to get married, and I'm really leaning toward saying yes, but that will mean change too. He says he doesn't care where we live, and he won't try to control my life or my time, but there's bound to be changes. I hate change. I like routines. I like knowing that every day I can rely on you and, in a pinch, the twins or Dawson can help out. I don't know. It just feels like everything is changing. Even good changes are still change. My book will get published in a few months, and while I'm excited, I'm also terrified. What if people don't like it? What if no one buys it and the publisher drops me? What if—"

"What if the sky falls tomorrow?"

I stared at my grandmother. "What?"

"Sam, there are no guarantees in life. Things change. People change. Your nephews are adults. They have to move on with their lives, and I know you wouldn't want it any other way. Your mom is moving to Australia, but you live in an age where you can talk on the phone or Skype, FaceTime, or use a host of other programs to look at each other daily." She smiled. "Just think, back when Lady Elizabeth was solving crimes, she had to rely on telephones or telegraphs."

I smiled. "I know, I'm being silly."

She came over and gave me a hug. "No, you're not silly. But the world is changing, and if it weren't for change, you wouldn't have your bookshop or Frank."

I put my head on her shoulder. "I asked Frank if we did get married where we'd live."

"And?"

"He said he would be okay with moving in here, but . . . would you be okay with that?"

"Probably not." She must have felt me start to object because she hurriedly added, "Now hold on. I like Frank. I really do, but I think the last thing a newly married couple needs is another person living there. You two will need time to get accustomed to each other."

"But I love having you here."

"I'll still help out in the bookstore, but there's no reason why I can't sleep in my own house. Freddie has been pressuring me to spend more time with him, so I might as well jump in and get over our own adjustment period."

"I hate change."

She squeezed me. "I know, dear, but you'll adapt, and you may find that you enjoy the unknown even more."

We sat talking for several minutes. It was good to unburden myself to my grandmother. She was such a strong force in my life. Before long, she had me laughing as we chatted about the fact that my mom, who was terrified of snakes, spiders, and all things creepy, was moving to the country with the largest number of venomous snakes in the world.

"Maybe I should get her something to catch snakes."

Nana Jo gave me a playful swat. "Now don't be cheeky. Your mom has never been particularly adventurous. Maybe experiencing a new culture will be good for her."

"Maybe you're right. Mom has always lived here, so I guess that's one reason the idea seemed so farfetched that she was actually moving."

"Now, I don't know that your mom will do much to help the koalas other than writing a check, but who knows."

Dawson came upstairs and stopped at the sight of Nana Jo and me sitting on the sofa. "I was going to get started on the cake, but if you need me to go open the store, I can—"

I glanced at my watch and then hurried up. "Happy baking."

Nana Jo and I went downstairs and opened the store.

Fridays were usually one of our busier days, and we both stayed busy most of the morning. I was shelving books when someone called my name. I looked up and saw Mildred Cloverton staring at me.

"Hello, I didn't know you liked murder mysteries."

Mildred glanced around. "I love books. I usually read technical books, nonfiction, and romance, but I sometimes enjoy a good crime novel every now and again."

"Great. Is there anything I can help you find, or would you prefer to look by yourself?"

"I didn't come to shop. I came to help. Remember, I told you I wanted to help you figure out who killed John."

I frowned. "I know you said you wanted to help, but . . . do you think you should? I mean, between preparing for the funeral and grieving, I just can't imagine—"

She waved her hand. "I think it would help to be active. Sitting at home is horrible. I just think. I don't want to think. I want to do something. I *need* to do something."

When Leon died, I don't know that I could have tracked down a killer, but I could understand the need to be busy. When you're busy, you don't have time to think. "We don't really have anything to do at the moment. We're not like policemen or private investigators who have all day to trail or interrogate suspects. Mostly, I've found that my grandmother and her friends have an extensive network. We can generally talk to friends and family to get information."

"Oh, I see."

I could tell she was disappointed. The girls, Nana Jo, and I had planned to meet for lunch at Frank's place, but I wasn't sure that inviting the victim's wife to our meeting was a good idea. What if she went rogue and decided to seek vengeance for John's death in her own way? No, I needed to think up something else for her to do. "There is one thing that you could help us with."

"What?"

"We've learned that the mayor's wife, Sharon, owed a lot of money at the casino and you and John were helping her pawn some of her smaller items to help pay down her debt."

Mildred's face switched from an eager beaver to a cautious sloth in two seconds. "What's wrong with that?"

"Nothing. I just wondered if you could find out from the tribal council how far she was in debt."

"You think Sharon killed John?"

"That's not what I'm saying. We have to investigate everyone that might have had a motive. This is just one of the lines of inquiry we're following. I doubt that the Pontoloma Tribal Council would provide that information if I asked, so I thought as John's wife, maybe you . . ."

"I see. Well, I suppose I could ask. Although John was the enrolled member of the Pontolomas, not me."

"What's an enrolled member?"

"Technically, anyone can claim an identity as a Native American, or any other ethnicity for that matter. My great-grandmother was Irish. So, technically, I can identify as Irish. However, recognized tribes like the Pontolomas, the Lakota, and the Apache have been granted special privileges and rights. To ensure that everyone doesn't claim to be a Pontoloma just so they can benefit from those rights, recognized tribes have an enrollment process."

"That's fascinating. What's involved in becoming an enrolled member?"

"Each tribe establishes their unique criteria for membership based on shared customs, traditions, language, and tribal blood. However, two common criteria are lineal descendants from the tribe's original membership and tribal blood. So, if you could prove you're a direct descendant of Geronimo, Sacajawea, or Crazy Horse, then chances are good you're going to meet the criteria to be an enrolled member."

"Fascinating."

She shrugged. "I guess. John was very proud of his Native American roots. Are you sure getting this information will help to find John's killer?"

"I can't see that there's a direct correlation, but we've found that once we get all of the evidence, that usually helps us figure out whodunit."

"Okay, well, I'll go and see if they'll give it to me." She

pulled her purse on her shoulder. "Is there anything else? Do you want me to come back here?"

"No, I can swing by your house later. We're also planning a going-away party for my mom, and I need to pick up some decorations."

I could see from the look on her face that I'd slipped about fifteen slots down in her esteem for my sleuthing ability.

She left, and I found myself breathing a sigh of relief. The last thing we needed was a vengeful wife looking for retribution in the middle of our investigation.

I felt guilty about taking up too much of Frank's time, so rather than meeting at his restaurant, we had arranged to meet here. I ordered a gallon of soup, sandwiches, and a gallon of tea from his restaurant online. That way, I could pay online and not have to argue with Frank, who was overly generous when it came to supporting me and my family.

Dawson said he'd pick up the food for us, but I was shocked when Nana Jo said she was going with him. Apparently, she planned to have it out with Frank about the bill for the party food. Frank refused to give us a bill and wanted to provide the food free of charge for my mom and Harold. However, Nana Jo was having none of it. She marched down to his restaurant with Dawson. I'm not sure what she said, but she came back with a price quote.

I sent Frank a text to see if he was okay. His response put a smile on my face.

"What are you grinning about?" Nana Jo asked.

"Did you really threaten to put Frank over your knee and spank him?"

"I did. Crazy fool winked at me and said he might enjoy it. I thought I was going to have to hog-tie him." She chuckled. "It won't be the first time, but he came to his senses and wrote a quote."

By teatime, everyone had arrived, and we piled into the

conference room that was in the back of the bookstore. Dawson arranged the sandwiches on a two-tiered plate along with tea cookies.

"When did you have time to make tea cookies?" I asked. "I thought you were baking a cake?"

"I'm practicing."

I popped one of the tea cookies into my mouth and moaned as it dissolved on my tongue. "Hmmm, these are delicious."

Nana Jo munched. "What are these things?"

"Russian tea cookies. The other day, Christopher and I were talking about Mrs. W.'s book launch party, and he suggested we have a tea-themed party with tea cookies, pastries, and tea sandwiches. You know, like a traditional British tea, like you had when you were in England. He thought since your books are British historical mysteries, that we could use that as a theme."

I reached over and pulled him into a hug. "That is so nice. I hadn't even thought about my release party. I think British tea is an excellent idea."

He smiled. "Great. I've got some time, but Christopher is really good with marketing, and he has tons of ideas." He halted. "I hope it wasn't supposed to be a secret."

"I'm sure it wasn't meant to be. After all, I will need to be there for it."

"Oh, yeah."

Dawson stayed a few minutes longer but then hurried back to take care of customers so we could get our meeting started.

Nana Jo sat at the head of the table. She pulled out her iPad and looked around the room. "Does anyone want to volunteer to go first?"

I raised my hand and filled everyone in on what I'd learned from Detective Pitt and also that Mildred Cloverton was going to the casino to see if she could get some data on how much Sharon Carpenter really owed. I also warned them that Mildred wanted to help, but I wasn't sure that was the best idea.

"Don't you trust her?" Dorothy asked.

"I don't know, I guess I've been more worried that she might take justice into her own hands."

We discussed it, and the general consensus was that I should trust my instincts. After that, Ruby Mae looked up from her knitting. "If no one else wants to go, then I'll go." She looked around, but no one else was itching to report. "Abigail told me that she got questioned by one of the members of the city council. Apparently, all of the publicity has the council asking a lot of questions. They're in the middle of auditing the chief of police's books."

"Wow!" Dorothy said. "Have they found anything?"

Ruby Mae leaned forward and lowered her voice. "Abigail says the councilman who questioned her implied that they were going to be getting a lawyer. They've been working with someone from the governor's office. It sounds like the governor is going to send down someone from the Auditor General's office and maybe even the reserves to maintain law and order in case the chief is removed from office."

"John Cloverton sure opened a can of worms," Nana Jo said.

We discussed this bombshell a bit more, but when the comments slowed down, Irma raised her hand. "I went out with Smithy last night. He's a real *hands-on* instructor, let me tell you."

Nana Jo rolled her eyes, and I think I heard Dorothy groan.

Irma reapplied her lipstick before she continued. "He didn't have much to add to what I've already told you, except that he thinks Chastity Drummond is on the verge of a nervous break-down."

"Because of Cloverton's murder?"

"I guess. He said she has memory lapses, and he's worried about her. She has large blocks of time that she can't account for. She was a very promising student, but her grades have slipped. He tried to get her to see a doctor, but she's refused. He's going to talk to a medical professional because he's afraid she'll harm herself."

"That's bad," Ruby Mae said. "That poor girl. I sure hope someone gets help for her."

"That's all I know. We're going out again tonight, so if there's any more news, I'll do my best to work it out of him."

Nana Jo mumbled, "I'll bet you will."

"I guess that just leaves me," Dorothy said. "I didn't find out much today. I talked to a friend who worked at an antique store. I described the items that your mom mentioned had been pawned. According to my friend, those items might have been extremely valuable."

"How valuable?" I asked.

"Now, she gave all types of disclaimers. She hadn't seen the items in person. They could be fake. Yada yada. So, I reached out to Grace to see if her friend had any details that might help identify the items. It turns out, she had taken pictures of them because she was going to have them insured."

"You mean they weren't insured?" Ruby Mae asked.

Dorothy shook her head. "Based on the pictures and *if* the items really were from companies like Tiffany and Company and S.T. Dupont, and *if* they really are vintage, then the emerald earrings could have been as much as fifty thousand dollars."

Nana Jo whistled.

Dorothy read from a list she pulled from her purse. "The glass dish was fifteen thousand, and the silver lighter could have been worth around five thousand dollars."

"That's a lot of money," Nana Jo said. "I'm sure a pawnshop wouldn't have given top dollar for the stuff, but surely Sharon Carpenter hadn't racked up debts to the casino in excess of that?"

"Hopefully, Mildred is able to get the number," I said, "but . . ."

"But what?" Nana Jo asked.

"If her debt wasn't that high, then why was she still making payments to the casino?"

By the time our meeting was finished, I had more questions than answers. My brain was swirling around like a washing machine, and I needed to steady things. I relieved Dawson from store duty so he could bake. The routine of the store helped settle my brain a bit.

At closing time, my guilt sent me to the party store to pick up decorations. Initially, I started to buy some generic items that would have been appropriate for a birthday, anniversary, or retirement party. However, when I wandered down the children's party aisle I found some really colorful Australia-themed decorations that included pin-up koala bears. Torn between fun and practical, I chose both and walked out spending twice as much as I had originally intended, and I still needed to get a gift.

I swung by Mildred Cloverton's gingerbread house on my way home. She opened the door and said, "I thought you weren't going to come."

Inside, I braced myself against sensory overload. I glanced around her overcrowded room with knickknacks on every flat surface. "I'm sorry. I had to wait until the store closed, and then it took longer than expected at the party store." I forced my voice to maintain a friendly, pleasant tone despite the fact that I felt like I was being interrogated.

I must not have been as good at hiding my emotions as I thought, because she immediately flipped a switch. Suddenly she was all smiles and pleasantness. "I'm sorry. I just want to help so badly, and well . . . you understand, don't you?"

Actually, I didn't, but I figured her question was rhetorical, so I ignored it. I glanced around, looking for a distraction, and my eyes bounced around from one knickknack to another. "What a fascinating home you have and so many amazing . . . heirlooms."

"Thank you. I collect Victorian antiques that go with the house."

"Hmm, I don't see any Native American influence. Was your husband into decorating?"

"John and I both liked nice things. Frankly, I wasn't interested in ethnic arts and crafts."

That got my back up. "I'm not an art expert, but I have seen some really amazing Native American artwork. A few years ago, my late husband and I attended an exhibition of Native American art and sculpture at MISU. It was breathtaking, and the last time I went to the Four Feathers I was astonished by a wood carving that looked as though it belonged in a museum. It was the most amazing thing I've ever seen."

She shrugged. "I'm just not into that . . . type of stuff."

Mildred's face indicated that anything that wasn't Victorian and expensive was beneath her, and I found it hard to look at her. I turned away. "Well, I should probably be on my way. Do you have the printout about Sharon Carpenter?"

"I thought we could have tea and talk. I want to know if you've found out anything else in your investigation?"

"I'm sorry, but I really can't stay. My mom is moving to Australia, and we're planning a going-away party."

Mildred didn't try to hide her disappointment as she headed toward the kitchen. "It's just in here."

I waited in the living room. In the corner of the room was a triangular curio cabinet that was built into the wall. I sidestepped an ottoman, a coffee table, and a floor lamp to get a better look. In the cabinet were some of Mildred's collectibles. One shelf held pocket watches, glass dishes, and music boxes. Another shelf was crammed full of old-fashioned black-and-white photos, while yet another held ivory letter openers, lighters, pipes, and tobacco tins. I felt uneasy and turned to find Mildred staring at me. "You have some amazing things. Oh, is that it?" I extended my hand.

Mildred gave me a hard stare but handed me the paper.

I took a moment and glanced at it and then folded the paper and put it in my purse. I smiled. "Thank you. I'll look it over more closely later, but now I'd better get home."

Mildred stepped back, and I sidestepped her along with the other large pieces of furniture crammed into the room to get to the door.

I opened the door but turned around to ask, "When is the funeral service?"

"Tomorrow at four." She mentioned a prominent South Harbor funeral home.

"If I can get someone to watch the store, I'll be there." I turned to leave. "Thank you so much."

Outside, I took a deep breath. I felt like I'd just been enclosed in a closet and was finally able to escape the claustrophobic monument to Victorian excess.

When I got home, I could smell the wonderful aroma of cake as soon as I opened the door. Dawson's exams were over, and he was excited to try some new technique he'd researched. There was a multitiered cake on my kitchen counter and multiple bowls of icing that he was experimenting with by making various designs.

I stared at a plate that held something brown that resembled what the poodles might have left outside. I raised a brow and stared. "What exactly . . . ?"

Dawson shook his head. "My first attempt at making a koala. I can't seem to get the color right. They're more gray than brown."

He looked stressed, and I didn't want to bother him. So, I dumped my bags on the sofa and made my way to my bedroom. My brain was churning. Something flitted around in my head, but I didn't know what it was or how to get it. I decided writing might help me sort through my brain clutter.

Thompkins entered the large kitchen. He couldn't help but compare it to the one at the Marsh estate, Wickfield Lodge. Even though the kitchen at Chequers was slightly larger, he noted that the Marshes' kitchen had been modernized with the latest equipment to make the servants' workload as easy as possible. The most recent addition was a modern icebox that worked without ice and the new cast-iron AGA stove, which Mrs. Anderson had initially railed against but now loved more than anything. The Marshes had even upgraded the entire mansion's plumbing and installed a telephone. Change was always tricky, but the new additions made working at Wickfield Lodge a pleasure.

Mrs. Ridley, the housekeeper Thompkins engaged on the duke's behalf, was a local woman. She was a widow. After her husband's sudden death, she found herself in need of money and was only suited for domestic service. This was one of her first positions as a housekeeper, and she was still a bit rough around the edges. When he entered the room, she stood. Thompkins's lips twitched at the thought of how the Marshes' housekeeper, Mrs. McDuffie, would react to seeing that. "Please, don't trouble yourself with formality."

Thompkins was prim and proper and believed in tradition and protocol, but over the years he'd learned to relax a bit and found that the staff was more open to sharing information when they were more at ease, and information was what he sought.

"Please, sit down. I'm hoping you could assist me with something."

Mrs. Ridley was a mature woman with curly gray hair, dark eyes, and a kind mouth. "Yes, sir. I'll be happy to help with anything I can."

"I was wondering what you could tell me about the area and the people here." Thompkins smiled. "You see, Lord William and Lady Elizabeth raised their nieces as their own daughters. So, naturally, they are anxious for her safety, and I'm afraid they've heard some alarming tales about lunatics running wild and killing people in the village."

Mrs. Ridley gave a broad smile. "Pshaw. You tell her ladyship there's no cause to worry. I've lived in Buckinghamshire my entire life, and I can tell you, it's a peaceful enough place."

The teakettle whistled, and she rose to get it. She brought a cup to the butler. "Would you care for a cup of tea?"

"That would be lovely."

She poured the tea and then brought over a plate covered with a tea towel. "I made a seed cake, and it's right tasty if I do say so myself."

When she was finished providing tea and cake, she sat. "I've lived here my entire life and never a safer place in all of England, but I do say there have been some strange goings-on since those young people started going over to The Park. My son, Errol, works there. He's head groundskeeper," she said with pride.

"I didn't know that. Congratulations."

She smiled. "Well, Errol tells me that it's just a lot of young folks working and having fun. He says there's nothing to be worried about. Some of the women . . . well, they come from the best families in England. My neighbor, Mrs. Hastings, she showed me the letter her boarder provided and the references." She shook her head. "Lady this and Duchess that, why, they were all members of the aristocracy, and her boarder is a lady herself. Why, I can tell you Mrs. Hastings was beside herself. She didn't know if she should curtsy to the girl or not." She laughed.

"Lady Elizabeth is well acquainted with all of the best families in Britain. She is, I think, going to invite the young ladies over for tea."

Mrs. Ridley smiled. "Ah, that's nice. I'll need to make sure we do her ladyship proud. It's a good thing I started baking the second I arrived."

"Please, let me know if you require any additional help with cooking or serving."

Mrs. Ridley thought for a moment. "I can handle the cooking, and with a small family, Elsie and I can handle the dusting and housework, but Elsie's never served ladies. Maybe we might want to consider . . ."

Thompkins nodded. "I can handle tea, but if His Grace decides to host a formal dinner, we will need to enlist additional help."

"Right you are."

"I assume you've heard that someone was murdered at Bletchley Park."

"I heard. It's a small village and news travels fast. Errol tells me they believe it was some type of accident."

"Did Errol know the young man?"

"He did. Errol thinks it might have been a joke. He says those young men are always playing jokes on each other. He thinks that was just a joke gone bad and the ones that did it are too afraid to come forward." She shook her head. "No, I don't believe there's anything to worry about at The Park."

Thompkins stared at her. "Do you feel there's danger elsewhere in Buckinghamshire?"

Mrs. Ridley took a long drink of tea. "There's definitely some strange things going on around the Shoulder of Mutton. Ethel is a cook there, and she's seen strange lights at night. Doors she knows were locked tight before bed are unlocked and sometimes even wide open the next day." She stared at the butler. "Something odd is going on at the Shoulder, that's for certain."

Thompkins stared. "Odd indeed."

"Marguerite, thanks for meeting me," Lady Clara said as she and Marguerite strolled through St. James's Park.

"I have to admit, I was surprised to hear from you."

Something in her friend's voice made Clara halt. "I know I was only supposed to reach out for an emergency, but . . . I was desperate."

"I'm sorry." Marguerite stopped and guided her friend toward a bench. "What's happened?"

Lady Clara pulled herself together. "There's been another murder. This time, we think the intended victim was Peter."

"Your policeman?"

Clara nodded.

Marguerite squeezed her friend's hand. "Do you think it's some crazy lunatic with a grudge against Scotland Yard?"

"Not likely. Besides, he's been reassigned to Buckinghamshire."

Marguerite stared at her friend. "Really? That's interesting."

"And you can stop being mysterious. I know the truth about Bletchley Park. In fact, I'm going to be working there."

"That's a relief. It's hard keeping secrets. It's so much easier when you can talk openly, but . . . that's just not possible right now. How can I help?"

"Was there anything Oliver said to you that might help us figure out who killed him?"

"Not that I remember." She paused and thought. "I've been working on remembering things as part of my special training. I might as well put it into practice." She closed her eyes and sat perfectly still. "I'm visualizing the room and taking myself back to that night. We talked about his family and his job. He used to be a physics major at Cambridge until his father died." Her eyes popped open. "Oh dear, I completely forgot."

"What? Oh, Marguerite, if there's anything, no matter how small . . . please. I'm so worried."

"He'd been telling me that he'd only been a policeman for a few months. He was a physics major, but then his father died. He mentioned his father had a bad heart. His grandfather, uncle . . . it ran in the family. That's why I didn't think anything about his sudden death."

"But you've remembered something?"

"I don't know if it'll be any good, but he recognized someone who was at the party. He couldn't remember where, so he was distracted. While we were talking, he remembered, and he said he had to go. He was very agitated."

"Did he say what he remembered? Or who?"

She shook her head. "No, but whatever it was, I could tell that it was important."

"It must have been someone he knew from Cambridge." Clara hopped up. "That narrows things down a bit. Who was at the embassy that also attended Cambridge?" She paced. "Billy Cavendish, John Cairncross, and Donald Maclean."

"But I don't see how any of them could have killed him. They were nowhere near him when he collapsed."

Lady Clara plopped back down on the bench. "It had to be poison, but how? No one came near the food. As much as I dislike the American ambassador, I doubt if he's trying to poison his guests, unless it was intended for Billy Cavendish."

"If it wasn't the food, then . . ." Marguerite stopped and stared at Lady Clara.

The two women came to the same conclusion at the same time.

"The champagne."

⁓

The revelation hit me at the same time as the characters I'd been writing about. "Poison."

I grabbed my phone and hurried downstairs. That's where

I found Emma. The store was closed, but she sat at the bistro table munching on cookies and reading *Strange Practice*, a medical mystery by Vivian Shaw.

Emma looked up. "This is amazing. There are literally mysteries about just about everything. This woman is a doctor who specializes in treating vampires, werewolves, and— What's wrong?"

"I know who killed John Cloverton." I held up a finger. "I have two things I need to confirm. I just want to make sure." I dialed the phone. "Jenna, how did John Cloverton die?" I nodded. "That's what I thought you said. I just wanted to be sure." I hung up, not waiting for her questions. I dialed my second number. "Detective Pitt, did you say Mildred used to be a pharmacy technician before you got married? . . . I thought so. Can you meet me down at the police station? I know who killed John Cloverton. . . . Okay, I'll wait here for you." I hung up.

Emma put down her book and leaned forward anxiously. "You figured out who the killer was?"

"Yes, I think so, but I need to get down to the police station and—" I looked up and found myself staring into the barrel of a very large gun.

# Chapter 22

"What are you doing?" I asked. "How did you get in here?"

"It was simple. I just told that big oaf of a football player that I had some valuable information about the murder."

I looked around. "Where is he? What have you done with Dawson?"

"He's taking a nap . . . for now. After I take care of you and Brad, then I'll finish him off."

"What did you hit him with?" I took several steps forward, but she pressed the gun into my chest. The crazed look on her face stopped me in my tracks.

"I had you figured for a dud, but I thought I should stick close by, just in case. What gave me away?"

I found it hard to think while staring down the barrel of a gun, but I knew I needed to keep her talking. "Detective Pitt kept saying you were jealous, and he kept calling you crazy, and my mind couldn't accept that anyone would be jealous of him."

She snorted. "I was never jealous of that slob, but John . . . he was special, and he made me feel special." She frowned. "That was until that tart thought she'd take him away from me. I could handle all of the other women. John tired of them quickly, but little Miss Chastity thought she could take him away from me." She laughed. "John thought he could trick me and the two of them could just skip town and run away together, but I fixed him. I'll take care of the tramp as soon as I finish with you."

"What will you do to her?" Emma asked. I was a bit more concerned with what Mildred planned to do with us, but anything to keep her talking was good.

"I mixed up a little special concoction and put it in her face cream. She's been absorbing it into her skin, and it's slowly making her insane. Eventually, she'll kill herself from the grief . . . at least that's what everyone will think."

"Detective Pitt mentioned that you used to work at a pharmacy," I said. "Then I remembered when you told us that your husband was killed, you said he'd been poisoned. How did you know that? The police hadn't released that your husband had been poisoned before he was shot. My sister didn't even tell me until I called to confirm. The police like to withhold certain details in every murder."

She smiled. "Did anyone else make the connection? That old busybody, for example?"

I shook my head. "Nana Jo hasn't guessed. I'm the only one. Please . . ." I squeezed Emma's hand. "Let us go. I promise we won't say anything. You can leave . . . go to another country. No one will ever find you. Please—"

"Leave? Why should I leave? I'm not the one who cheated on my marriage vows. Not this time anyway." She shook her head. "No, I don't think so. Out of curiosity, what was it you saw in my curio cabinet that you found so fascinating?"

"Sharon Carpenter has a gambling problem. According to the sheet you got from the Pontolomas, she owes the Four Feathers casino five thousand dollars."

She shrugged. "So what?"

"The S.T. Dupont silver lighter in your curio cabinet is unique and worth more than five thousand dollars. Even if a pawnshop only gave her half of what it's worth, she wouldn't have to continue pilfering her husband's family heirlooms. The items that her mother-in-law saw her giving to you were worth a lot more than five thousand dollars. If you were truly intent on helping her, then she should have been able to pay off her debts, but you weren't helping her. You were stealing from her."

She threw back her head and laughed. "You are so right, but how else could I get the dirt I needed on Mayor Carpenter?"

"Why was it so important to you?"

"If John was going to be mayor, I had to stir things up. This town would never have elected an Indian for mayor." She scowled. "Vipers. Heathens and vipers. That's what they are."

If I hadn't already figured out that she was crazy, this confirmed it. Her eyes were wild, and she waved her gun around. I frantically searched my mind to figure out how to get Emma and me out of this. The only thing I could think about was to keep her talking until someone came. *What was taking Detective Pitt so long to get here?* "How long have you been tapping Detective Pitt's phone?"

She gave me a slightly crazed look of respect. "How'd you know about that?"

"You got here too fast. You had to be tapping one of us."

"I've been listening in on Brad's calls for weeks. I heard him and John talking. John wanted to have me committed to an asylum, and he wanted Brad's help. That's why Brad showed up to arrest him, the fool. John owed a lot in parking violations. When I heard them, I knew I needed to make them pay. They were both working against me, but I fixed them. I killed John and arranged it so Brad would get the blame. It was perfect. I knew Brad kept a gun in his nightstand. He always followed the same routine, night after night. Come home. Go to the bar and drink for an hour and then home to watch television." She smirked. "It was so easy to sneak in there and get his gun. He always keeps a bottle of water by his bed. Routine. I just put a mild tranquilizer in the bottle, and he was out like a light. After I killed John, I put the gun back where I'd gotten it."

"Millie, put the gun down." Detective Pitt had come in through the back door. "It's over."

She shook her head. "No. It's not over. I'm the one with the gun. I hold all the cards. Now, you go over there." She used the gun to indicate she wanted him standing next to me.

Detective Pitt held up his hands and moved slowly over next to Emma and me. "You can't get away with this."

She gave a maniacal laugh. "But I can. I've been poisoning that tart Chastity. She's going to find a large lapse in her memory where she can't remember what she's done. She's going to wake up here, covered in blood with this gun . . . John's gun in her hand. If they don't hang her, she might just take her own life. Either way is fine with me."

"Chastity won't come here," I said. "She doesn't trust you."

"She doesn't need to trust me. She just needs to trust you. Didn't I mention that you left a message for her asking her to come by your store?"

We all heard the bell on the door at the same time and turned. I was about to scream for help when Mildred took the gun and pointed it at Emma, and I froze. Fortunately, Detective Pitt didn't.

"Hit the ground," he yelled as he lunged for Mildred.

Detective Pitt and Mildred wrestled for the gun.

"Call the police," I yelled to Chastity. She hesitated a split second and then hurried out of the bookshop.

"You too," I yelled at Emma. "Go get Frank."

I could tell she didn't want to leave me, but she took off.

I looked around for a weapon. The only thing close at hand was a broom. I grabbed it and cracked it across my leg to get the bristle end off. I planted my feet and held the stick like a bat. I thought of Dawson and anger welled up inside me, and I knew I could easily bash Mildred's skull to smithereens.

I heard the sirens, and the front door flew open.

There was a loud explosion as the gun fired.

Frank flew through the back door. He saw that I was okay and then reached down and grabbed Mildred's hands. She still held on to the gun, and he twisted until she screamed. The gun fell to the floor, and he held her down.

"Are you okay?" he asked.

"Yes, but I don't think Detective Pitt is."

A puddle of blood poured out of his stomach, and he went completely white. His eyes rolled into his head, and he passed out.

# Chapter 23

"Call for an ambulance," Frank said.

The police burst through the front door with their guns drawn. Frank quickly filled them in while I ran to my cell phone and dialed 9-1-1.

Emma pushed her way through the crowd. When they tried to hold her back, she yelled, "I'm a medical student."

She dropped to her knees and felt for a pulse. "He's still alive, but his pulse is weak, and he's losing a lot of blood." She looked around. "I need some towels."

Frank went to the bistro and grabbed all the tea towels he could find.

Emma pressed the towels into the wound. "Hold these down. Apply as much pressure as you can."

Frank did as he was told.

Emma turned to one of the officers. "Give me your belt."

The officer quickly removed his belt and passed it to her.

Frank must have anticipated what she wanted, because he said, "You're not going to be able to lift him. Let me."

She nodded. "On three. One . . . two . . . three," she quickly counted. She handed him the belt and took over applying pressure to the wound.

Frank raised Detective Pitt and slid the belt around his chest. "Is this okay?"

Emma looked up and nodded. "Pull it as tight as you can."

Frank pulled the belt ends together as tightly as he could and buckled them.

The ambulance screeched to a stop in front of the building, and two EMTs ran in.

Frank backed away while Emma and the EMTs worked on Detective Pitt.

"Dawson!" I said, and ran through the back of the store.

He was sitting on the floor with his head in his hands. I dropped to my knees and pulled him into a tight hug.

When I went back inside the store, my entire family was there, along with what felt like the entire North Harbor Police Department.

Detective Pitt was being rolled out and taken in the ambulance to the hospital. Emma wasn't allowed to go with them. She walked over to Zaq, and he wrapped his arms around her. She put her head on his chest and wept. After a few moments, she pulled herself together. "He saved my life."

"Mine too." I shuddered at the thought, and Frank hugged me.

The paramedics quickly assessed Dawson and pronounced him fit, but they suggested he come to the hospital to be checked out.

A tall African-American man with a mustache and light gray eyes approached. "I'm acting Chief of Police Daryl Stevenson."

"Stevenson?" I said. "Are you related to . . . ?" I glanced at Ruby Mae, who was beaming.

"Yes, ma'am. She's my great-aunt. Now, can you tell—"

"Acting chief of police?" Nana Jo said. "What happened to Chief Zachary Davis?"

"He's been placed on temporary suspension pending an investigation into financial impropriety. Could you—"

Mom rushed in and hugged me. "Oh, Sam, I'm so glad you're okay."

"I'm fine. How did you all get here so quickly?"

"Nana Jo called us and told us to get our butts over here quick; you were in trouble," Jenna said.

"Could someone please tell me what happened?" Chief Stevenson asked.

I told him everything I'd figured out based on the information everyone had discovered. I hadn't noticed that Chastity Drummond was still there until she spoke.

"She's been poisoning me?" She stared wide-eyed. "I thought I was losing my mind."

"That's what she wanted you to believe," I said. "Detective Pitt kept telling me Mildred was nuts, but . . . I just thought he was bitter because she'd left him for John Cloverton."

Dorothy turned over the list of items that Mrs. Carpenter had given her, and I told him where I'd seen them in Mildred's house.

After what felt like hours, Chief Stevenson left, but not before walking over to Ruby Mae and kissing her cheek.

"He's cute," Irma said. "I wouldn't mind getting arrested by him."

Ruby Mae shot her a look that would have crushed walnuts. "Don't even think about it."

Emma and Frank were covered in Detective Pitt's blood. Zaq took Emma home to change. It took a bit of reassurance before I convinced Frank that I was really okay before he was willing to leave.

Nana Jo gave me a once-over. "You look tired."

"I suppose I am. I'm finally crashing from the adrenaline high." I yawned. "I think I'm going upstairs to take a long hot bath before getting some sleep."

"You do that, and don't worry about anything."

I accomplished the bath. I stayed in the tub until my skin started to pucker. Sleep was more elusive. Rather than fighting it, I went to my laptop.

Lady Elizabeth sat on the sofa near the fireplace and pulled out her knitting. "I think we've all had a busy day." She glanced at her husband. "Perhaps you'd like to go first, dear."

Lord William coughed. He took out his pipe and refilled the bowl. "Sent a message to Nigel Greyson at the Home Office. Met me for lunch at the club." He lit the tobacco and puffed. "Bright man, Nigel. He confirmed what James told us. Chester was a maths genius, but apparently, they were more interested in his friend . . . Alan Turing. The two men were . . ." He glanced at Detective Inspector Covington and coughed. "Rather close. He's concerned that the attempt might have been meant for Turing and somehow got mixed up." He puffed. "Nigel did say they were concerned about infiltration. So far, there doesn't seem to be any leakage about what's really going on up at Bletchley. They suspect Bolshies trying to recruit over at Cambridge. Afraid it's just a matter of time before the Nazis are trying to do the same."

James Browning paced. "It's a big concern for MI5, but it's hard. England's a free country. We can't just arrest people because they think differently. So far, it's just a few idealists who believe socialism is preferred over free enterprise, and that's not a crime."

Lord William puffed. "That's all Nigel was able to tell me. The rest is hush-hush."

Lady Elizabeth sighed. "Well, I had tea with eight former debutantes who are now all working at Bletchley Park. Bright girls. The only thing they were able to tell me that might be of any use is that Philip Chester and some of the other boys liked to play practical jokes. They believe it's a practical joke gone bad, innocent fun that got carried a bit too far. Although the girls have taken to carrying a brick in their purses, just in case."

"Sounds like a good idea, although it has to make their purses heavy," Lady Clara said. "Maybe I'll do the same."

"It certainly couldn't hurt," Lady Elizabeth said, smiling.

Thompkins coughed. "Excuse me, your ladyship. I found out mostly the same thing from Mrs. Ridley, the housekeeper." The butler summarized his conversation with the housekeeper.

"Well done, Thompkins."

"How did things go with Uncle Winnie?" Daphne asked.

Lady Elizabeth finished a complicated stitch before continuing. "Winston bellowed about the safety of the empire for a good five minutes. Eventually, he told me that Bletchley was critical to the war effort. Things are . . . progressing very rapidly, and he feels Britain will be at war before the year ends. If the enemy manages to infiltrate Bletchley Park, then England won't stand a chance."

Lady Clara gasped.

"I can't repeat most of what he had to say about Lady Nancy Astor." She colored slightly. "The two don't agree on anything, but even still, he didn't feel her capable of murder or being a spy. He felt when the rubber meets the road, she'll get in line and support the nation. His feelings about the American ambassador were a lot more coarse."

Lord Browning smiled. "I can imagine they were."

"He's of the opinion that Mr. Kennedy will be recalled to the States soon. The man's become an embarrassment and is harming relations. He doesn't think very highly of Ambassador Kennedy, saying the man lacks integrity and will stoop to any lengths to get what he wants. However, he doesn't feel Kennedy has the . . . intelligence or the stomach to murder someone himself. He felt pretty much the same way about the German ambassador. Both men are idiots." Lady Elizabeth stopped knitting and looked up. "He wasn't well acquainted with John Cairncross or Don Maclean, but he instinctively felt that if there was a murder, then those two were in the middle of it."

Detective Inspector Covington sat on the edge of his seat. "Based on what evidence?"

Lady Elizabeth shook her head. "Nothing that you would find useful in issuing a warrant against the men. I'm afraid Winston doesn't trust Cambridge."

Lady Clara sat up. "I might be able to help when it comes to evidence." She shared what her friend Marguerite remembered from the embassy dinner. "There were three men present who attended Cambridge: John Cairncross, Donald Maclean, and Billy Cavendish. If Oliver Martin remembered something about Cambridge, then it had to be one of those three people."

James Browning glanced at Lady Elizabeth, who gave him a slight nod. "Perhaps I should share my special assignment." He stood in front of the fireplace. "I was tasked with following my dear friend Detective Inspector Peter Covington."

The detective stared. "Me? What in the devil would make you do that?"

Lady Elizabeth took a deep breath. "I must confess that he did it at my bidding. Please understand that it was solely for your safety."

"Yes, old man. If someone was trying to kill you, then we thought it would be better if we intercepted them first."

Detective Covington acknowledged the truth and nodded. "Well, you must have done a good job, as I'm still here." He smiled. "Did you discover anything?"

"I learned that I'm not cut out to be a policeman. Too much walking. But I didn't notice anyone following him."

"Normally, I spend a fair bit of time with paperwork, but today I did a bit of running around, and it's faster to walk or take the Tube than drive in London sometimes." He smiled. "Next time you're following me, let me know and I'll slow down."

"Did you find out anything in your investigations?" Lady Elizabeth asked.

"I couldn't find any connection between Oliver Martin and Philip Chester, other than the fact that both attended Cambridge University. However, both men were poisoned. It's common enough to find in most homes . . . arsenic. Like Clara, I think Cambridge is the link connecting both murders."

Lady Elizabeth stared at her niece. "Daphne, you've been very quiet."

"I'm sorry. I was just thinking. I talked to the vicar and Mrs. Price, the head of the Ladies Aid. I really don't believe any of the locals are suspicious of Bletchley Park, but Mrs. Price did mention that several of the farmers have mentioned seeing suspicious lights out in their fields at night."

James frowned. "What kind of suspicious lights?"

"It's silly, but she said the farmers believe there are aliens." She laughed.

"Not as silly as you might think." James rubbed his chin. Eventually, he stood up. "It could be signal lights, or they might be using Morse code to pass messages to the enemy."

"Morse code?" Lady Clara said. "Don't you need a telegraph machine or something for that?"

Lord Browning shook his head. "Messages can be sent using a variety of methods. It's basically a language using dots and dashes." He pulled out his lighter and demonstrated by opening and closing the lid. Sometimes the flame was only shown for a brief second, and others it was allowed to flash longer.

Lord William watched intently. When the flashing ended, he said, "Clara."

Lord Browning nodded confirmation.

Lord William stuck out his chest. "Never forget my military training."

"Someone is sneaking out into the night and sending messages with lights," Lady Clara said.

"The critical part is *who* is sending the messages and *to whom* are they sending them?" Lady Elizabeth said.

"Mavis, I'm going to walk to the village," Lady Clara said as she strolled the grounds of Bletchley.

"You going to meet that dishy copper?"

"I wish. He's all work and no play mostly, but if I'm lucky, maybe I'll just happen to run into him."

"Well, be careful. I'm sure Philip's death was probably just some darned fool accident gone bad. I mean, who would want to kill him?" She shook her head. "Regardless, Mr. Knox, the boss, wants all of us girls to be extra careful."

Lady Clara bent down and picked up a brick that had come loose from the wall and slipped it into her purse. "I'll be careful."

In the village, Lady Clara caught sight of Peter. She raised her hand to get his attention but dropped it when she noticed two familiar figures leaving the Shoulder of Mutton: John Cairncross and Donald Maclean. The two men got into an automobile and drove off.

Clara hurried into the pub's reception area and spoke to the owner.

"Hello, I don't know if you remember me from the other day, but my name is Lady Clara Trewellan-Harper. I was here with my cousin, Lord Browning." She leaned across the desk and smiled brightly.

The pub owner stood up straight. "Of course, your ladyship. What can I do for you?"

"I thought I saw a friend of mine in here, and I just wondered if you could tell me if Lord Hardcastle was staying here?"

The pub owner frowned. "I don't rightly recall a Lord Hardcastle."

"Darn it. I was sure I saw him. Would you be a duck and check the register?"

"Of course, your ladyship." He pulled out the register, and Clara glanced over the counter. "No. I'm afraid there's no Lord Hardcastle checked in."

"Thank you so much for checking." Lady Clara smiled and walked away.

When the owner got called back to the pub, Lady Clara seized her chance. She raced around the corner and up the stairs. She found the door she wanted. To be safe, she knocked first. When she didn't get a response, she reached up and pulled a hairpin from her hair. She stuck the hairpin into the lock and fidgeted until she heard a *click*. She glanced over her shoulder and then opened the door.

Once inside, she rummaged through drawers and searched under the mattress. She was just about to give up when she noticed a foil wrapper sticking out from under the bed.

Clara dropped to her knees and pulled out the scrap of foil. By holding it up to the light, she was able to detect the embossed name of a chocolate company. She also found a large suitcase.

*Now, why would they keep this suitcase under the bed?* She pulled the suitcase out and opened it, discovering a wireless receiver and a massive torch inside. She closed the suitcase and rushed to leave, taking the evidence with her. Just as she opened the door, she bumped into Donald Maclean.

The two locked eyes.

Lady Clara recovered her wits and tried to push

past, but Maclean was too quick and brandished a gun from his pocket.

"Lady Clara, didn't anyone ever tell you it's not polite to take things that don't belong to you?" He wrenched the suitcase out of her hand. "Back in the room."

Lady Clara took one step backward and then swung her purse as hard as she could.

The brick connected to Maclean's head, and he dropped like a rag doll.

"I can't believe that worked." Lady Clara grabbed the suitcase. "Now I'd better get out of here before your partner returns."

She ran down the hall and turned the corner toward the stairs. She was almost out of danger when she ran straight into a solid wall of flesh.

# Chapter 24

A pair of arms wrapped around her, holding her in place.

She struggled to free herself.

"Clara! What are you doing?"

She looked up into the face of Detective Inspector Covington and nearly collapsed with relief.

"Peter, it's Maclean and Cairncross. Maclean grabbed me and tried to—"

"Did he hurt you? Where is he?"

She smiled. "Actually, I think I might have hurt him." She pointed toward the room.

"Stay here."

"Not on your life." Clara followed the detective.

They heard the squeak of someone coming up the stairs.

Detective Covington shoved Clara behind him and prepared to pounce on the intruder, but James Browning appeared around the corner.

Peter released a sigh. "Still trailing me?"

Lord Browning looked from Peter Covington to

Lady Clara. "I didn't mean to interfere."

The detective blushed. "Wait. It's not what it looks like."

Lady Clara colored slightly. "Let's go into the room, and then I can explain." She led the way down the hall to the room where Donald Maclean was still lying in the doorway. "I might have coshed him harder than I thought. He isn't dead, is he?"

Detective Covington bent down and checked Maclean's pulse. "He's still alive, but what did you hit him with?"

She held up her purse and pulled out the brick she'd added earlier. "Turns out, Mavis was right."

Peter and James slid Maclean back into the room and closed the door.

Clara quickly explained what had happened, and although Detective Covington looked as though he wanted to throttle her, he remained quiet. When she was done, she opened the suitcase with the wireless equipment and handed over the foil wrapper. "I was just on my way to find you when he came back."

They revived Maclean and interrogated him.

However, he refused to say anything.

Eventually, the detective gave up. "We may not be able to prove treason, but you're going to hang for killing Oliver Martin and Philip Chester."

"I didn't kill anyone," Maclean said. "I swear it. Look here, I'm not a traitor. I work undercover for the British Secret Intelligence Service. My job was to infiltrate the Russian spy ring. I've been working undercover for nearly three years."

"Then what happened?" Detective Covington asked.

"We met Oliver Martin at Cambridge. I tried to recruit him to the GBCP, that's all."

"What's GBCP?" Lady Clara asked.

Lord Browning said, "The Great Britain Communist Party."

"He seemed like the right type of chap," Maclean said. "Young, idealistic. Once he joined the party, the next step would be convincing him to spy for Russia, but Martin refused."

"Is that when you killed him?" Covington asked.

"I didn't kill him."

"Then who did?"

"I've wondered that too. John swears that Ribbentrop did it." He rubbed his head. "He believes Ribbentrop put the poison in the champagne."

"Why would Ribbentrop kill Oliver Martin?" Lord Browning said. "Don't tell me the German foreign minister is a member of the Russian Communist Party too."

Maclean shook his head. "No idea, but John thinks Ribbentrop wanted to cause problems between Britain and the United States. A British citizen, better still, a policeman, is murdered in the American Embassy? If the newspapers got hold of that, well . . . John thinks Ribbentrop is stupid enough to believe that might prevent the U.S. from joining the war, but who knows. Ribbentrop is an idiot."

"Ribbentrop may be an idiot, but starting an international incident is a cunning plan," Browning said.

Maclean stared at the duke.

"If Ribbentrop killed Oliver Martin, then why were you trying to kill Peter?" Lady Clara said, holding up the foil. "And don't say you weren't."

Maclean sighed. "John was certain Martin told him what he knew about the GBCP before he died. Then you showed up here, near Cambridge, and his superiors in Russia said you were a danger to the organization and ordered him to . . . finish you off."

Lady Clara shivered.

"Frankly, I tried to convince them that you'd be much more valuable alive and suggested they try to recruit you, but your reputation worked against me. Apparently, you're too bloody honest. That's when John tried to murder you. He sent those poisoned chocolates with the love note." He rubbed his head. "I hoped to get to The Park ahead of you. I drove like a madman. That's when I nearly ran you off the road. Unfortunately, I was too late, and Chester had snagged the chocolates. I'm sorry about that."

Detective Covington grabbed him by the arm. "Well, that's a nice story that paints you in a slightly better light, but it'll be up to a jury to decide. Come on."

Maclean stared at the detective. "You don't honestly believe any of this will ever make it to a jury, do you?"

"What are you talking about?"

Maclean turned to Lord Browning. "Ask your friend."

"What's he talking about, James?"

Lord Browning paced. "I need to make a call." He left the room for a few minutes, and when he returned he said, "Release him."

Later, Detective Covington, Lord Browning, and Lady Clara sat in the Shoulder of Mutton's private alcove.

"I'm sorry, Peter," Lord Browning said. "My boss

at MI5 will make sure that Scotland Yard is alerted. Within hours, both Oliver Martin's and Philip Chester's murders are to be declared accidents, and the files closed."

"What if Maclean is lying?" Covington said.

"What if he's telling the truth?" Lady Clara asked.

"If he's telling the truth, and he really is a double agent, then he will be useful when the war starts. If he's lying . . ." James shrugged. "Either way, they'll keep a closer eye on him. They'll make sure that he doesn't have access to any information that could harm Britain or her allies. Unfortunately, that's the way this game is played. We're entering a different world now, and the old rules no longer apply. The days when you knew exactly who the good guys were are gone."

Lady Clara looked from James to Peter. "Well, I think I know who I can trust."

# Chapter 25

Saturday morning, I slept late for the first time in years. I stretched, and my muscles felt sore. Ten pounds of poodle was curled up on my chest, which might have been part of the reason I was sore, but then I was accustomed to sleeping with the ten-pound weight on my chest.

I rolled over and dislodged the sleeping poodle and got out of bed.

Snickers moved to the spot I had just vacated, turned around twice, and then curled up in a ball to continue her nap. Life was hard.

I spent longer than normal in the shower and allowed the hot water to pelt my skin. Reluctantly, I got out of the shower and finished dressing. Fully dressed, I tried to coax Snickers to come take care of business. However, she ignored me. Eventually, I picked her up and carried her out of the room. Oreo preferred sleeping in his crate, and as soon as he saw Snickers and me leaving he followed.

I was drawn into the kitchen by my two favorite scents—coffee and bacon.

Nana Jo handed me a cup of coffee and pushed the

creamer and packets of artificial sweetener toward me. "I'll take them out. You eat." She took Snickers from my arms and headed downstairs.

I downed half the cup of coffee before I realized I hadn't thanked her.

When she came up, I made up for it.

She slid a copy of the *River Bend Tribune* in front of me. "You might as well get this over with."

I read the account of yesterday's events and tried not to cringe at the old picture the paper had found to print of me. "Good thing we're closed today."

"That hasn't stopped the reporters. They've been taping outside the door and calling the bookstore phone, trying to get a quote."

I read on. "It says Mayor Carpenter couldn't be reached."

"He chose the wrong time to go to Portugal, but I'm sure he will be able to clear his name when he's back." Nana Jo stretched. "Ruby Mae got her daughter to agree to clean the bookshop. I'd better go let her in."

"Clean?"

Nana Jo frowned. "Detective Pitt . . . I don't think the rug can be saved, but they have a lot of experience with crime scene cleanup."

"Have we gotten any word on how he's doing?"

Nana Jo shook her head. "I'm not family, so the hospital won't tell me anything other than he's still in critical condition. I sent flowers from both of us and figured we could go to the hospital and see what we could find out."

I glanced over at the decorations that I'd bought for the going-away party. "Do you think we should still have the party? I mean, it might be a bit macabre."

"I think we should still meet, at least for dinner, and wish your mom and Harold well."

Dawson was downstairs supervising the cleanup and preventing any overzealous reporters from getting too close. He'd checked out fine at the hospital and, apart from a headache, seemed no worse for the wear.

When he saw me, he hurried to the back room and came out carrying a box. "Mrs. W. This box came yesterday, and in all of the excitement, I didn't get a chance to tell you."

I was confused. This was a bookstore, and boxes of books arrived almost daily.

Nana Jo smiled and pulled out her phone and started recording. "Go ahead, open it."

I looked at the label, and that's when recognition hit. "Oh my God!" My hand shook as I tried to pull the tape from the box. Dawson handed me a box cutter, and I was able to get through the layers of tape. I unfolded the top and looked down at a box full of my book, *Murder at Wickfield Lodge*. I pulled out a copy of the book and stared at it while tears flowed. "I can't believe it. That's my book. That's my name on the cover." I cried. "I wish Leon were here to see this."

Nana Jo put down the phone and hugged me. "He is here. He's never left. He's right here with you."

The books were stamped with a bright label that proclaimed them *Advance Reader Copies*.

When Nana Jo and I went to the hospital to visit Detective Pitt, I took one of the copies of my book. Chief Stevenson was there talking to a doctor. The chief smiled when he recognized us.

"You have perfect timing. Detective Pitt has just regained consciousness. His condition is being moved from critical to stable."

I heaved a sigh of relief. "I'm so glad." I extended the book. "Would you please see that he gets this?"

Chief Stevenson looked at the doctor, who gave a nod. "Why don't you give it to him yourself?"

"I thought only immediate family were allowed?"

"Yep. That's why I think you and your grandmother should go in. You believed in him when no one else did." He grinned. "That sounds like family to me."

"He's still very weak," the doctor said. "Two minutes."

We tiptoed into the room. Detective Pitt looked weak and was wearing one of those cotton hospital gowns.

Nana Jo whispered, "That's got to be the first time I've seen him wearing anything except polyester."

His eyelashes flickered, and he opened his eyes and looked at us. "You okay?"

"I am. Thanks to you. You're a hero."

He tried to smile but winced. "All part of a day's work," he said softly.

"Thank you." I reached out and squeezed his hand. "This is my book. I wanted you to get the first copy." I held it up so he could see.

"I'm not much of a reader."

"No worries. I just wanted to give you something to let you know how much I appreciate what you did."

Nana Jo moved forward. She looked down at Detective Pitt and smiled. "You did good, Bradley. I'm grateful, and I'm very proud of you."

Detective Pitt stared, and a small tear fell from the corner of his eye.

We turned to leave but were stopped when Chief Stevenson moved forward. "Detective Pitt, I want you to know that as soon as you're better, I'll expect to see you back on the job."

We all left Detective Pitt to rest.

The going-away party was more low key than we originally planned. We skipped the streamers and koala-specific decorations and instead just had a meal with family and friends.

Emma was excited to hear that we'd seen Detective Pitt

and that his condition was stable. She was also excited to share a bit of her own good news. "I got them. Last night, when I got back to the dorm, there they were." She held up the letters and screamed. "I got into Columbia's and Northwestern's medical schools!"

We cheered and hugged.

"Those are both excellent schools," Harold said. "Which one will you choose?"

She gave a slight glance in Zaq's direction and then said, "Northwestern."

Dorothy smiled and hugged Jillian. "My granddaughter has some good news to announce too."

Jillian smiled. "I got the Bolshoi scholarship. I'm going to be spending my summer in New York."

Harold stood and raised his glass. "This calls for a toast."

Everyone picked up their glasses. "We have so many wonderful things to be thankful for. Grace and I are starting our new adventure in Australia. Christopher and Zaq have new jobs in Chicago. Jillian is going on a new adventure with the Bolshoi in New York, and Emma is starting her new adventure at Northwestern University's medical school."

"Don't forget Sam's new book," Nana Jo yelled.

"We cannot forget Sam's new book." Harold smiled. "Let us all raise our glasses to family, friends, and new adventures."

We drank.

The food was delicious. Dawson's cake was not only beautiful but also moist, delicious, and everything that a cake should be.

When we finished eating, I grabbed Frank by the hand and slipped outside. I handed him a copy of my book. "I wanted to give you this."

He hugged me. "I am so very proud of you. This is amazing. Did you sign it?"

"Of course."

He started to open it, but I stopped him. "Before you do that. I wanted to say thank you."

"For what?"

"For the party. The food. For being so kind and understanding and patient. For always being there whenever I needed you, especially yesterday. I don't know what I would have done if you hadn't been there."

He pulled me into his arms. "You won't ever have to find out. I'm not planning to go anywhere."

I snuggled into his chest and thought about how nice and cozy it was to be here with my friends and family nearby. My bookshop and a man who loved me. After a few moments, I pulled away. "You can open it now."

Frank opened the book and flipped to the front. There was only one word:

YES.